The Dowry

The Dowry

A Novel of Ireland

WALTER KEADY

Thomas Dunne Books
St. Martin's Press ✄ New York

To Kate, and in memory of Patricia

ACKNOWLEDGMENTS

My sincere thanks to the following:
Eugene Carney, whose humorous anecdote provided me with the genesis of a story;
Carolyn Palmer for reading the manuscript and offering many insightful suggestions;
Taconic Writers for their unfailing support and constructive criticism; Regina Ryan,
for her many helpful suggestions, and for continuing to believe in me.

THOMAS DUNNE BOOKS.
An imprint of St. Martin's Press.

www.thomasdunnebooks.com
www.stmartins.com

Library of Congress Cataloging-in-Publication Data

Keady, Walter, 1934–
     The dowry : a novel of Ireland / Walter Keady.—1st U.S. ed.
        p. cm.
     ISBN-13: 978-0-312-36191-4
     ISBN-10: 0-312-36191-2
     1. Marriage—Fiction. 2. Ireland—Fiction. I. Title.

PS3561.E16 D69 2007
813'.54—dc22

                                                              2006101701

First published in Great Britain by Robert Hale Limited

First U.S. Edition: March 2007

10 9 8 7 6 5 4 3 2 1

GLOSSARY OF UNUSUAL TERMS

-a stor	my dear
-amadhan	fool
-bad cess	bad luck (literally, bad taxes)
-begor/begob	by God
-bob	shilling
-bodagh	lout
-boreen	lane
-bowsy	malicious fellow
-cailin alainn (colleen awlin)	beautiful girl
-ceilidh (kayly)	social evening with Irish dancing
-chancer	dishonest person
-ciarog (keerogue)	beetle
-codding	joking
-colcannon	casserole made with potatoes and cabbage
-craic (crack)	entertainment
-doing a line	dating
-eejit	idiot
-flaithiul (flohool)	generous
-gobdaw	gullible person
-gobshite	despicable person
-gom	simpleton
-gossoon	boy
-gurrier	uncouth fellow
-Holy Hour	afternoon compulsory closing of pubs for an hour
-hooley	celebration, usually with alcohol
-hoor	whore; often used as a gender-neutral derogatory term, sometimes affectionately
-jar	a drink

-jax	toilet
-Lough Derg	a place of pilgrimage where severe penance is performed
-make a horse's collar of	make a mess of
-make a hames of	make a mess of
-nipper	young person, boy or girl
-Pioneer	abstainer from alcohol
-plamas (plawmawss)	diplomacy, soft talk
-puck	billy goat, hence randy young fellow
-quid	pound (money)
-rashers	bacon
-raimeis (rawmaysh)	nonsense
-rí-rá (ree-raw)	uproar, devilment
-Roman collar	frothy head on a pint of draught stout
-Sassenach	English person (derogatory)
-scut	contemptible individual
-seafoid (sha-foje)	nonsense
-sidecar	jaunting car
-sorra	sorrow (interjection); sorra much = not much
-spalpeen	seasonal hired labourer
-streel	slattern
-tramp-cock	a small haystack
-wick	fun
-yob	lout

1

It was the sudden onslaught of lust that convinced Brideen Conway she had to get married. Soon. She had been in love for some time and was enjoying the mixture of happy anguish and despairing delight that the tender passion holds out to entrap its victims. But though she was twenty-six years of age she had never, until that Saturday evening, allowed herself to experience an unrestrained blast of carnal pleasure.

Brideen was a teacher, in charge of the three lower classes at Coshlawn Crann National School. At home she kept house for her invalid mother and her brother Liam who, since their father died, worked the family farm on his own. Kieran McDermott, the man she was daft about, slaved seven days a week on *his* father's farm, so the courting of Brideen and Kieran was limited to Saturday and Sunday evenings. On Saturdays they'd walk back the road, or sit by Brideen's fireside and talk; on Sundays they'd cycle to a dance or the pictures in the town of Lahvauce. Activities that allowed them closeness without offending the ethical rules prescribed for the unmarried. For this was a time – 1946, the aftermath of World War II – when insular Ireland was priest-clean pure and the strictures of Catholic moralists placed the requirements of chastity before the demands of nature. *There is no trivial matter where purity is concerned,* was a constant admonition from pulpit and classroom. *The slightest carnal pleasure deliberately entertained is mortal sin and merits Hell for the unrepentant sinner.* Since Brideen and Kieran had been brought up in the piety of fear of Hell-fire they were nervous of anything that might place their salvation in jeopardy. Or they were until that fateful Saturday night.

The day in question began without warning of how it might end. Kieran came over to help Brideen and her brother save hay. 'The drying is good,' Liam said, as they surveyed the neat rows he had cut with a borrowed mowing machine the previous afternoon. 'It's ready to be turned.' They worked at it for a couple of hours, flipping over the still-green grass with wooden rakes. Liam and Kieran talked football incessantly, as they always did.

After the distant church bell rang the noon-time Angelus, Brideen returned to the house and made scones. While waiting for them to bake, she helped the mother take care of her personal needs: Mammy had Parkinson's disease, which was why Brideen had left her job in Dublin a year earlier: the other four siblings had gone to England as soon as the war ended, leaving Liam alone to take care of the farm and Mammy. Coming home had been painful: she loved teaching and she loved Dublin where there were boys to flirt with and dances to go to. And if food was sometimes a bit scarce while the world was still at war, and the digs weren't too comfortable, still the city was a more interesting place for a young woman than back-of-beyond Coshlawn Crann. But Mammy needed her. Daddy was dead, gored by a bull several years earlier. To her surprise, and as if God decided to reward her virtue, a teaching position became available in Coshlawn Crann soon after she came home.

She talked to Mammy now as she helped her: about school, the new young priest, her horrible Principal Teacher, her fellow. 'Kieran is here today; he came back to help us with the hay. And he was bragging because he brought his own rake and it had no missing teeth. "I hope you can say the same about yourself", I said to him.'

The corners of Mammy's mouth twitched, the nearest she ever came nowadays to a smile. She mumbled something, of which Brideen caught the single word *marriage*. Mammy was forever nudging her to get married, though Brideen knew well that when she did her leaving home would be traumatic for the mother. Many a night sister and brother had spent discussing how she'd be cared for after the wedding, until Liam mentioned the problem to Julia Ryan, *his* fiancée, who said there was no problem: *she'd* take care of Mammy. It was understood that Liam and Julia would get married as soon as Brideen moved out.

'No,' Brideen told Mammy now, 'we won't be getting married for a long time yet.'

'Why not?'

'Because we can't afford to, that's why.'

Mammy conveyed her contempt for that excuse with an extra wave of her hand, accompanied by something that sounded like 'bloody eejits'.

When the scones were baked, Brideen made tea in a large tin can. She fed her mother, then prepared a basket and headed back out to the hay field. Kieran grabbed a scone and bit into it. 'Where did you get the raisins?'

'I have my sources.' Maura Prendergast, her friend and fellow teacher, was married to a Garda in Lahvauce who had a way of acquiring commodities that were still available only on the black market. Brideen smiled at Kieran; she had met him shortly after she began teaching in Coshlawn Crann. Maura Prendergast made library books available to the parish by bringing them up from the County Library and spreading them out in her classroom after the Sunday masses. Brideen and Kieran touched hands there one morning when they reached for the same book at the same instant.

'Sorry,' she said.

'Sorry,' he said. 'Go ahead, you take it.'

'No, you can have it.'

'But you were first.'

'I think we touched it at the same time.'

'Let's cut it down the middle; you can have the even pages and I'll take the odd.'

That made her laugh. 'Since we're allowed to keep books for two weeks, why don't I read it first and give it to you next Sunday.' He was good-looking without being pretty, nicely built without being tall, and there was an aura about him that made her tingle.

'I'm Kieran McDermott from Cloghmor.'

'And I'm—'

'Everyone knows who *you* are.'

It hadn't occurred to her that the whole parish would recognize her because of her job. 'I'll be seeing you here next Sunday then.' She dreamed about him all week, read the book in a hurry, and couldn't wait for Sunday. Of course she arrived late: it wouldn't do to let him think she was anxious to see him. After she handed him the book she made as if to move on, but he blocked her way.

'I was thinking.' He was staring at the floor. 'There's a dance in Lahvauce tonight. Did you know that?'

'You're a goldmine of information, I must say.'

'I was wondering if maybe you'd like to go?'

'I'd love to.' It wasn't in her to be coy. He came to her house, they cycled into town and danced together all night. At times she felt giddy from the pleasure of being near him. When the band stopped playing at one o'clock he accompanied her home and shook hands at the gate. He was getting on his bike when he wondered out loud if she might like to go to the pictures the following Sunday evening. She said yes again, and from that time on they were going steady.

Sun and wind dried the hay quickly, and in the afternoon they turned it again. She made dinner, and while her brother was milking the cows, Kieran helped her feed the pigs and chickens. Afterwards they watched Liam perform his Saturday evening shaving ritual before the small mirror on the wall near the back door. Stropping frequently, he pulled the straight-edge across cheeks and throat, and damned and blasted when he nicked himself. After a careful examination to ensure all stubble was removed he washed face and hands and arms, and his feet in the same water. Then he disappeared into his room, emerged in Sunday clothes, and returned to the looking glass to comb his hair.

'I'm off to see a man about a dog now.'

'Say hello to Julia for me,' Brideen said. Shortly after, the mother got up from her wicker chair and shuffled into her bedroom. Brideen followed and helped her into bed. When she returned, Kieran was sitting by the fire. She pulled up a chair and sat beside him.

He patted his knee. 'Come and sit here.'

'Ah no; I couldn't do that.'

'Why not?'

'You know very well why not. It wouldn't be right, that's why.'

'Arrah what's wrong with it anyway?'

'Ask our new curate what's wrong with it; he'll tell you quickly enough.'

'Feck the new curate. Feck all curates. Not one of them has ever kissed a girl in his life, I'll bet.'

'What's got into you at all?' *You must be strong, girls,* Sister Timothy used to say. *Boys are such weak helpless creatures, blown every which way by the winds of passion. It's up to you to preserve your chastity, and theirs. Above all, you must never let them touch you in indecent places.*

'Don't bother so.' He stared hard at the fire, as if defying Hell itself to touch him.

It was their first disagreement. She wanted to cry. Why did she have to be so scrupulous? Kieran would never touch her indecently anyway: he was too much of a gentleman for that. She stood, as if impelled by a force outside herself, lifted his hands off his knees, perched lightly on his lap, and put an arm around his neck. 'Like this?'

His face turned bright as a new-lit lamp. 'You're beautiful.' He kissed her cheek.

Which peck was to Brideen like a spark to a furze in a dry March wind. She bent her head and kissed his lips with the hard lingering press of burgeoning passion. *Prolonged kissing,* Sister Timothy warned, *easily engenders unchaste gratification and must be religiously eschewed.* The sensation was quite new. Not that she'd never felt unchaste gratification before: from puberty on her imagination had learned to roam forbidden streets, and in Dublin, dances and flirting and brief kissing at parties had frequently resulted in bubbles of arousal. Those experiences, however, were merest tittles compared to the charge that coursed through her now. Was she on fire? It was like fire indeed, except that the pain was pleasure. But like anger, too, in that she was out of control, feeling only the frustration that demanded fulfilment. Where was her control anyway? But the question was only a tease to conscience: for once in her life she was mistress of that sourpuss ogre. And, though she'd pay for it later, for now she didn't care.

Their mouths remained pinched and pressed, like bees sucking nectar from a rose. His hand dropped down to her knee and glided up her thigh. She ought to have stopped him then; *you ought indeed,* said Sister Timothy. Instead, when her frock, taut from sitting, prevented the hand from moving further, she stood and hiked the dress loose. The hand roamed steadily upwards, across her belly and over her sternum, till the fingers encompassed a breast. Another new sensation. She'd caressed her breasts many times herself, but never experienced what the touch of his hand gave now.

The fingers retreated, probed her navel, slid under her knickers. She had to stop him now of course. *Most certainly, Sister T.; right away this very instant.* So why didn't she? His fingers were caressing her most indecent parts. And she was allowing him. And, oh God, was she ever enjoying his touch?

Then, just when she felt she was about to explode, the hand withdrew. He heaved like a man in a retch and moaned like a bullock in pain while he clutched her waist with the claws of a drowning cat. She held him tight, though the ecstasy she had almost reached turned to ache; into ashes all her lust. His head lay dead on her shoulder. Were it not for his exhausted breathing she might have thought he was dead. Vaguely she remembered reading that sexual climax was called the little death. So *he* had achieved it. And she had caused it. But why did he have to stop? A little more touching and she, too, would have been there. Was this what her friend Marie in Dublin meant when Brideen met her after the honeymoon? 'Oh *he* had a bloody great time, but I can't say it was much fun for me.'

Kieran raised his head and looked at her. His face was flushed, and pleased, and tender. He kissed her hard, then his hand burrowed back into her knickers. She made a feeble effort to restrain him but he persisted. Some infinity later her whole being enraptured.

Did we fornicate, Sister? She lay with her head nestled into his neck, tingling, content, enervated. Sin it certainly was, and in time she must repent. But for now the euphoria must not be spoiled. 'Where did you learn to do that?' She herself knew nothing about making love: Sister Timothy's instructions did not include lessons in the passionate art.

'Martin told me about it. Of course *I* never actually did it before.' Embarrassment etched in his murmured words. Everyone knew his older brother was a rake.

'You're a very fast learner, I must say.'

'I didn't hurt you, did I?'

She had to laugh at that idea. 'I wouldn't exactly call it hurt.' Her sense of well-being was overwhelming. She continued laughing till the tears came to her eyes and the laughter got away from her. Was she becoming hysterical? Then suddenly she was weeping, equally out of control, gasping for breath.

'What's the matter?' He held her tightly. She couldn't answer for the choking sobs. 'Are you all right?' He was stroking her back, her head, kissing her forehead, hugging her, murmuring. 'Everything will be all right. Not to worry. It's going to be OK.'

When she recovered, she removed herself from his lap, dried her eyes, smiled down at him. 'I'm all right now.' She sat in her chair and stared into the fire.

'I shouldn't have done it.'

'No, you should not.'

'It was a terrible thing to do to you.'

'But it was wonderful.'

'I thought it was fantastic myself.'

'Only now we'll have to get married. And soon.'

'I wish to God we could.'

'Well, why can't we? Don't you like me any more?'

'But how can we? I'm as poor as a church mouse.'

'I make enough to support the two of us.' It was only recently this thought had crossed her mind.

He folded his arms and looked at her crossly. 'It's a husband's job to support his wife.'

'And who made that law, may I ask?'

'I think it was God. Anyway, that's the way it is.'

'So how are you going to do it?'

'I'll go to England for a while to make some money.'

That hit her with the dull thump of expected pain, like a slap from Sister Timothy's cane. Though it was the first time he had mentioned leaving, the fear of it had stalked her ever since they had became serious. Emigration was the Irish solution to poverty, the traditional alternative to economic deprivation, the last desperate hope for a better way of life. So it was natural for him to see it as the response to their predicament. She herself, however, had always rejected that expedient. 'I'd rather starve here than live in England,' she had said more than once to friends who talked about going. Now she clawed for words to dissuade him. 'No! Don't. Please. We'll get by somehow. Anyway, it's not that easy to make money in England. I've heard stories. By the time you pay for digs and travel. And there's terrible food rationing as well.'

'I'm not happy about it either. I truly hate the thought of going. But—'

'Then don't.'

'What other choice is there?'

'Remember, if you go to England you'll wait a long time to repeat tonight's performance.'

That shook him, she could see by the look on his face. 'Ah Christ!' He reached over, pulled her to him, and kissed her.

She drew back. 'Anyway we can't do this again unless we're married first.'

'Why not? Martin does it all the time, he says.'

'Well, you're not Martin, and I'm not one of his loose women. Besides, what am I going to tell the new curate when I go to confession?' That thought brought home the horror of what they had just done. 'Oh my God! I have to go to confession. What am I going to tell him? He'll think I'm the scarlet woman of Babylon.'

'Go to the old canon in Lahvauce. Martin says he's half deaf. And he doesn't ask any questions.'

'Anyway, we have to get married. And the sooner the better.'

2

Had the new curate of Coshlawn Crann overheard her, he'd have applauded Brideen Conway's urge to marry. Not just because marriage would deliver her from a proximate occasion of serious sin – though as a celibate priest he, of course, abhorred all carnal congress committed beyond the connubial bed – but also because by entering the holy state she'd be furthering the rehabilitation of rural Ireland. An act that was sorely needed as the flower of youth flocked to post-war England in search of work, and when those who stayed home could afford to marry only late in life, if at all. Father Donovan was appalled at the devastating abandonment of the Irish countryside. As a priest he feared for the salvation of emigrants to the pagan world of the Sassenach. As a patriotic Irishman he mourned the hemorrhage of its sons and daughters from their native soil. On the day of his ordination four years earlier he had dedicated his priestly life to redressing the evils of emigration, late marriages, and no marriages at all. Less than a year later, an event occurred which deepened that commitment. Eamon De Valera, Ireland's political leader, spoke paternally to his nation on St Patrick's Day, 1943, while the guns of war caused death and destruction across much of the earth.

> *The Ireland we have dreamed of would be the home of a people who valued material wealth only as a basis of right living, of a people who were satisfied with frugal comfort and devoted their leisure to things of the spirit; a land whose countryside would be bright with cosy homesteads, whose fields and villages would be joyous with the sounds of industry, with the romping of sturdy children, the contests of athletic youths, the laughter of comely maidens; whose firesides would be forums for the wisdom of serene old age. It would, in a word, be the home of a people living the life that God desires that men should live.*

There were those who alleged that wily old Dev had only in his mind

an upcoming election and that this speech was intended to divert attention from harsh wartime austerities. But to Father Donovan's idealistic
mind, the leader's vision of what rural Ireland should be was nothing less
than an interpretation of the first Beatitude, attuned to the needs of the
present time. The following day he cut out that portion of the speech
from the newspaper and pasted it to his prie-dieu. Thereafter he never let
a day go by without reading it, and many's the night he fell asleep imagining what he'd do to implement it when he was appointed to a parish –
after ordination he had been assigned to teach Latin and History at the
diocesan junior seminary. Three years later, to his great delight, the archbishop sent him to Coshlawn Crann, once a thriving parish but now
because of emigration reduced to the status of a curacy and ruled by
Canon McCarthy, parish priest of the neighbouring town of Lahvauce.

'We have to unite the athletic youths and the comely maidens,' Father
Donovan told Brideen Conway when he visited the school on the
Thursday after her sin-laden tryst with Kieran McDermott.

'Sorry, Father; what was that?'

'Marriage, Brideen! Marriage is the key to the future of this parish.
We have to get people married. Will you look at your half-empty classroom. How else are we going to get children to fill it?' He gazed at the
small boys and girls in front of them: three classes and a total of only
twenty-five pupils.

'Indeed. But how are you going to do it? Half the parish is over in
England trying to get enough money to marry. And then they stay there,
and they and their children become Sassenachs, so all we're doing is
adding to the population of the old enemy.'

'It's my opinion that most people are too caught up in the things of
this world. If they would value material wealth only as a basis for right
living and be satisfied with frugal comfort, as Mr De Valera has so well
said, there would be no need for them to go traipsing off to England. At
the risk of their eternal salvation, I might add.'

'In my family we don't think too highly of Mr De Valera, Father. Isn't
it because of him and his bankrupt policies that people are so poor they
have to go away?'

If she had been a fellow priest, Father Donovan would there and then
have mounted a spirited defence of his hero. But having been warned in
his pastoral studies class to never argue politics with his flock he
contented himself with a 'be that as it may, we have to find some way to
keep our people here and get them married.'

'Money and jobs, Father. And better pay. That's what we need. Take my own situation, for instance. My poor fellow, Kieran, works for pocket money on his father's farm, without a hope of getting the place until the old man kicks off; which likely won't be till Kieran is old and grey and stooped and lame and no longer any good to a woman.'

'Something will have to be done.'

'And things are going to get worse. At the present birth-rate I'm going to be out of a job here in another five years.'

'Something will definitely have to be done.'

'But what, Father?'

That question haunted the new curate for the remainder of the day. It spoiled his boiled egg and brown bread tea, and kept him awake for hours into the night. How could you have sturdy children romping if you couldn't get the athletic youths and the comely maidens married? Money and jobs and better pay, she said. But providing such things was beyond the scope of a priest's remit. On the other hand, here was his opportunity to fulfil his own and De Valera's dream. He raised the subject on Monday with his friend Paddy Burke when they met at the latter's house for lunch.

'The land,' he said, 'belongs to the people. And the people belong to the land.'

'Begor, Ger,' Paddy said, 'that's a slogan De Valera himself would be proud to use. Especially at election time.'

'It's a terrible thing that's happening around us: all our young people getting up and going to England as if they were fleeing the plague. And where do they wind up? Working long hours in filthy factories and living like rabbits in city slums.'

'True for you, lad. But, of course, you're preaching to the choir here. I'm well aware of the problem. And just as concerned about it as you are.'

'Sorry. I got carried away.'

'Here, have another drop.' Paddy emptied the second bottle of wine. They were indulging in their usual post-prandial philosophizing on the states of parish, county, country, and world. This particular session differed from previous ones in that it was the first since Father Donovan had been appointed curate. Thanks to that assignment, and to the effects of the drink, he was feeling that his pronouncements today carried a greater authority than they had hitherto enjoyed with his friend.

'Frugal living, Paddy; frugal living. That's the answer. The flight from the land could be halted tomorrow if only people would listen to De Valera.'

'I'm afraid we've both had too much to drink, Ger, to talk much sense right now.'

'I intend to lay down the law to my parishioners. Frugal living. And a living wage. It's a crying shame that farm labourers aren't paid a living wage. Pope Leo—'

'True for you Ger, and I applaud your enthusiasm. But if I were you, I'd sit back for the first year and study the lie of the land before I'd say too much. Especially as regards social issues like the living wage. You'll be a lot safer to leave that matter to the bishops. Their lordships are very wary these days of anything that might even remotely smack of social-ism, because that comes close to atheistic communism. And we all know what they think of that.'

'You're right, of course.' For Ger Donovan Paddy Burke was always right. A brilliant man, he had short-cut the promotion path by studies in Rome and teaching in Maynooth, where he had been Ger's professor of Church History. Three years ago, he had been appointed parish priest of a big urban parish, long before his time. Last year he had been desig-nated a monsignor at the unprecedented age of forty, and he was now being tipped as the next archbishop.

Nevertheless, Father Donovan chafed at the thought of remaining silent on his pet subject. That night in bed he recalled his conversation with Brideen Conway. A pretty girl, that dark-haired, green-eyed teacher with the gorgeous skin and ravishing smile. Not that her good looks should make any difference to a celibate priest. Though it was her complaint that caused De Valera's vision to shine with renewed lustre before his eyes: *the laughter of comely maidens.* But when you got down to it, after all the dreaming and imagining, what could he really do? Not even Eamon De Valera himself had been able to make headway against the country's grinding poverty and enervating emigration.

Still, after much hashing and rehashing the problem, the germ of an answer came to Father Donovan that very night. Prayer. That was the solution. Storm the gates of Heaven with the pleas of the comely maid-ens and athletic youths. And the cries of their not-yet-conceived babbies. How could Almighty God and his Blessed Mother refuse to hear such prayers? He'd organize the parish in a mighty petition to the powers of Heaven. They'd pray and they'd pray, by night and by day, till their needs were granted, for what they were seeking had to be the will of God.

He recognized, even as he formulated his heroic resolve, that this wasn't necessarily so. God's ways, said every theological sage, were myste-rious: not for His children to know the depths of His thinking or the subtlety of His plans. On the other hand, it might well be the will of God that they pray for relief from their distress, and that their prayers were the condition of their deliverance. A parish novena, perhaps: nine days of prayer by every man, woman, and child. With fasting; that'd show how sincere they were. Then, his imagination taking wing, he saw other parishes latching onto his idea, till soon the whole nation was rattling the gates of Heaven pleading justice for the poor of Ireland. His problem solved, Father Donovan lay back and slept the sleep of the just.

The dull sobriety of a rainy morning, however, tempered his night-time enthusiasm. He'd never be able to coax his parishioners into nine days of prayer and fasting. Seven, maybe? Though even a week seemed an awful lot. Three days they might go for. If he left out the fasting. A triduum. In the evening, after the day's work was done. With rosary, sermon, and Benediction. He'd preach God's command to increase and multiply. A delicate subject for a young priest to give to a mixed congregation. Maybe separate them: one triduum for the women and another for the men. And what of the children? The prayers of the little ones were precious in the sight of God. Have them pray for their older brothers and sisters, and themselves, too, that they wouldn't have to go to England.

'What do you think, Cait?' he asked when his housekeeper came in to clear away the breakfast dishes.

'What do I think of what, Father?' She stacked cup, saucer, plates, and cutlery in a single pile, then picked them up with one hand while the other grabbed the milk jug.

'I'd like your opinion.'

She stopped to listen, though her pose – body half turned to the door – suggested a trace of impatience. When he told her of his plan, the clouds of doubt suffused her thin plain face. 'I'll tell you the God's honest truth now, Father. People in this parish don't go too much for anything new. I'd say you'd get a few to come, but if it isn't of obligation you won't get too many. If you know what I mean.'

'In that case we're going to have to coax them, aren't we?' He mustn't be deterred from his great undertaking by the pessimism of his housekeeper.

'And how do you suppose you might do that, Father?'

'I'll have to think about it.' As she was walking out the door he shouted after her, 'If you have any ideas yourself I'd be glad to hear them.'

Cait still intimidated him a bit. His predecessor's housekeeper, on the day of his arrival she had taken for granted that she'd be his, too. Indeed, he had the impression that it was she who was judging *his* fitness for *his* job. She briefed him, unasked, on parish affairs, in great detail both as regards activities and persons, and then told him that due to the poor state of the economy she wouldn't be asking for an increase in wages. At least her years – late middle age, he guessed – and physical attributes – thin, angular, and sour-faced – made her canonically suitable for the post: she'd pose no threat to his chastity.

She returned in a couple of minutes while he was still at the table. 'A thought just occurred to me, Father.'

'Terrific.'

'You'll need help. Coaxing these people to come is going to be a terrible job.'

'It will indeed.'

'And the best people to help you are them that have the most to gain from it.'

'I'd say that's true all right. So who do you think they are?'

She looked at him, with a kind of sly smile. 'The teachers, Father. Aren't they the ones that'll have the most to lose if there are no childer left to teach?'

'Indeed. You're absolutely right. I'll certainly ask them for help.' Brideen Conway would be no problem. And he had formed a good opinion of Maura Prendergast when he visited her classroom. On the other hand, although he had encountered the Principal, Alphonsus Finnerty, it wasn't at all clear he could count on him: a cold, forbidding man he appeared to be.

3

Adventurous fowl scratching for tidbits in the road scurried squawking back into farmyards as Brideen Conway cycled by. She was on her way home from school the afternoon of her conversation with Father Donovan. Poor naïve little priest: De Valera and his stupid notions indeed. Weren't they poor enough already? What she and Kieran needed was land and a house, not lectures on frugal living.

It was then the solution came to her, with clarity and certainty, product of her anger, and furious pedalling. Once recognized, it was so obvious that she marvelled she hadn't thought of it before. Kieran could get Tom McDermott's farm if he'd only be assertive enough to ask for it. Hadn't he told her that his father often said he wanted to go and live like a gentleman in Lahvauce? And hadn't he complained to her many times that his older brother Martin had no interest whatever in farming, that he was always leaving his work for Kieran to do while he was off chasing girls or taking part in sports meetings on his fancy racing bike? Never mind the tradition by which the oldest boy got the farm and the rest had to fend for themselves. That bad old law of primogeniture was brought in by the Sassenach, and it was time for a free Ireland to get rid of it. Kieran would just have to tell the old man that he was getting married and that he needed the place signed over to him. And if Brideen Conway had any say in the matter he was going to do it very soon. She recognized that he wasn't great at speaking up for himself: much too modest and self-effacing for his own good was what he was. So she'd have to persuade him. Her frown changed to a smile at that thought: she was good at persuading.

When she arrived home, her mother was sitting in her wicker chair, staring into the fire that was almost gone out. 'Where's Liam?' Brideen asked after she had got the fire going again and made the tea and fed the invalid.

'Kieran.'

Of course. It was sheep-shearing day at the McDermotts, and Liam had promised he'd lend a hand. 'I'll take a spin over to help them.' Recollections of Saturday night's ecstasy had intensified her longing for Kieran. 'I'll be back in time to do the milking.'

When she crested the hill that led up to the McDermott house she saw the men in the field at the side of the hay shed, the unshorn sheep penned in a corner where the walls were high, guarded by Marco the sheepdog. She left her bike up against the side of the house, walked down the muddy yard, and opened the iron gate by the side of the pig sty. 'God bless the work,' she called out.

The four men who were clipping looked up. 'You, too.'

'Will you look who's here?' Martin was rolling a fleece into a ball. 'The most beautiful girl in the parish of Coshlawn Crann, by God.' He was a big man, much taller than Kieran, with dark wavy hair, and he was terribly good-looking.

Kieran looked up at her and smiled. 'Grab a sheep for the girl, Martin, and give her a pair of clippers.'

She walked over to Packy O'Brien. 'How many have *you* done so far?'

Kieran's friend grinned. 'Damn near all of them. These other jokers here would take half an hour to shave a duck's backside.'

'Give me another.' Liam let go the sheep he had been clipping and threw the fleece at Martin.

'Easy does it.' Martin caught the fleece and began tying it with ends of wool from the fleece itself.

Brideen grabbed the sheep crook from the ground, pulled a sheep out of the flock by the hind leg, and dragged it over to Liam. He upended it and began to clip its underbelly.

Martin finished tying the fleece and threw it into the nearby cart. Then he filled a mug from the half barrel of Guinness that rested on the back of the cart. 'Have some?' He held out the mug to Brideen.

She wrinkled her nose. 'I can't stand the taste of that stuff.'

'It's not good for women anyway.' He quaffed it himself. 'Puts them in heat, they say.'

'Martin!' his father shouted. 'For God's sake will you get me another sheep, or we'll never get out of here tonight.'

Martin winked at Brideen. 'The oul fellow is in rare mood today.'

Brideen stayed with them till they finished. Then all went into the house where Rosaleen had dinner served up on the kitchen table: a slab of bacon, a bowl of cabbage, a mountain of potatoes, and tall glasses of milk. Rosaleen was the youngest of Tom McDermott's three children. The mother had died giving her birth and he had married again. Then the step-mother died when Rosaleen was fifteen. 'You'll have to stay home from school now and keep house for us,' her father told her. And that was the end of her formal education.

'The new priest came to the school today,' Brideen told them as she peeled a potato.

'Another cross old bugger like his predecessor, I suppose.' Martin forked a huge helping of cabbage onto his plate.

'If you had been to mass last Sunday you'd have seen that he's younger than yourself.' Tom McDermott scowled at his eldest.

'It was kind of hard to see what he looked like from the back of the church.' Martin winked again at Brideen.

'He thinks all us young people should get married straight away,' Brideen told them. 'And have lots of children. And be content with frugal living.'

'Good man himself,' Packy said. 'Some of us wouldn't mind getting married straight away if he'd just give us enough frugal to live on.' He smiled at Rosaleen.

'Speak for yourself, Packy.' Martin poked a finger into his neighbour's shoulder. 'Remember, the fun is over the day you tie the knot.'

'He said that marriage is the key to the future of the parish.' Brideen gazed across the table at Kieran. 'I told him that half the parish was over in England trying to get enough money to get married. And do you know what he said?'

'He said he was going to get married himself to give us a good example.' Martin ignored his father's glare.

'He said that if people would value material wealth only as a basis for right living and be satisfied with frugal comfort, as Mr De Valera advised, there would be no need for them to go traipsing off to England.'

Tom McDermott waited till he finished chewing before commenting. 'So he's a Dev man, is he?'

'From the way he talked today, I'd say he worships the Long Fellow.'

'Well in that case, sorra much he'll get from me at Christmas and Easter.' Tom McDermott put a piece of potato in his mouth, then stopped chewing long enough to add, 'De Valera is the ruination of this country, so he is.'

'Father Donovan is right about one thing:' Brideen said, 'we do need more children in the parish. Otherwise I'm going to be out of a job in a few years.'

'There's always England,' Martin said. 'Plenty of work to be had over there. Your man here wouldn't like you to go, of course.' He nudged Kieran with his elbow.

'I hate England.' She gave Martin a black look. 'I wouldn't be found dead going there.'

'America is better,' Packy said. 'I wouldn't mind going to New York myself.'

'Don't ye all have plenty to do where ye are right now?' The old man cut himself another piece of bacon.

'Plenty of work but damn little pay,' Kieran said. 'Right, Packy?'

'Damn right.'

'You'll come into your own place in good time, Packy.' Tom McDermott's tone was comforting.

Packy's laugh was sour. 'But when? A sister to be married out first, and sure Mick O'Brien will live to be a hundred. I'll be an old codger myself by that time.'

'When are *you* going to hand over *this* place?' Martin asked his father.

'When I'm good and ready.' That sharp rejoinder put an end to the conversation for the time being.

After dinner, Liam went home to do the milking. Brideen stayed and helped Rosaleen with the dishes while the McDermott men took care of their evening chores. 'I've something to tell you.' Rosaleen's head was down as she scrubbed the big black pot. She was several inches taller than Brideen, had red hair, and was inclined towards plumpness.

'What?' Brideen was drying the cutlery.

'Packy and I got engaged.'

'Rosaleen! That's great. When did it happen?'

'He asked me today after I brought the tea out to them.'

'In front of everyone? Isn't he the lad?'

'No. Of course not.' Rosaleen smiled, showing her beautiful dimples. 'He followed me back to the house. Said I needed help with the basket.'

'That's wonderful news. I'm delighted for you.'

'We're keeping it a secret for now. God knows when we'll be able to get married: Packy doesn't have a penny to his name. So don't tell anyone. Except Kieran, of course.'

'Maybe your father will give you a dowry?'

'We can't count on Daddy. He's a terrible old skinflint altogether.'

Of course, if he did give her a dowry there would be all the less left for Kieran. Which ominous thought redoubled Brideen's determination to galvanize her fiancé. So afterwards, when the two of them were strolling back the road in the slow descending dusk, she said, 'Why don't *you* ask him for the place?'

He stopped and gazed into her eyes. 'You've been reading my thoughts again, Miss Conway.'

'You're going to do it?'

'As soon as I can figure out the right way to pop the question. My father is a wily old bugger – you heard the answer he gave Martin a while ago.'

'I liked that. It meant – to me anyway – that he doesn't want to give the place to Martin.'

'He keeps saying he wants to live like a gentleman in Lahvauce. So why doesn't he do it, for Christ's sake? He's got plenty of money.'

'Maybe find him a rich widow with a house in town.'

'I've thought of that. But I don't think it would work. He's marriage-shy at this stage.'

'Maybe if he found the right woman. . . ?'

'I know for a fact that he asked several women to marry him after my stepmother died. And they all shot him down.'

'Why? He's still a good-looking man and, like you said, he has plenty of money.'

'What woman in her right mind would want to marry a farmer these days? Nothing but hard work in muck and dirt. They'd all rather be off in Dublin working in the Civil Service. Except yourself, of course.' Kieran grinned at her.

She glared at him. 'I'll have you know that I'll be a teacher married to a farmer. Which is a very different thing altogether. You can get someone else to feed your bloody pigs.'

'Anyway, the question is, how to talk Tom McDermott into giving up his farm to me?'

'Tell him to do what his father did for him – he must have got this place when he was quite young.'

'Indeed. But he didn't get it from his father.'

'I always assumed he did.'

'My grandfather was very poor, living off fifteen acres, and with nine mouths to feed. My father was the youngest of four boys. He told us many times that he knew he'd have to make his own way in life. And he did. With the help of God, he said. And the bit of luck of course: you had to have the luck on your side, too, he always said. Since he had nothing of his own, he decided he'd have to marry a girl who had a place coming to her. So he went to work for Mick Joyce, a well-off farmer with an only child, Kathleen, who was four years younger than himself. It was a long shot, he said. Who would have guessed that Kathleen would fall for him?

Or if she did, that her father would let her marry a mere spalpeen?'

'Kathleen was your mother?'

'The Lord have mercy on her soul.'

'Wasn't he the lucky man? And her father signed over the place to him like that?'

'Not quite. Shortly after the wedding my grandfather got himself and my grandmother killed driving their new Ford car into town – they hit a cow that wandered onto the road. So my mother got the place. And when she died, my father got it.'

'So now he should hand it over to you.'

'He should. But will he?'

'Tell him to buy himself a car and drive it into Lahvauce. There are plenty of cows on the road these days.'

Kieran chuckled. 'You're a wicked woman, Brideen Conway.'

'Why not just ask him?

'I'm thinking about it. But if I ask and he says no, then I'm done for.'

'And if you don't ask, you're done for anyway. Don't let I dare not wait upon I would.'

Kieran looked puzzled. 'Let what?'

'That's what another woman said one time to a fellow when he wanted something but didn't have the courage to do anything about it.'

'I *have* the courage, I just want to do it right. What I'm afraid is that he'll hand the place over to Martin when he decides to go to Lahvauce.'

'Arrah he will not. You've said yourself that Martin has no interest in farming.'

'Never mind that. Martin has always been the favourite. I remember when we were growing up he could do no wrong in my father's eyes.'

'You're the farmer and you know it. And your father knows it, too.'

Kieran kicked a loose stone on the road and sent it scudding into the bank. 'Martin got to go to a fancy boarding-school, and I had to make do with the Christian Brothers in Lahvauce.'

'It obviously didn't do the rake much good.'

'He was the one that got the new Raleigh when he barely passed the Leaving Cert. And what did I get when I got seven honours? My father's old crock.' He kicked another stone.

'Never mind the past; just think of the future. Our future.'

'Martin was taken to the Galway races every year. I never once got to go. But I was the one who always did the most work.'

'Will you stop feeling sorry for yourself, for God's sake? What matters now is that your father knows you're the better farmer.'

'But I'll bet he'd still prefer to give the place to Martin.'

'Would you rather go to England? And be wondering every day while you're breaking your back hauling bricks if maybe you'd have got the place if you'd had the courage to ask for it?'

'So you think I might have a chance?'

'I honest-to-God do. Not that I have any ill-will towards your brother, but I'm tired of seeing you only twice a week.'

'It would be nice all right, wouldn't it?'

'And especially now that we—'

'Ah, but he'll never give it to me.'

'You won't know unless you ask him.'

'Ah Jeez! He'd bite my head off, that's what he'd do. The man has a terrible temper, you know.'

'Oh come on. Don't be such a coward. You're a grown man now, not a child.'

'Oh, I'm not afraid of him, but all the same. . . .'

'If me no buts, as the fellow said. The question is, do you want us to have a future together or not?'

'Oh God, yes. More than anything in the world.'

She pinched his arm. 'Well then ask him. Right away. No more procrastinating.'

He kicked another stone. It skidded away down the hill. He stood still in the middle of the road for the longest time. Eventually he said, 'All right. I'll ask him tonight.'

She stood in front of him then and offered her lips. He wrapped his arms around her and kissed her until she pulled away. 'Remember, there'll be even better things than this every day as soon as we get married.'

4

After Brideen left, the enormity of what he had to do registered with Kieran. Easy for *her* to say, 'ask him for the place', but it wasn't as simple as that. He'd be asking his father to flout the unwritten law that the eldest son should inherit the farm. On the other hand, if he didn't at least ask, he could lose his Brideen.

When he came into the kitchen Rosaleen was sitting on the sofa reading. His father was on his throne – the comfortable stuffed armchair near the stove – removing his boots and listening to the news. The wireless was Tom McDermott's special pride, since only a few houses in the parish had one. Kieran picked up a newspaper from the table and sat next to Rosaleen. After the weather forecast was given for the next day, with rain promised, the old man turned off the set and got to his knees. 'We'll say the rosary now. I don't suppose the other fellow will be in until after hours.'

Kieran picked his beads off a nail in the wall, pulled a chair out from the table, and knelt before it, his elbows leaning on the seat. Rosaleen was already on her knees, bolt upright by the sofa. Tom, hunched over his throne, intoned the opening prayers, announced that the Joyful Mysteries would be the subject of meditation, and launched into the first decade: *the Annunciation.*

Brideen was right, of course. He had been working hard for his father for the past eight years, with nothing to show for it except calluses. And he was the better farmer, so he deserved the place. Obviously, Martin wouldn't see it that way, so there was going to be a royal donnybrook when he found out. And whereas Martin loved a fight, he himself was non-contentious by nature. He should have taken that Bank of Ireland job when it was offered him after the Leaving Certificate; he'd have enough money to get married now. Daddy had encouraged him to take it: get away from the muck and dirt, he'd said, wear good clothes and polished shoes every day. But he'd have died counting dirty money in that bleak building in Lahvauce. To work the land was what he wanted; all he needed was the farm. And, dammit, he had a right to this one. Martin had no interest whatever in the land. The only enthusiasm he ever showed was for racing the low-handlebar bike he had cajoled the old man into buying him three years ago as a bribe for getting down to serious work. But after he got the machine he did even less than before. All he could think about were the sports meetings around the county where he'd win races and medals and cups and prize money, and the admiration of the girls. He was good at the racing – as long as he stayed sober. But if he didn't kill himself by falling off the damn bike he was surely going to drown himself in Guinness. He'd—

'Kieran, wake up, will you!' His father summoning him to give out the second mystery: *the Visitation*. That stern tone reminded him of the awful commitment he had made to Brideen.

'Our Father, Who art in Heaven . . .'

Hell! Forget about asking and go to England: there was a lot of money to be made over there, with the country trying to rebuild after the war. Then he'd come home in a few years and build a house for himself and Brideen. And he wouldn't have to fight with his brother. *And be wondering every day while you're breaking your back hauling bricks if maybe you'd have got the place if you'd had the courage to ask for it?*

Shite! He'd either have to fight Martin, or have a row with Brideen. Of the two, his brother was less fearsome.

'Glory be to the Father and the Son. . . .'

Rosaleen led the third decade: *The Nativity*. Wasn't Jesus born into a family without a place to live? So what was he complaining about? But that was then and this was now and he did want a decent home to bring his wife into. Suppose he asked, and got the place, where would Martin and Rosaleen go? No way would he want Martin in the house. Apart from them not getting along, there was Martin's eye for the ladies. He'd trust Brideen, of course, but he couldn't leave her open to his brother's advances. Rosaleen's engagement to Packy, about which he had just learned from Brideen, wouldn't make things any easier: Packy's father had told him he couldn't bring a wife into the house until his oldest sister Teresa was taken care of. God! It was all so bloody complicated.

The rosary dragged on with the slew of trimmings that Tom and Rosaleen always added: prayers for this one and that, remembrance of this deceased and that invalid, help for this cause, preservation from that evil. Eventually the old man said his final *Amen* and they all got off their knees.

The moment was at hand. His father picked up the *Farmer's Journal.* Rosaleen went to bed. Martin was still out. Such an opportunity would be difficult to duplicate. But did he have the courage? *Oh come on. Don't be such a coward. You're a grown man now, not a child.*

'I have a question for you, Dad.'

Tom McDermott lowered the paper and looked at him over the top of his glasses. 'If it's about those bullocks, they're not ready to be sold yet.'

Dammit to hell! His father was always presuming to read his mind. 'It's not about the bullocks.'

'Go ahead then.' The old man kept on reading.

'How old were you when you got married?'

'Twenty-four.'

'I'm twenty-six now. And I'd like to get married.'

The paper was lowered again. 'Well, good on yourself. Brideen, I suppose.'

'Of course.'

'She's a fine girl. Good stock.'

'She is indeed.'

'And she said yes to you?'

'She'll marry me all right. But I'll need to be able to support her before we can go to the altar.'

'You will, of course.'

'And right now I have no means of support.'

'If you had taken the Bank job that time you'd be on the pig's back now.'

'I'm a farmer, Dad. What I need is a farm.'

'It won't be easy to buy one these days.'

Kieran wanted to shout that on what he was being paid he couldn't afford to buy a henhouse, never mind a farm. He said, mildly, 'I was hoping to inherit one.'

'Ah! The blessings of God on you, my boy.' The old man nodded. 'Aren't you the cute one. So what are you going to do about Liam?'

'Liam?' What had Liam to do with it?'

'When the mother gives Brideen the farm, Liam will have to get something, won't he?'

Bloody man! He could be thick as the wall when he wanted. 'I wasn't thinking of the Conway farm, Dad. That'll go to Liam, of course. I was hoping you might sign *this* place over to me.'

The old man laughed then, a gentle pitying kind of chuckle, as at the antics of a drunken eejit looking for a fight on a fair day. 'God bless your innocent heart, lad. What put a thought like that into your head?' He resumed his reading.

Kieran *felt* like the drunken eejit at the fair. What on God's earth made him think he had a hope? But the thought of Brideen urged him on. 'Haven't you often told us you'd like to get a house in town for yourself? Maybe this is a good time to do it.'

The paper came down and the glasses came off. 'True for you. I would indeed like a house in town. But where's the money coming from to buy it? And to support me after I get it? I'd have to sell this place to afford it.'

The door opened, Martin came in. He appeared less than sober as he crossed the kitchen and plopped onto the sofa next to Kieran.

'Have ye said the rosary yet? I was thinking all the way home that with a bit of luck I'd be in time for the nightly prayer.' He looked around. 'Where's Rosaleen?'

'She's gone to bed,' Kieran told him.

'Well, if Rosie's gone to bed then the rosary's been said. Amn't I right? She'd never ever go upstairs before the rosary, so she wouldn't.' He leaned his head against the back of the sofa and closed his eyes.

'Amadhan!' Tom McDermott muttered. Kieran sat there, too numb to leave. Before he had asked, there had been hope. Now hope was gone. He'd have to go to England. Leave Brideen. Which he desperately didn't want to do, even for a short time. And it wouldn't be a short time.

'Listen to me now, Kieran.' His father lowered the paper. 'I'll need two thousand pounds before I can buy a house in town. A thousand of that has to go into the bank as a dowry for Rosaleen if she ever decides to get married. You're not to tell her that, of course. So, when you find two thousand for me, the place is yours: house and farm and livestock.'

'For God's sake, where am I going to find two thousand pounds?' It could take him five years working in England to earn that much. By which time Brideen would have married someone else.

'The Conway's farm would fetch a fair bit if they could get the mother to sell it. Brideen would get half. You'd be off to a good start with that.'

'According to the father's will, the farm goes to Liam when the mother dies. Brideen got an education, and that's all she's getting.'

'Wait a minute! What about me?' Martin sat up and looked across at his father. 'Amn't I the heir apparent here, the Prince of Wales of Cloghmor? What's the big idea of telling the nipper he can have my inheritance?'

The father glared at him. 'Martin, you're not a farmer, you never were a farmer, and you never will be a farmer. So get out of your head any thought of inheriting the place.'

Martin leaned back and closed his eyes. The old man returned to his paper. Martin straightened up again, leaned across Kieran, jabbed a finger in his father's arm. 'Listen! You told the nipper that if he came up with two thousand quid you'd give him the place. Supposing *I* come up with the spondulicks first, won't I be entitled to it then?' He winked at Kieran.

The old man continued reading, giving no indication he had even heard the question. Martin began to snore. Kieran, feeling the weight of the day's work on his body, decided to go to bed. He was getting to his feet when his father said, loudly, as if speaking to the half deaf, 'Listen to me, the two of you.'

'I'm all ears,' Martin said, without opening his eyes.

'I'd move into town tomorrow if I could afford to. So whichever of you gets me the money first gets the place.'

'Just give me one week,' Martin said. 'I'll find the pot of gold.'

'But if neither of you gets it inside of two years, I'm selling the place.'

Kieran went to bed trying to repress a wish that Martin, or his father, or both, would drop dead.

5

The following Thursday when he visited the school, Father Donovan invited the teachers to drop by his house after class; he had something to discuss that was of serious import to them all. Brideen Conway and Maura Prendergast immediately said yes of course, they'd be there by a quarter past three. Alphonsus Finnerty hesitated, frowned, stared at the floor, opened his mouth to speak, thought better of it, frowned again, and eventually conceded that it was just possible he might be able to attend. 'But only for a short time.' Tall, thin, with rimless glasses, he wore a grey waistcoated suit, wrinkled white shirt, food-stained tie, and an expression of perpetual misery. The strap was in his hand and a boy stood before him, and the sharp sound of leather on palm reached the priest after he closed the door going out.

At a quarter past three Cait showed the teachers into the parlour and smirked satisfaction at Father Donovan.

'Thanks so much for coming,' the priest said. 'I think you'll all agree when you hear what I have to say that the matter is of great urgency, and that it affects not only all of us here but the future welfare of the parish as well.'

'That sounds terribly serious, Father.' Maura Prendergast was short and chubby, with a round face and a quick smile. 'Are we all in danger of losing our jobs?'

Father Donovan did his best to assume a non-committal expression 'If you don't mind, I'll wait till Cait brings the tea before getting started.'

'We're in no hurry at all,' Brideen Conway said.

Alphonsus Finnerty pulled out his pocket watch and made a show of squinting at it. 'I need to be on my way at four o'clock.'

Just then Cait came with the tea and poured for them. 'The subject of my concern,' said Father Donovan after she had left and closed the door, 'is the falling birth rate in the parish. It means fewer children in school, and consequently a threat to your own jobs as teachers.'

'True for you,' Brideen said.

'It's been on my own mind for some time,' Maura Prendergast acknowledged.

'It's part of a nation-wide trend.' Alphonsus Finnerty rubbed his nose. 'The population of Ireland is falling like apples from a dying tree. In time the tree will be bare and dead and there won't be a single soul left in the entire country.'

'Ah now, isn't that a bit pessimistic, Alphonsus?' Maura said. 'I think myself these things go in cycles. Sometimes the population rises and sometimes it falls. I imagine now that the war is over people will start getting married again and in a few years' time we'll have a lot more nippers running around. My concern is that it should happen before the school loses another teacher.'

'Do I suspect you have a plan to do something about it, Father?' Brideen's eyes were wide with happy expectation.

'I do indeed have a plan, and that's what I've asked you to come here to talk about.'

'And we'll all be most happy to do that. Right away.' Alphonsus Finnerty looked at his watch again.

'Marriage,' Father Donovan said, 'is the key to population increase. So the question is: how do we get more people to enter the holy state? The parish is full of spinsters and bachelors who haven't a thought in their heads of going to the altar. I'm talking about those of marriageable age, of course. The older ones are beyond hope.'

'Some of us would be only too glad to get harnessed,' Brideen put in. 'But we have to be able to afford it first.'

Finnerty nodded. 'Those who want to get married emigrate to where they can make enough money, leaving at home only those who are resigned to their single state.'

'Like yourself, Alphonsus.' Maura Prendergast winked at her principal.

'I'm not at all convinced,' the priest said, 'that lack of money is the principal barrier to marriage. If people would be satisfied with frugal comfort and devote their leisure to things of the spirit, as Mr De Valera has so rightly said, then we'd soon have a countryside bright with cosy homesteads, whose fields and villages would be joyous with the sounds of industry, with the romping of sturdy children, the contests of athletic youths, the laughter of comely maidens.'

An awkward silence descended. The teachers sipped their tea and stared at the floor. Father Donovan waited in vain for even a single nod of agreement. Eventually Maura Prendergast said, 'That sort of talk is all very well for Dev, Father: he doesn't have to live on spuds and buttermilk for his dinner. But it's no help at all to the lads who work seven days a week in dung and dirt, and have to come to mass with patches on their pants and cow-shite on their boots. You can't live more frugally than those lads, but they still have no hope of ever getting a place of their own to get married into and raise a family.'

'The Irish farmer is doomed to extinction.' Alphonsus Finnerty surveyed his teacup as an augur might study the entrails of a chicken. 'Centuries of serfdom under the yoke of English landlords have destroyed in him the will to better his miserable lot. I see it every day in the faces of his children: in their inability – or unwillingness – to learn even the fundamentals of reading, writing, and arithmetic.'

'They might learn a lot better if they weren't so terrified of being beaten.' Brideen's face reddened.

Father Donovan found himself in a delicate position. Not only were his teachers not in sympathy with Mr De Valera's visionary hope for rural Ireland, now he had two of them at loggerheads over corporal punishment. His sympathies on the latter subject lay with Miss Conway, for he himself was a kind-hearted man who could never beat a child. On the other hand, he needed all three teachers' support for his triduum campaign, so he mustn't say anything to antagonize the principal.

'What I had in mind is a campaign of prayer by the entire parish. God alone can remedy the failure or inability of our young people to marry. So I'm going to conduct a series of triduums to invoke His aid.'

'By the time the children reach my classroom they're already well behind, because learning can only be beaten into them, and the teachers in the lower classes are not nearly strict enough.' Finnerty waved a finger at Brideen. 'Failure to use the strap is a guarantee of failure to learn.'

'I think that's a wonderful idea, Father,' Maura said.

'I will never use a strap on a child,' Brideen said. 'I find that my children learn very well if I make the material interesting.'

'I'll have one triduum for the men, another for the women, and a third for the children. On Monday, Tuesday and Wednesday evenings for three successive weeks. With rosary, sermon, and Benediction.' Father Donovan gazed at each teacher in turn to make sure he had their attention. 'I'll preach on the theme of *increase and multiply*.'

'Well it can't do any harm,' Brideen said.

'That's for sure.' Maura agreed.

Alphonsus Finnerty took out his watch again.

'What I'd like you all to do for me,' Father Donovan said, 'is to canvass the triduums with me to make sure everyone attends.'

'Naturally,' Maura said. 'I'll be most happy to tell the children that they're to remind their parents and older brothers and sisters.'

'Me too,' Brideen added.

Alphonsus Finnerty said nothing.

The priest felt himself redden as he prepared to make his daring proposal. 'I thought that maybe you'd be willing to share with me the burden of visiting every house in the parish and asking each family member to take part. There's nothing like the personal touch, you see.'

'You mean, for each of us to visit a certain number of houses?' Maura asked.

'That's what I had in mind.'

Alphonsus Finnerty looked aghast. 'You're joking.'

It struck the priest that the principal never addressed him as Father. 'I know what I'm asking is beyond the call of duty, and I wouldn't normally ask it of you. But they say that desperate situations require desperate remedies, and it is imperative that the entire parish take part in storming Heaven to gain our most necessary ends.'

'Why wouldn't you visit all the families yourself?' Finnerty gulped down the remainder of his tea. 'That kind of thing would seem to be a strictly priestly duty.'

'A fair question indeed, Mr Finnerty. And the reason is time. The problem is urgent: I feel that Almighty God is calling us to undertake this harvesting of prayers as quickly as possible. So I intend to announce the triduums at next Sunday's masses and begin them a week later. That won't allow time for me to visit every house myself. Besides, an invitation coming from a teacher carries its own special weight. People have the greatest respect for you all.'

'I'll be happy to help you,' Brideen said.

'You can count on me,' Maura Prendergast told him. 'I'm a firm believer in the power of prayer. Shall we divide the parish into four quarters and take one each?'

'We'd need to start on Monday, wouldn't we?' Brideen said.

Alphonsus Finnerty laid his cup and saucer on the tray. 'As you all know, I do like to help out whenever I can. I think I can safely say I have always been a good parishioner. However, this is not the sort of thing I would consider at all appropriate for a teacher to engage in.' He stared at Brideen and Maura in turn.

'Arrah for God's sake, Alphonsus, what's wrong with it?' Maura's tone awash with asperity. 'Is it ashamed you are to knock on people's doors and ask them to come out and pray for something they know is vitally important for the future of the parish?'

Finnerty cast a scathing glance at Maura. 'I won't even deign a response to that unseemly statement.'

Father Donovan had been accused of being too soft on backsliding students when he was teaching in the junior seminary. 'Too much velvet glove, you see, and not enough steel hand,' was how the testy dean of discipline had put it to him. Nevertheless, he felt he was quite capable of showing his steel when the occasion demanded. And such an occasion was at hand right now.

'Mr Finnerty, you are well within your rights if you don't want to participate in our crusade of prayer. And although I'm the school manager I wouldn't dream of trying to coerce you into helping us with this cause, however important it may be for the future of the school and its teachers.'

Alphonsus Finnerty nodded agreement.

'On the other hand, when the number of pupils falls below the level that can support three teachers, I'm the one who will have to decide which of you is to go redundant.'

Finnerty's head shot up. 'I've been teaching here for twelve years and I've been the school principal for the past ten. You can't . . .' His voice trailed away as he caught Father Donovan's uncompromising stare.

'School managers,' said the priest, 'have extraordinary latitude in the matter of appointments and redundancies.'

The principal pulled out his watch. 'I have to go now.' He got to his feet and headed for the door. As he opened it he turned and looked back at the priest. 'Let me know which quarter of the parish you want me to cover.' And then he was gone.

6

By the time Liam left for his date with Julia, Kieran was half an hour late. Brideen was annoyed, her longing having reached lusting point much earlier in the day. After she helped her mother into bed and another half-hour went by, vexation changed to anxiety: since they had started going steady he had never once failed to come over on Saturday evening. At ten o'clock, with Mammy sleeping soundly, she got on her bike and hurried back to Cloghmor in the early twilight. She needn't have worried: Kieran had been balked by an expectant cow. The old man decreed that he stay with the animal, as it was her first calf and there could be complications. When Brideen arrived, the cow was lying in a stall chewing the cud; Kieran was sitting on a milking stool reading a Penguin in the dim light of a storm lantern.

'You see?' She picked up the other stool and sat next to him. 'You're always the one who gets the dirty work.'

He stuffed the book into his jacket pocket. 'I already asked him.'

'Well! What did he say?'

'He didn't say yes, but he didn't say no either.'

'Don't be so mysterious. What did he say?'

'He said I can have it if I give him two thousand pounds.'

'Stop your codding. Tell me what he said.'

'On my solemn oath.'

'He wants you to give him two thousand pounds?'

'Martin or myself. Whoever comes up with the money first gets the place.'

'I don't believe it. What does he want two thousand pounds for? Everyone knows the man is rolling in money.'

'He wants to live like a lord in Lahvauce. The extra money will buy him a coach and four.'

'He might as well have turned you down altogether. Where on God's earth are you going to find two thousand pounds?'

'No bother. I'll wait till I spot a rainbow, race to the end of it, grab hold of the leprechaun, and won't let him out of my sight till he gives me his crock of gold.'

'Your father, if you don't mind my saying so, Kieran McDermott, is the meanest rottenest man I've ever come across in my entire life.'

'He'd put Shylock to shame, that's for sure.'

'Scrooge could take lessons from him.'

'He'd skin a flea for its lousy hide, so he would.'

'He'd scrape the cross off an ass if he could sell it.'

'He's tighter than a fat woman's corset.'

'He's meaner than a dog in the manger.'

'He's a disgrace to – oh God, here he comes.'

The shed door opened and Tom McDermott stepped in, carrying a lantern. He came forward and looked at the cow. 'She hasn't done anything yet?'

'I'd say she mightn't calve till morning.'

'All the same, it's better to—' It was only then he spotted Brideen sitting on the far side of Kieran. 'How are you, Brideen? What brings you here this time of night?'

'It's our courting night. Since Kieran couldn't come to see me I came to see him.'

'You won't be needing me then, Kieran, as long as you have herself to help you.' Tom McDermott turned and walked out.

'I thought that—' Brideen began, when the door opened again.

'Kieran,' the old man shouted from outside, 'bring some milk over to Barney Murphy in the morning, like a good lad. His cow has gone dry.' The door closed again.

'Why can't you do it yourself?' Kieran muttered.

'Because you let him walk all over you, that's why.'

'What am I to do? You can't argue with that man. It's either do as he says or get out.'

'I'll tell you one thing, Kieran McDermott: I'm never coming to live in this house as long as he's here.'

The cow stirred and moaned. Kieran rubbed her back. 'It's OK, Bessie, just relax and take it easy.'

'Two thousand pounds,' Brideen said. 'Do you know how long it would take me to *earn* that much, never mind save it?'

'Not as long as it would take me working here for the old skinflint.'

'It would take me six years.'

'At a pound a week it would take me forty.'

'Well, I can tell you this, Mr son of skinflint McDermott, I'm not waiting for you for forty years.'

'Why not? I'll have a nice grey beard and a stoop and a walking stick. Won't that be worth waiting for?'

'We're getting married by next summer or not at all.'

Kieran patted the cow again. 'We could sell you, Bessie; you should be worth at least forty quid. Then all we'd need would be another one thousand nine hundred and sixty.'

Brideen leaped up off the stool. 'That's it, that's it! Eureka! I've got it.' She did a couple of twirls of a dance around the stall.

'Will you calm down, girl; you'll frighten the poor cow, and then we'll have serious trouble on our hands.'

'Listen. I have the solution. And it's so simple.'

'You mean other than the leprechaun's crock of gold?'

'How many cattle does your father own?'

'Let me see. Eighty-four bullocks, four milk cows, two heifers, and three calves. That makes ninety-three altogether.'

'There you are. That's our solution.'

'You're thinking of stealing them? May I remind you, Miss cattle-rustler Conway, there are laws in this country against that. They mightn't hang you from the nearest tree, like in the old West, but they'd certainly put you in jail.'

'Listen, Kieran, listen.'

'Anyway, how far do you think you'd get with a herd of cattle before you got caught? And who would you sell them to, even if you did get away?'

'Will you shut up and listen.'

'If you think I'm going to marry a cattle thief you better think again. I'm a respectable farmer, so I am.'

She came behind him and put her hand over his mouth. 'Listen, you yob. You told me your father said that whoever comes up with the money gets the farm and the house and the livestock. Am I right?'

He took her hand from his mouth and kissed it. 'That's what the man said.'

'And you said Bessie is worth forty pounds. In which case all the cattle together are worth a lot more than two thousand. Not to mention all those sheep you just sheared. So all you have to do is tell your father that he can sell two thousand pounds' worth of livestock and keep the money when he gives you the place.'

He stared at her for a minute, then pulled her down onto his lap and kissed her. 'You're a bloody genius, Brideen Conway. Now I know why I want to marry you.' He made to kiss her again, but she pulled away and stood back from him.

'No unseemly shenanigans in front of the young cow, sir. But don't you think it'll work?'

'It's stupendous.' He stroked Bessie. 'Though it's too much like the three card trick. Let me tell you something: you have to get up very early in the morning to pull the wool over Tom McDermott's eyes.'

'It's a straightforward deal: he gives you the place – house and farm and livestock – and he gets his two thousand pounds from selling some of the livestock that he's given you.' She did another little dance. 'This is going to work, Kieran; I know it's going to work. And then we can get married.' She pirouetted. 'And then we can make love every day.' She wiggled her hips. 'So what do you say to that, Farmer McDermott?'

He got to his feet, stretched his arms over his head. 'I don't want to be pessimistic, but—'

'Then don't be. There's only one way to find out if this will work, and that's by asking the man.'

'I'll think about it.'

'You will not think about it. You will go to him right away and put it to him.'

'He's gone to bed already.'

'Well, first thing in the morning so. When you tell him about the calf.'

'Speaking of which, will you look.' There were indications from Bessie's nether regions that the McDermott herd of cattle was soon to be augmented.

The calf arrived shortly after midnight, without complications. After cleaning out the stall Kieran accompanied Brideen home, so it was almost three o'clock before he got to bed. He was up again at eight to inspect the new calf, and to milk, without help, her mother and the other three cows: Martin could never be got out of bed on Sunday mornings and his father no longer did milking. Rosaleen had his breakfast ready after he put the milk away. The old man, in Sunday clothes, was still eating.

'I'll leave ye to it,' Rosaleen said. 'I have to get ready for mass.'

Now was a good time to broach the subject. His general annoyance at the lack of help with the morning chores fuelled Kieran's courage. 'I have a proposition for you, Dad.'

'Did the cow calve?'

'She did, and they're both doing fine. What I wanted to propose to you was—'

'I'm glad to hear it.'

'You said the other night that whoever comes up with two thousand pounds first gets this place: farm and house and livestock. Right?'

'That's what I said.'

'So when I get the place I'll own all the livestock?'

'Why wouldn't you. The farm wouldn't be much good without livestock.'

'So listen to this.' Kieran rested his elbows on the table and leaned across towards his father. 'Why don't you sign over the place to me now, and then I'll sell two thousand pounds' worth of livestock and give you your money.'

'Well, aren't you the cute lad.' The old man raised his cup. 'Get me some more tea like a good boy.'

Kieran went to the stove, picked up the teapot, and filled his father's cup. 'So what do you think?'

Tom McDermott put two spoons of sugar in his tea and a large dollop of milk, then stirred it slowly. After he put the spoon back in the saucer he looked up. 'Listen to me now, Kieran. I'm going to need a lot of money to live in Lahvauce. If I hand over the place, and I said *if*, it'll be *after* I've sold part of the livestock to give me some of that money. You'll need the remaining animals to keep the place going. The two thousand I'm expecting from you or your brother will be in addition to the money I'll get from the sale of livestock. Do you understand?'

Kieran repressed his anger. 'What I understand is I'd have to work in England for five years to save two thousand pounds. And you want it in two years.'

'Rosaleen tells me she just got engaged to Packy.'

'I know that.'

'And they'd like to get married soon. So my suggestion is that you marry Brideen at the same time, and then Brideen can take Rosaleen's place here as the housekeeper.'

This time, anger overcame Kieran. 'Brideen is a National School teacher, not a housekeeper. Anyway, she said she'll never come into this house as long as you're here. And she's right. Look at the way you treat us. As if we were your slaves.'

The old man pushed back his chair and stood. 'You should have taken that job at the bank, like I told you.'

He went out the hall door; Kieran heard his footsteps on the stairs. He'd have to go to England. Maybe Brideen would go with him. It wasn't their dream, but it was useless waiting here expecting anything from that bloody bastard. He was still eating, and fuming, when the old man came down again, this time wearing his bowler hat.

'You better hurry up or you'll be late for mass.'

'If I'd had some help with the milking I'd be on time.'

'Don't forget to bring some milk back to Barney Murphy.'

'Why don't you give it to him yourself when you pick him up for mass?'

'I haven't time to get it now.' Tom McDermott was heading briskly out the back door when Rosaleen came rushing into the kitchen.

'Can I have a ride to mass in the sidecar, Daddy?'

'I won't be coming home afterwards. I'm going to the gymkhana in Lahvauce.'

'I'll take the bicycle so.'

'He's a terrible man,' Kieran told her. 'He wants Barney Murphy to get milk, and here he's taking him to mass in a few minutes, but nothing will please him except that I bring the milk back to him.'

'Ah sure there's no use fighting with him. We'll all be out from under him soon, with the help of God.'

'It can't be soon enough for me.'

Brideen and Kieran went dancing that night at the Town Hall. As they shuffled around the dimly lit floor to the music of a foxtrot, Kieran told her about his failure to persuade his father to accept her plan. 'What's more, he wants us to get married at the same time as Packy and Rosaleen, so that you can take Rosaleen's place as his housekeeper.'

Brideen stopped dead in the middle of the floor and stepped away from him, as if he had just informed her he had the bubonic plague. 'And what did our brave Kieran say to that?'

'I told him what you told me the other evening: that you'd never move into the house as long as he was in it.'

She frowned. 'Maybe you shouldn't have told him that. Now he's going to hate me, and that'll put an end to any chance of your getting the place.'

'I was so mad I couldn't think. So I said the first thing that came into my head.'

She put her arms around him and started dancing again. 'Never mind. We'll get along without him.'

'I was thinking.' Their cheeks were touching.

'Good lad yourself. It always pays to think.'

'Since I'll definitely have to go to England now, maybe you'd come with me.'

She stopped again. 'You know I hate the idea of *anyone* going to that place.'

'We could get married before we go.'

'I like the idea of getting married. But we could stay here and live on my salary.'

He made a face. 'You're dead set against England, aren't you?'

'Just as you're dead set against living on my pay. Anyway, didn't you learn any history at school? About all the suffering England caused us for seven hundred years?'

'That's all in the past. We're free now, aren't we?'

'Ah but you see, we can't stop hating them for a long time yet.' She smiled at him. 'Another seven hundred years at least. Anyway, a fat lot of freedom we have if we're still beholden to the old enemy for our livelihoods.'

'Unfortunately, we need the work. And that's the only place we can get it.'

'And look at the work they give us. The kind they can't get Englishmen to do. I've heard all about it. Back-breaking labour, hauling bricks and mortar. Dangerous construction work where no one cares if you get hurt or killed. Long working hours. Crowded digs. Sharing dirty beds with strangers. The worst food – no meat except maybe a piece of cat. Ugh!'

He held her close: there was no persuading her where England was concerned. But, if they didn't go, their prospects for future happiness were bleak indeed.

7

Thursday evening, Martin McDermott, suffering from a mighty thirst, was getting ready to cycle back to Glynn's public house. His foot on the crank of the bike, he was clipping his left trouser leg when the Morris Minor turned in the front gate. 'Holy shite, I better get out of here quick.' He hurriedly clipped the other leg, jumped on the bike, and was barrelling head down for the road by the time the priest emerged from the car. He almost escaped.

'Hello there,' came from behind, as he reached the gate. He slid to a halt and turned his head, one foot on the ground. 'Oh, hello, Father.'

'If you're not in too much of a hurry I'd like to have a word.'

'Shite,' said Martin again, inaudibly of course. Audibly, he said, 'Why wouldn't I have time.' He leaned the bike against the pillar, and walked back.

'I won't keep you but a minute.'

'Ah sure there's no hurry at all.'

'And you are. . . ?'

'Martin McDermott, Father.'

'Martin.' The priest extended his hand. 'Father Donovan. I'm new here, as you probably know. Just getting to know everybody.'

'It takes time to get to know us all.'

'I came back especially to remind you about the men's triduum next week.'

'Ah yes.' What the hell was that?

'You heard me talk about it at Sunday mass, of course.'

'I did to be sure, Father.'

'But I thought it would be best if I reinforced my plea from the altar with a personal invitation to each parishioner.' The young priest gazed earnestly into his eyes. 'You *will* be coming, won't you, Martin?'

'Oh, begod I will, Father. Wouldn't miss it for the world.'

'And I expect a strapping young fellow like yourself is already seriously thinking about getting married.'

'Oh indeed. I've been thinking about it all right.' Fooking hell, he had. What kind of a gobdaw did the man think he was? Is it saddle himself with a wife and a bunch of nippers? That'd be the end of the fun for sure.

'And you have a particular young lady in mind, I suppose?'

'Ah well, nothing definite yet, Father. But I'm working on it. It isn't always easy. You know how it is with the young ladies?'

'Well that's grand. So we'll be seeing you at the triduum on Monday evening?'

'You will for sure, Father.'

'I'll let you go then. The family is at home, I suppose?'

'They are. And I'm sure they'll be delighted to meet you.'

Just as he was getting on his bike the priest called out again, 'Martin!' Shite! Shite! Shite! 'Yes, Father?'

'We'll be looking forward to seeing you at the altar with your bride in the not too distant future.' The priest waved an expansive hand in front of his expansive smile.

Austin Glynn was polishing glasses when Martin McDermott hustled into the bar. 'A pint, quick,' the lad shouted, before he had even shut the door. It was still early drinking time, with only half-a-dozen patrons present.

'Begob, you have the hurry on you of an Arab coming out of the desert.' Austin surveyed him, as he pulled the drink. 'What happened to you at all?'

'I got one hell of a shock just now.' Martin placed a hand over his heart and panted like a dog. 'It'll take a few of these to restore equilibrium, I'd say.' He took a long draught of the Guinness.

'You fell off that yoke of a bike again?' Martin was a dangerous man on that low handlebar, tail-in-the-air contraption of his. Last year he'd taken a toss at the crossroads and given himself a concussion.

'Divil a fall. But tell me, what's this triduum thing?'

'Triduum?' The word had a foreign sound to Austin Glynn.

'The priest said he talked about it at mass on Sunday.'

'Ah yes.' Austin hadn't been to mass himself on Sunday, but now he recalled fellows discussing the triduum that evening. 'If you'd been paying attention to your priest at mass instead of eyeing the girls you'd know what it was about.'

'Well, tell us.' Martin slapped his hand on the counter.

'You tell him, Ned.' Austin winked at Ned Canavan, standing next to Martin.

'Be the holy fly, 'tis you young fellows are in for it now,' Ned said.

'In for what, for feck sake?' Martin was reddening with temper.

'The priest wants all you young hooligans to get married. So he wants you up in the church on Monday night on your bended knees begging the Almighty to send you a missus. That's what you're in for, me lad. No more scamping around the countryside chasing girls, let me tell you.'

'Fooking hell!' Martin downed half his pint. 'You're pulling my leg again?'

'No codding this time, on my oath.' Ned looked around. 'Amn't I right Josie?'

'He's not fecking getting me tied to no woman.' That young man scowled into his drink. 'Josie Ryan is staying the way he is.'

'Twill be good for your business anyway, Austin.' Jack Kelly smirked. 'They'll be all flocking in here like ducks to a pond to get away from the missus.'

Austin picked up another glass and polished it with vigour. The sight of Martin and the mention of the triduum brought to the fore an idea that had been rattling around the back of his mind for some time. Though a bit wild, and said to be a wicked man for the ladies, Martin McDermott mightn't be half bad at all for Aideen. He'd have preferred a man with a bit more refinement, but that maybe wasn't to be. Anyway, Martin came from good stock, he was a fine cut of a lad, and he was heir to a prosperous farm; all in all about as favourable a match, unfortunately, as Aideen was likely to get, with her lack of good looks and her terrible temper. Though she was the apple of his eye and he wouldn't want her any other way than what she was, nevertheless he had often thought it a pity that she didn't take after the mother, who was tall and slender and a great looker in her day, instead of being the image of himself – short and round, with a crooked nose. The result was that though he had given her a fine convent education, the best clothes that money could buy, and made it known that she'd have a substantial dowry when she married, not a single suitable man had ever sought her out. Oh, there had been a few lads all right – farm labourers and poor farmers' sons in search of easy money, but not one that would get his own seal of approval even had they survived his daughter's scrutiny, which none of them had. Aideen, despite her own shortcomings, was as hard to please as if she were the Princess Royal. Tall, dark, handsome, rich as Midas, and entirely devoted to her, were the qualities a suitable husband must have. A fierce reader of romantic novels, she wanted nothing less for a spouse than young Prince Charming himself.

'Listen, Martin,' Austin said now, 'come over here a minute; I'd like to have a word with you.' He moved to the end of the bar, away from the other customers.

'He's going to hear your confession, Martin,' Josie Ryan shouted.

'Never mind that blackguard. Listen to me now.'

Martin drained his glass. 'I'm all ears, as long as there's money in it.'

'Isn't it time you were thinking of getting yourself married?'

'That's what the priest said to me just a while ago.' Martin looked into his empty glass. 'Fill her up again.'

Austin pulled him another pint. 'This one is on the house.'

'So what's on your mind?' McDermott pocketed his money. 'You haven't turned matchmaker, have you?'

'I might.' He lowered his voice so that it was barely audible. 'For my daughter.'

A wary look came over the lad's face. 'You want me to marry Aideen?'

'You could do a lot worse. She's a fine girl.'

'She is indeed.' McDermott's knuckles were white around the rim of his glass.

'And she'll bring a fat dowry to the man who marries her.'

'You don't say?' The lad lowered some more Guinness, then plunked the glass on the counter with a bang. 'How much?'

Hooked, by God! Now to reel him in. But not hurriedly; that way he'd likely yank himself free again. 'If you're interested, we can sit down and have a chat at a more convenient time. We wouldn't want to talk now with all those ears cocked.'

'Maybe I'll drop back tomorrow then, during the Holy Hour.'

'You do that.' He picked up Martin's glass. 'Have another one on the house.'

8

The following afternoon, while they were building tramp-cocks in the long meadow, Martin stuck his fork into the ground and headed back towards the house. 'Where are you off to now?' the old man shouted.

'I have to go get fags.' Since his father smoked only a pipe and his goody-goody brother didn't smoke at all, neither would have one to offer him.

'God help us,' Tom McDermott muttered. 'You and your bloody cigarettes. Well, don't take all day.'

Martin didn't answer. He'd take as long as he bleddy well pleased. This was no casual trip to get a pack of Woodbines: the entire future of Martin McDermott was at stake. Far into last night he had examined, like a jobber circling a prospective heifer, the awful possibility opened up by Austin Glynn. And all his waking hours today had been taken up with trying to decide. Here was an opportunity that could turn Martin McDermott, penniless rake, into Martin McDermott, respectable farmer and man of substance. There was a price to pay for the transformation, of course, but wasn't that always the case when something of value was offered? The question he had to answer was whether the reward was worth the cost. As if to spur him on, the old Percy French song about a farmer's offer of a heifer as dowry with his homely daughter had been humming in his head all morning.

> Now there's no denying Kitty was remarkably pretty,
> Though I can't say the same for Jane;
> But still there's not the differ of the price of a heifer
> Between the pretty and the plain.

He knew lots of pretty girls around Coshlawn Crann and Lahvauce, but not one who had the kind of money he needed. So it came down to a simple question: was marrying plain Aideen Glynn a fair price to pay for Tom McDermott's farm? Which, of course, raised the more fundamental question: did he really want the farm? *Martin, you're not a farmer, you never were a farmer, and you never will be a farmer.* The old man's words might indeed be true, but they had hurt him deeply. Especially with his young scut of a brother sitting there gloating behind that pious puss. St Kieran the good, who always did the right thing: excelled at school, worked hard on the land, never answered back, never got drunk, went to his monthly sodality, was considered the best footballer in Coshlawn Crann. Well anyway, Martin had settled one score with his racing bike: *there* was something in which he excelled that Kieran couldn't compete with. But why did people always compare him unfavourably with his brother? It was something he felt more than heard, but he knew it was there. He had seen it in the sidelong glances of old men chatting with his father at fair days in Lahvauce. He sensed it in the rough laughter of his fellow footballers that ceased when they saw him coming. It came home to him last year when a neighbour asked Kieran for a day's help with the oats, but didn't ask him. He'd never live it down if Kieran got the farm.

So that was his answer then: he had to prevent the brother from taking what was rightfully his. And he had to do something about it soon because Kieran, too, was trying to get his hands on that two thousand quid. Hadn't Martin heard him trying to make a deal with the old man on Sunday morning? He was coming down the stairs to get breakfast when he heard his brother put the question: '*Why don't you sign over the place to me, and then I'll sell two thousand pounds' worth of livestock and give you your money.*' Fortunately, the old man refused to consider that wily suggestion, but who knew what the nipper would try next?

Still, he needed to ask himself the question: was the place worth the price? Actually Aideen wasn't really a bad sort once you got past the face. And the figure. And the temper. Oh shite! He should stop right now and let Kieran have the bleddy place. Go to England and start a new life. No, he couldn't, he'd choke on the very thought. So take your choice, Martin: give in to Kieran, or put up with Aideen?

He crossed the narrow bridge that spanned the Lahvauce river, pedalled past Barney Murphy's donkey grazing on the side of the road; in a couple of minutes he'd be back at Glynn's. Then he'd have to choose one or the other. Remember that the lad in the song waited too long and lost his chance. What if he vacillated now and Austin Glynn found someone else for his daughter? Anyway, he'd had his fun with pretty girls for the past ten years, hadn't he? Maybe it was time to get married. They said that after a while you didn't notice whether the missus was pretty or not, you got so used to looking at her. Besides, who said he couldn't have fun with a pretty girl *after* he got married? Now there was a thought. So a married future mightn't be that grim after all.

The pub was a thatched lean-to against the slate two-storey house that Austin Glynn had built after he bought the place. Pub and house had originally been one long low thatched structure. Glynn had replaced the house but kept the pub intact: it would change the luck if he built a new one, the old people said. Austin Glynn had an abiding faith in the sayings of the old people.

When Martin arrived, the pub was closed for the Holy Hour. He went straight to the front door of the house and knocked. Mrs Glynn opened it. 'Is himself in?' he asked.

'I'll get him for you.' She didn't invite him in. Christine Glynn wasn't known to be a friendly woman.

Austin appeared in a minute. 'How are you, Martin? What can we do for you?' A quizzical look on his face as if Martin's presence at this time was a surprise.

'I came so we can talk some more.' He shouldn't have to explain anything after what the publican said last night.

'I'm always happy to talk to a man like yourself, Martin.' Glynn let him in. 'We can sit in the bar without being disturbed. There's no one home anyway, except the missus: Aideen is gone to town.' He winked. 'There's a lad in Lahvauce has an interest in her.' When they were perched on high stools he said, 'I'd offer you a drink only there's a new garda in town is keeping an eye on the place. It wouldn't do to get caught with a pint in your hand during the Holy Hour.'

' 'Tisn't the Guinness I came for.' He didn't like the idea that Aideen was seeing a fellow in Lahvauce. 'I've been thinking about what you said last night.'

'Ah indeed. And what would that have been?' Glynn scratched his head, as if trying to recall. 'I do say a lot of things when I'm standing behind the bar.'

'You said it was time for me to get married.'

'Did I now? Sometimes I say the damndest things. But sure 'tis, I suppose. Our new priest would think so, anyway.'

'And you said you had a fine girl waiting for me.'

'I did?'

'You were talking about Aideen.' Martin could feel the temper coming up in him.

'She's a grand girl, our Aideen.'

'And you meant it?' What was he up to anyway? Maybe thinking the fellow in Lahvauce a better prospect?

'Mind you, 'tisn't any lad I'd let her go to; I'm very particular in that regard. She's a great girl and she deserves the best. But I've had my eye on you, Martin. "Now there's a lad," I said to the missus, "that might make a good match for our Aideen".'

'I do believe I would. And I'd marry her tomorrow if I could afford it.'

Austin Glynn stared at him. 'Arrah why couldn't you afford it? Isn't Tom McDermott a rich man? Sure everyone knows he has a bundle under the mattress.'

'If he does, sorra much of it his sons get to see. But there is a way I can get him to hand over the place to me, lock, stock, and barrel.'

'You don't say?'

'Right away,' Martin added, in case the fellow from Lahvauce was serious.

'Well then, the matter is settled. Naturally, you'll need to talk to Aideen. She'll have to agree to the match, of course. And I don't know now about this fellow in town that she's gone to see.'

'There's just one hitch.'

The publican yawned. 'Sorry. I always do get sleepy this time of day.'

'My father wants money from me before he'll give me the place.'

Glynn stared again. 'Does he now?'

'And I don't have any, of course.'

'You wouldn't, I suppose.'

'You mentioned last night that Aideen will have money coming to her when she gets married?'

'I did, faith. You can't send a girl out on her wedding day without some change in her pocket. 'Twould be hers, of course, to do whatever she wanted with it.'

'In that case, I'm afraid I can't afford to marry her.' He got down off the stool.

Austin Glynn remained seated. 'How much does Tom McDermott want?'

'Three thousand.' Deciding on the spur of the moment to throw in an extra thousand for himself.

'Does he now? There isn't a hope for you then, I'm afraid. One thousand was all I had in mind for Aideen.'

'A thousand is no good. He wants three.'

The publican came down off his stool. 'Maybe if I talk to him myself he'll take fifteen hundred.'

'He won't, no, no way. But he might settle for two. Anyway, there's nothing to be gained by talking to him about it.'

Glynn continued to stare at him for so long that Martin felt uncomfortable. 'Two is more than I can really afford, but for a man like yourself I'm prepared to go the extra five hundred.'

'And the money goes directly to me?'

'That can be arranged.' Glynn held out his hand and Martin took it. 'You'll need to talk to Aideen first, of course, and get her consent.' The publican's eyebrows went up. 'Which she may or may not give you; she's a mighty particular girl when it comes to suitors for her hand.'

Martin visualized the mortified look on his brother's puss. 'I'll come back later, when she's home. You *do* think she'll have me, don't you?'

'That remains to be seen, doesn't it?' Austin Glynn took a watch from his vest pocket. 'We can drink to the hope of it anyway; the Holy Hour is over.' He shook his fist at the window. 'So you can go home now, Garda Higgins, and get pissy drunk yourself.'

9

'I'm not a happy man.'

Though it seemed to the bank manager that the remark was addressed to his companion's whiskey glass, he took the liberty of presuming it was intended for himself. 'You've shot better rounds, Fonsie. Today wasn't one of your best.'

Alphonsus Finnerty finished his glass at a gulp. 'It isn't the golf I'm out to drown, Dick. It's that bloody priest.'

'You don't say?' Dick Fogarty took a slug of his pint, then brushed his moustache with a couple of fingers to remove any lingering froth.

'Happiness, Dick, is a myth, and that's a fact now. People just pretend it's real, the way the old folks believe in fairies and leprechauns.' Finnerty raised his glass to get the bartender's attention.

'What's the problem with the priest?' The bank manager sensed a lick of scandal.

'Reality, Dick, is unrelentingly painful, so it has to be peopled with myths to make it bearable. Do you understand me? Misery is a staple of human existence.' He raised his refilled glass and sipped with closed eyes. 'It takes this stuff to survive the dissonance of an insufferable world.'

'It does, I'd say, all right, Fonsie. But 'twas the priest that made you unhappy?'

'How did you know that?' Finnerty glared suspiciously at him.

'You just said it yourself.'

'I did?' The teacher looked around the clubhouse lounge. Three men sat in a far corner, talking in low tones; otherwise the place was empty. 'Priests are the bane of Irish society; take my word for it, Dick. Bishops are worse, of course.'

'So what did the priest do to you?'

'A bloody triduum of prayer, he calls it. And demands that I promote it for him. Can you believe that?'

'Indeed.' No scandal here; just the griping of a man in his cups.

'Mind you, it's not at all, as the bloody fellow insinuated, that I'm ashamed to ask people to come out and pray. What bothers me is canvassing for something I don't believe in. As you well know, Dick, I'm not a pious man. *Au contraire*, I consider all forms of religious practice to be archaic superstitions, completely at variance with the advances of modern science.'

'I'm aware of that, Fonsie. And I disagree with you. You know that, of course.'

'It wasn't just the religious bit that bothered me, Dick. I have a particular aversion to the subject for which he's seeking his so-called divine assistance.'

'I see. And what is that subject?'

'He should know bloody better than to ask Alphonsus Finnerty to promote a triduum of prayer in support of marriage. You know how I feel about marriage, Dick, don't you?'

Was there anything more pathetic than the pleading eyes of a drunk? 'Take it from me, Fonsie – I've said it before to you and I'll say it again – you're a hell of a lot better off single than married to the wrong woman. And you're looking at a man who knows what he's talking about, let me tell you.' Fogarty finished his pint. 'I have to go home now or I'll be in worse trouble than usual.' He winked at the teacher and took his leave.

Finnerty, too, finished his drink, then shambled out of the Lahvauce golf links clubhouse and into his car. It was Friday night and time to start writing. He drove home fuzzy-brained, but cheered at the thought of his secret world: the one sane thing about the mad universe he was trapped in. He chuckled. Who, in all the parish of Coshlawn Crann, would ever believe that their crusty schoolmaster could do such a thing? That Alphonsus Finnerty, principal teacher and confirmed bachelor, could also be Laura Devon, author of such romantic novels as *Moonlight Kisses* and *Sundered Sweethearts*? He had five such sentimental sillies to his credit. And he'd have had more if the bloody war hadn't interfered with the publishing business, cutting off his market to the housewives and shop girls and factory workers of England. Now that that wretched business was over, Laura Devon would be in demand again. This weekend he was going to write the reconciliation scene of *Madeleine Amorosa*, a work in which he would scale heights of sexual boldness that had hitherto daunted him.

He'd have to hire a housekeeper again: the kitchen was filthy; the whole house was dirty. What he needed was a wife, but since he'd never been able to find one he had to settle for housekeepers. The last woman went to England a year ago and he thought he could manage by himself. But he was a terrible cook and a woeful cleaner, and his respectable house on the best street in Lahvauce was beginning to resemble the Dublin tenement of his childhood. The floor was littered with detritus of meals, old newspapers, turf mould, mud. The walls were shedding their faded paper, the ceiling was dark with smoke, the table top was stained and sticky.

He fried rashers and an egg over a cast-iron stove, cut slices from a loaf of white bread, and got a plate of butter and a jug of milk from the dingy pantry. When the kettle boiled he made a pot of tea and ate his supper. Afterwards, leaving the dishes unwashed, he went to his writing desk in the parlour.

The irony was that if had married he'd probably never be Laura Devon. Only once had he even come close to the altar – when he was twenty-six and teaching at St Patrick's National School in Dublin – and it was that particular would-be bride, a ravishing young woman who worked as an ice-cream girl at the Drumcondra Grand cinema, who gave him the idea of writing romantic novels.

'Hollywood film stars are only trotting after them, Fonsie: the heroes are such smashers and the heroines are so gorgeous; and they're all so lovey-dovey, they make me wet me knickers.'

To show what she meant she insisted on his reading a dog-eared copy of a slender paperback. He was appalled at the banality of the writing and the naïvety of the story. But when Maisie told him how popular that particular book was, the idea came to him that he could write much better himself, and maybe make some money in the process. He was a natural story-teller, the woman editor to whom he submitted his first draft acknowledged. And such a romantic soul, she added, when she accepted *For Love of his Ice-cream Girl* for publication. But though his sentimental writing wrung the hearts of his readers, and his heroes wooed and won their luscious brides, no such fortune ever came the way of their sad sack creator.

He wrote till two in the morning, then fell into his unmade bed and slept till after ten. Waking sober with a headache, he remembered Father Donovan's imposition. In school on Thursday he had managed to sidestep the issue, but what if the man should ask him point blank next week if he had canvassed? Much as he hated teaching grimy boys and ignorant girls, his profession gave him stature in the community. And though his writing alone might give him a living, he could never publicly admit to being romantic Laura Devon. So he shouldn't risk the priest manager's ire that might result in the loss of his post. He could fib, of course, but it was against his principles to do that if the lie could be exposed. On the other hand, he certainly wouldn't humiliate himself by going from house to house calling people out to pray. 'Ah, the hell with him,' he yelled to his image in the bathroom mirror. However, after wrestling some more while he made himself toast and tea he reluctantly decided to make a gesture that he could later point to if necessary. So in the afternoon he drove the Vauxhall through his allotted quarter of the parish, with the idea of stopping to chat with whomever he met and casually bringing the conversation around to the new priest and his bloody triduum. Such understatement would be more appropriate from the National School Principal than the brow-beating undoubtedly committed by his fellow teachers.

The first person he saw was a tall, powerfully built young fellow coming through a gate onto the road carrying a scythe on his shoulder. He pulled the car alongside, stopped, rolled down the window. 'Hello, young man.'

The fellow stooped to look in at him. 'Be Jasus it's you, isn't it?' He lowered the scythe, removed his cap, and scratched his head.

'Do I know you?' The lad looked vaguely familiar, but he couldn't put a name on him.

'By hell you ought to. Josie Ryan. Jesus Christ Almighty! You raised enough welts on my palms with your bloody strap, so you did.'

'It made a man of you though, didn't it, Josie?' He remembered him now, a terribly stupid boy altogether.

'Fook you, Finnerty. Take your bloody arse out of here before I swipe your fooking head off.' The fellow raised his scythe in a threatening gesture.

Alphonsus Finnerty rolled up the window, put the car in gear, let in the clutch, and didn't stop till he was safely back in Lahvauce.

10

Aideen Glynn had indeed gone to town that Friday afternoon when Martin McDermott came calling. But although she had cycled in to see a man, as her father said, the visit was by no means romantic. Timmy Walsh was more than fifty years of age, married, with seven children in family. He was the supplier of an ale not brewed by Arthur Guinness but popular with a number of Glynn's customers. Austin himself couldn't be seen talking to the man because if the word ever got back to the great brewer's salesmen that he was patronizing a competing brand of liquid refreshment, his supply of Guinness porter and stout might be severely curtailed, or even cut off altogether for a while. Aideen went to the Walsh back door by way of another back door, that of her dressmaker's shop on Sycamore Street. Her mission was to tell Timmy that a specified number of bottles were to be loaded onto a certain farmer's cart that would be left in his yard during next Monday's sheep fair. Under a covering of sacks they'd be transported to Glynn's drinking establishment in Coshlawn Crann, with no one being any the wiser except the farmer who owned the cart, himself a connoisseur of the brew in question.

Aideen returned from her mission just as Mammy was putting the evening meal on the table. They always ate at six, a custom of which the drinking clientele was well aware: it was considered the poorest of poor taste for anyone with however great a thirst to invade the premises at that hour. She had peeled a couple of spuds and was warming up to her lamb chop when her father put the question to her.

'What do you think of Martin McDermott?'

She had her mouth full, so she couldn't answer on the spot. Her mother said, 'That lunatic with the racing bicycle? Everyone says he's mad as a hatter.'

'Ah now, Christine, let the girl answer for herself.'

'Actually I think he's not a bad sort.' She'd say that anyway to spite her mother. But in fact she did rather like the wild man of Cloghmor. 'He can be great wick when he's half jarred.' And with his good looks and tall strong body he was a lad to fantasize about on the way to sleep at night.

'He came in today asking for you.'

'The nerve of him,' Mammy said.

'He said he wants to marry you.'

'That's not funny, Austin. Even by your standards.'

'He said that, Daddy? Oh my God! I don't believe you. He never said that?'

'He meant it, too.'

'Well I hope you showed him the door in a hurry.' Mammy made a face.

'Holy Jesus! Are you codding me, Daddy?'

'Aideen!' Mammy said sharply. 'Watch your language.'

'No codding, Aideen. The man is serious.'

'But why did he ask *you*, Daddy?' Suspicion replaced amazement: her father had once suggested making a match for her, so anxious was he to have grandchildren. She had scotched that idea with a temper tantrum that neither of them would forget.

Daddy chomped on a piece of meat. 'You'll have to ask him that yourself, a stor.'

'If you'll take my advice, Aideen, you'll run a mile from that rogue,' Mammy said.

Aideen could tell by the look in his eye that her father was being evasive. The thought of that blackguard approaching Daddy instead of herself – or of Daddy approaching the blackguard, which was even worse – ignited a flaming anger inside her. She stopped eating. How dare they? What was she, a heifer to be bought and sold? Only in this case it was the buyer who'd get paid: Martin McDermott would get money from Daddy for taking his homely daughter off his hands.

'How much did you offer him?'

The dad's eyes were fixed on the spud he was peeling. 'Offer? What would I offer him? I didn't offer him anything. I just told him that if he wanted to marry you he'd have to ask you himself. And he said he would. He'll come back another evening when you're at home, he said.'

She didn't believe a word of it, but there was no use saying anything more for now. By God, though when Mr Martin McDermott came to see her, if he ever did, he'd have to explain to her satisfaction why his first proposal was to her father and not to herself. Still, in spite of her annoyance, she dreamed of his coming for the rest of the evening. It wouldn't actually be the first time she'd had a proposal. There had been several

shortly after she came back from the convent boarding-school, all from
uncouth country lads urged on by fathers greedy for Austin Glynn's
money. But after she sent those lads packing, the word went around that
Aideen Glynn, though she might be no beauty, was no streel of a girl,
either, waiting to be carried off by the first gobdaw that came along. And
since then sorra lad had ever even asked her to a dance, except for the time
that Packy O'Brien took her to the Town Hall in Lahvauce a couple of
years ago. A decent poor lad, Packy, but, of course, not educated enough
for a girl like herself. Anyway, he had never followed up on that one date.

Martin McDermott was something else. A well-educated fellow and
a great talker, he had a reputation as a charmer of good-looking girls.
'Short lines and long legs,' was how she once heard a lad in the bar
describe his girl-chasing. When she asked her friend Carmel Quinn, who
had once done a line with Martin for a few weeks, what exactly that
meant, Carmel had blushed. 'I'd be ashamed to tell you,' she said.

'Ah, go on.' They were strolling up Castle Street in Lahvauce on a
Saturday afternoon, looking in shop windows.

'He likes girls with long legs. But he only does lines with them for a
short time.'

'Why? Does he get tired of them, or what?'

'Sort of, I suppose.' Carmel stopped to stare at a dress in the draper's
window.

'Why did *you* stop doing a line with him?'

Carmel blushed again. 'I heard before I ever started going with him
that if the knickers didn't come off by the third time out, the line was off.
I didn't believe it at the time, of course, but I found out that it was true.'

Well, at least he'd know what to do on the wedding night – if it should
come to that. She had heard stories at school of lads who didn't know
which side was up on their first visit to the nuptial bed. That she knew
anything about the business herself was due entirely to a girl at school
whose Protestant mother had given her a thorough run-down on the
facts of life. Her own mother had never said much about sex beyond
admonitions that boys were to keep their hands off her. Not that she ever
had a problem with that.

As a voracious reader of romantic novels she was convinced that love
was the *sine qua non* of marriage; a lacklustre suitor in *Moonlight Kisses* was
rejected because he failed to cause the beautiful heroine's heart to flutter.
So the question was, what to do if Martin McDermott should propose?
While she liked him in a casual sort of way as a cheerful lad who could
make her laugh when he'd had a few jars, he didn't cause her heart to flut-

ter. On the other hand, she wasn't a beautiful heroine, a sad fact she had come to accept, and with which acceptance had died any serious expectation of getting a decent marriage proposal. So now if she did get one, albeit from a fellow who was more of a Don Juan than a Prince Charming and whose motives were unrelated to romantic love, shouldn't she accept it? She'd have to assume that if she turned it down she'd most likely never get another. She'd live with her parents till they died, then live on her own till she, too, went the way of all flesh. Was that what she wanted from life?

She leaned towards accepting. Strongly. Loneliness, which she had already begun to experience, was a terrible state in which to live. She knew too many old maids whose lot she didn't want to share. Better a mediocre partner than none at all. Anyway, behind Martin's wildness she had often sensed a little boy wanting to be taken in hand. There was a plaintiveness in his bravado that said look at me, Mammy, aren't I great? She could tame him if she worked at it. And she would. Everybody admitted that she was a strong woman who took no nonsense from anyone. And, by God, she'd take none from Martin McDermott once they were married. There would be no more chasing long-legged girls, or drinking too many pints. She'd have his children, lots of children, and he'd settle down to being a solid provider, a faithful husband, a loving father. She'd see to that, so she would.

It was decided then: she'd marry him if he gave her the chance. But she wasn't going to let him see she was anxious. Heroines always treated suitors with pretended disdain while they tested their mettle. So Aideen Glynn was going to test Martin McDermott's sincerity before she accepted his proposal of marriage. He might be doing it for the money but he'd have to at least pretend he was doing it for love.

He came on Saturday evening. They had finished dinner and washed the dishes. Daddy was in the bar and Mammy was over in the church arranging flowers on the altar for Sunday mass. Aideen was reading a book in the parlour, when the knock came to the front door.

'How are you, Martin!' She greeted him cordially, as she always did in the bar, the only place they had ever talked.

'Good morrow, Aideen.' Though he smiled his face was strained, with a look that almost suggested fear.

She waited for him to say something more, but he stood there looking at her, as if she was supposed to know what he wanted. 'I take it you don't want to go into the pub.'

'I don't.'

'That's a surprise. Have you taken the pledge or what?'

'Do you know, I was thinking that one of these days I might do just that. But this evening I came around to see yourself.'

'Did you now?' She made no attempt to reciprocate his smile. 'What about?'

'Oh, something I'd like to discuss with you, you know.'

Despite the grin, she could see he was rattled. No doubt he expected she'd have heard of his proposal and would be fawning all over him. Well, he had another think coming. 'I suppose you better come in then.' But even the way she held the door for him bespoke her grudging permission. And when he was inside she turned her back on him and led the way into the parlour. 'Sit yourself down.' He picked the sofa, no doubt hoping she'd sit next to him. She perched on the chair furthest away.

'Lovely sitting-room.'

'It's too dark.' She was feeling better, now that he seemed uncomfortable. 'I don't like those curtains at all. But that's the way Mammy wants it.'

He stared at the curtains. 'They're a bit dark all right. So what kind would you like yourself?'

'I'd prefer something that was translucent and had a bit more colour.'

'Ah, indeed.'

'Something that would let in more light.'

' 'Twould be better all right with more light. When you have your own house you'll be able to do it whatever way you want.'

God! She had fallen straight into that trap, hadn't she? 'I'm perfectly happy where I am.' But she hated the primness of her snotty retort.

'Why wouldn't you? 'Tis a grand house.' He crossed his legs and leaned back. 'All the same, 'twould be nice to have a place of your own.'

'Would you like something to drink?' If he wanted to marry her he was going to have to ask her straight out. None of that oblique stuff, like the farmer she heard of who proposed by asking the girl if she'd like to be buried with *his* folks.

'I'm a bit thirsty all right.'

She got to her feet. 'Tea or Guinness?' She had to hold back a smile at the thought of Martin McDermott choosing tea over Guinness.

'Guinness, if you please.'

'I'll be right back with it.' At the door, she turned. 'Would you like to talk to Daddy? I can see if he's busy.' That should shake him up.

'Ah no, not at all. It's you I came to talk to.' The reddening of his cheeks reassured her that Daddy had not been pulling her leg. In the bar she pulled a pint and poured a glass of sherry.

Daddy came up behind her. 'You've got company?' She nodded, her back to him. 'I told you, didn't I? Be nice to him,' he added, as she was leaving.

She handed Martin his pint and retreated again to the furthest chair. 'Slainte.' He raised his glass in a toast.

'Health and happiness.'

'I like your frock. It's very pretty.'

'Mammy made it. I hate it. The colours are awful.'

'I was wondering if maybe you might marry me?'

She gaped at him, then exploded. 'Jesus, Mary and Joseph!' Despite her expectation, his timing took her by surprise, so that her screech of laughter was genuine rather than affected. She stood in a hurry, holding her glass at arm's length. 'You made me spill sherry all over my new frock.' She swatted the hem of her dress.

'I wasn't trying to be funny.'

'Well, I thought it was awfully funny.' She perched again on the edge of the chair. 'You're a fierce comedian altogether, so you are.'

'What's funny about asking you to marry me?'

'What isn't funny about it? Why would you want to marry *me*, for God's sake?'

'Because I think you'd make a great wife.'

'Do you now?' She was suddenly angry at him, though not knowing why.

'On my solemn oath I do.'

She stared into her glass. '*I* know I would,' she said eventually. 'But why would a Casanova like you want to marry someone like me?'

'Why not?'

'The stories I've heard about the girls you've chased, and the girls who've told me they'd love to marry you. You're up to something, Martin McDermott, aren't you?' She glared at him, but he held her gaze without blinking.

'Honest to God, Aideen, for once in my life I'm not up to anything. I want to marry you because I'm looking for a good woman who'll make a great wife; someone who'll be a kind mother to my children and a trusted companion for myself.'

'I don't believe you.'

'Don't so. But it's the God's honest truth.'

'You really want to marry *me*?'

'I really want to marry *you*.'

'What about all the other girls?'

'What about them?'

'Rita Kelly is cracked about you; she told me so herself. And she's gorgeous.' She got to her feet and looked down at him. 'Look, Martin, I have no illusions about myself; I'm short and fat and not considered a marriage prize. Not one of them lads who come into the pub has ever asked me out, including yourself. Except once with Packy O'Brien.'

'It's like this.' He stood, too. 'There's the sort of girl that's good for a coort, and there's the sort that'd make a good wife. Now, can you imagine Rita Kelly feeding pigs or carrying water from the well?'

'So that's what you want me for?'

'I'm a farmer, Aideen, and I'll always be a farmer, and my wife will be a farmer's wife. So I want a woman who'll stand by my side through thick and thin, when there's work to be done as well as when there's good times to be had.' He stared into the remainder of his drink. 'Of course, if you're not interested in that kind of life, then there's nothing more to be said.'

'You've a way with words, Martin McDermott; I'll say that for you.' She looked hard at him, as if trying to peer into the recesses of his brain. 'I suppose I'll have to give it some thought.'

'Arrah what's there to think about? What you're getting is an honest proposal of marriage from an honest man who wants to get married as soon as he can. Didn't Father Donovan himself tell me only a few days ago that it was high time I took the plunge? And I promised him I'd do my level best. So here I am, on bended knee, asking you to marry me. And I'll be taking over my father's farm as soon as I take my bride to the altar. Best damn farm in Coshlawn Crann parish, let me tell you.'

'You know, I'd *like* that.'

'You'll marry me then?'

'No. I'd like you to ask me on bended knee. That's what you said, wasn't it?'

'It was just a way of speaking, of course. But I'll do it if you'd like me to.'

'Would you?'

'I most certainly will.' He cleared his throat. 'Aideen, my love—'

'Don't forget to kneel down.' She put her glass on the table, sat on the sofa, joined her hands in her lap. 'I've always dreamed of having a man propose to me on his knees. I've seen it done that way in the pictures and it always struck me as being fierce romantic altogether. Don't you think it is?'

'It is to be sure.' He put down his drink and slid to his knees and took both her hands in his. 'Aideen, my love, my life will not be complete without you. So I beg you to make me the happiest man in the world by consenting to be my wife.'

'Jesus God!' She let a howl of merriment out of her that could have been heard in the bar. 'Clarke Gable himself couldn't have done better than that. You'd make a great film star, Martin, so you would.'

'Only I wasn't acting.' He squeezed her hands. 'I really want you to marry me.'

She took a deep breath, closed her eyes. 'I will so, if your proposal is serious.'

'I'm dead serious.' He got off his knees, sat next to her, cupped her face in his hands, and kissed her. A bit disappointing: though his lips were strong and demanding, she felt only the pressure of them. But no doubt passion would burgeon at a later stage.

'You're a powerful kisser,' she told him anyway: the heroine in *Sundered Sweethearts* had flattered her lover after she surrendered. Then she jumped to her feet. 'Let me go and tell Daddy. I'll be right back.' Daddy would be pleased as Punch. Mammy, on the other hand, would not be happy. Maybe let Daddy break the news to her.

11

At the very moment that Martin McDermott was going down on his knees to propose marriage to Aideen Glynn, his brother Kieran was inviting Brideen Conway to perch on his lap. Brideen had almost as much misgiving about complying as Aideen had about accepting. Though for vastly different reasons.

'I was at confession last Saturday afternoon,' she said.

'Did you go to the canon in Lahvauce, like I suggested?'

'I did.'

'And you told him everything, I suppose?'

'Of course.'

'And what did he say?'

She smiled. 'He didn't say a cross word.'

'Didn't I tell you? The man's as deaf as a doorknob.' Kieran patted his lap by way of renewing the invitation.

Brideen didn't move from her chair on the other side of the fire. 'But I made a promise of amendment just by going, didn't I? Isn't that what confession is all about?'

'And you did amend, too, by God. All we did last Saturday night was help the cow to calve.'

She laughed, then driven by a fierce desire for him she got up and sat on his lap. When his hands began to grope she said, 'Not here; Mammy might hear us.' She led him across the kitchen into her bedroom and closed the door. They sat on the bed and set to kissing in earnest. The pleasure and the pain were almost too much to bear. Yet when he began to unbutton her dress she forced herself to say, 'We really shouldn't be doing this, you know.' Knowing full well that there wasn't an iota of conviction in her tone.

'We won't so, if you don't want to.'

'Oh, go ahead.' She'd die if they didn't. He unbuttoned her dress down the back. She stepped out of it, slipped the galluses off his shoulders and removed his shirt. He undid her brassiere and his hands caressed her breasts. She unbuttoned his fly and let his trousers drop. He removed her knickers and stood before her to lower his shorts. But here her fear overtook her passion. 'Better leave those things on; you wouldn't want to get me into trouble, would you?' *If you don't have protection let them do everything except intercourse*, Nuala Caffrey, a rather scandalous colleague in teacher training college, had once told her. She had been shocked at the time: Nuala was a Dublin girl who liked to show how sophisticated she was. However, Brideen had recently recalled her advice and decided to follow it.

They took their pleasures then, urgently sweaty and ultimately ecstatic, after which they dressed and she made tea, and they discussed their future again. No, she would not go to England, and neither should he. However, they came to no conclusion about what they should do. At midnight, after Kieran had gone home, her residual passion still excluded guilt. This latter would come later. As would confession: she'd have to acknowledge some form of unchaste touching, even after stretching euphemism to its utmost boundaries. And then she'd have to promise not to do it any more, knowing full well that at the very next opportunity she'd be up to the same old devilment again. But how could she not? She and Kieran were daft about each other, and the more intimate they got, the more her lust for him grew. Asking her to keep her hands off him now was expecting her to deny her very nature. Which of course was exactly what was being asked of her: the church was quite explicit about it. Hadn't she been told at every retreat she ever took part in that self-denial was the key to holiness? How, then, resolve the awful dichotomy between what her body craved and what her church forbade?

She ended her interior monologue with the consoling thought that her sin would end when they married, and that she was doing her level best to make that marriage happen as soon as possible. So wasn't that, then, her promise of amendment?

Had Father Donovan, by some unholy revelation, been apprised of Brideen Conway's lustful behaviour that evening, he would have suffered not only priestly sorrow at her offence against God, but a most unpriestly jealousy at her betrayal of himself. He'd have rejected, of course, any suggestion that she was his beloved: he was a celibate priest forbidden by his vow to form any such emotional attachment. Nevertheless, Brideen Conway was now firmly nestled in the deepest recesses of his emotional being. Deny it how he might, Father Donovan was in love. For the past couple of weeks thoughts of her had been invading his idle moments, and even intruding his recital of that most priestly prayer, the divine office. Chaste thoughts of course, at least at first: recollections of her infectious laugh, her Madonna-like face, the sparkle in her green eyes. However, that very evening as he heard confessions for the men's sodality, less seemly images had forced their way into his mind, distracting him from his priestly duty: the form of her undraped flesh, the shape of her soft red lips, the sensuous sound of her laughter. As if he, like Kieran McDermott, had been infected by her tidal lust.

She was still in his mind, unsought but not rejected, when he went to bed that night. As he was dozing off in her delectable company, a loud hammering disturbed the silence. Before he could decide to seek its cause Cait knocked at his door. 'There's a sick call for you, Father.'

He rolled out of bed, lit a candle, and dressed quickly. A young man whose face was vaguely familiar, stood outside the door.

'I'm Packy O'Brien, Father. Something terrible's happened.' Even in the dim light the priest could see shock on the lad's face.

'What is it?'

'I was on my way home just now when I found Martin McDermott's bike on the road by the bridge. The front wheel was smashed in. What I'm afraid is Martin must have hit the wall and been thrown into the river.'

'Good God!'

'I went looking for him with my lamp. I climbed the wall and slid down the bank and searched for a hundred yards on both banks. But not a sign of him.'

'Perhaps he just damaged the bike and left it there and walked home?'

'Is it Martin leave his bike on the road like that? Not a chance, Father. We're always codding him that he's permanently attached to the thing, he's that fond of it.'

'So what do you think happened?'

'What I'm afraid of is that he tumbled into the river and drowned. The water is deep at the bridge and it moves fast. If he fell in he'd have been carried away very quick.'

'Was he – is he – a swimmer?'

'One of the best, Father. But sorra much good it would have done him if he hit his head on the wall on the way in. Oh God!'

Father Donovan paused a moment to think. The gardai needed to be informed. But first the young man's family had to be told. 'You didn't stop by his house, in case he might have made his way home?'

'No, Father. I thought you might be better at doing that, just in case. . . .'

'Ah!' So that was why the lad came to tell him. The priest was always the preferred person to bring bad news to a family. 'Let me get the car key.'

Packy accompanied him. At the bridge they stopped, and in the car's bright headlights they examined Martin McDermott's bike. It lay forlornly on the roadside, the front wheel buckled and one handlebar twisted out of shape.

'I always thought the wall here was too low,' Packy said. 'He must have gone flying over it.'

'You'd wonder how he could have smashed into it, though,' Father Donovan observed. 'He must have swerved just when he got on the bridge.' They put the bike into the boot of the Morris Minor, with most of it sticking out.

'Good God Almighty!' Was Tom McDermott's comment after they roused him out of bed and Father Donovan told him what they had discovered.

'He hasn't come home, I suppose?' Packy asked.

'Saturday nights he doesn't come in till early Sunday morning. But I'll check his room anyway.' The farmer returned a minute later. 'We'd best go looking for him.' He showed no emotion.

Rosaleen came racing down the stairs. 'What's the matter?' She looked from one to another, fear and bewilderment in her expression.

Packy told her, then put an arm around her when she started to cry.

'I'll take you all in my car,' the priest said.

'Wait till I get my shoes on.' Rosaleen dashed up the stairs again.

'I'll get the storm lantern.' Her father went into the kitchen.

'Where is Kieran?' Father Donovan remembered that Brideen's fiancé was brother to the missing man.

'Visiting his girlfriend, I suppose,' Packy said. 'He's always late on Saturday night.'

'Poor lad; it'll be a terrible shock for him.' But what the priest felt most at that instant was a sharp ugly jab of jealousy.

At the bridge, the light from the newly risen moon created a patchwork of shadows. Tom McDermott lit his storm lamp; Packy turned on his carbide lamp; Rosaleen had a flashlamp.

Father Donovan said, 'I suppose I better go for the gardai.'

'You do that, Father,' Tom McDermott said. 'We'll stay here and search.'

★

Aideen Glynn had gone to bed early on Saturday night so as to be out of the way when Mammy came back from the church: she didn't want to be present when Daddy broke the news of her engagement. Naturally, there was no chance that she'd sleep, with her head a babble of conflicting voices debating her impulsive commitment to marrying a man she didn't love. Though Daddy had denied it, and in the end she didn't have the courage herself to challenge her fiancé, how could she doubt that Martin had wooed her for her father's money? Why else would a man who could have any woman he chose be bothered with her? She had wanted to believe what he said about her making a good wife, but after even a moment's reflection wasn't it obvious that he was just putting her on? What really happened, of course, was that Daddy had offered the Cloghmor Lothario a mighty sum of money to take her off his hands. That realization annoyed her so much that she was tempted to leap out of bed that very minute, cycle back to his house, and reject out of hand Martin McDermott's mercenary proposal. What stopped her was her honest acknowledgment that, at twenty-five years of age with no prospect of another suitable mate, it behoved her to treat with respect any serious offer of marriage from any halfway suitable candidate, regardless of his motive. Besides, she did like Martin; he had always been pleasant to her. She even told herself that in time she might come to love the lunatic.

In the morning, she came downstairs at five to nine, groomed and dressed, ready for first mass. It was the Sunday morning ritual: her mother would be already in church and her father would be in the kitchen singing as he prepared his breakfast. This morning she felt light-headed and giddy, thrilled and terrified. She had thought of nothing since she woke except the weirdly wonderful thing that had happened: she was engaged. At one time hoped for, many times dreamt about, lately despaired of, it was now a reality. She did the last three steps in a kind of a skip.

Both parents were sitting in the parlour. Their sombre faces and downcast eyes told her she was in for it: Mammy had taken the news badly.

'Come on, Mammy.' She'd try to brazen it out. 'It's almost nine. You'll be late for mass.'

'Sit down here, Aideen.' Her father moved over on the sofa.

'Aren't you having any breakfast this morning, Daddy?'

'Come and sit with me, please. We have something to tell you.' His tone was sepulchral.

'Well, it was your idea, Daddy.' Bad enough having Mammy on her back, without him joining in.

'Something has happened to Martin.' The despondency in Mammy's voice chilled her to the marrow. She sat abruptly next her father.

'I don't know of any easy way to say this, pet.' Daddy put his arm around her shoulder. 'Martin is dead.'

She heard the words, she knew what they meant, yet they had no immediate effect. 'That's a rotten joke, Daddy.' Automatic response to the unbelievable.

'He got drowned last night on the way home. He was thrown off his bike into the river.'

As if explanation could make the impossible real. 'But he was just here . . .'

'Sweetheart.' Mammy, the most undemonstrative woman she knew, rose from her chair, slid onto the sofa, and put her arm around her.

'But he can't be.' As long as she could deny she'd keep him alive. Only when she admitted the fact would he be dead. And he mustn't be dead. He had no right to be dead. After years of despair she had found a man. And even if he wasn't Prince Charming, he was her passage to womanly pride and respectability. 'Who said he was dead, anyway?' She heard her own voice; it sounded hysterical. But she wasn't hysterical; she was just keeping Martin alive.

'I met Cait on the way into the church just now. Father Donovan was called out last night. Packy O'Brien found Martin's bike at the bridge, all smashed up and Martin was nowhere to be found. They haven't located his body yet, but the gardai are quite sure he drowned.'

Aideen broke down then.

12

Martin McDermott did not drown. Even as Aideen Glynn was mourning his loss he was lying in Josie Ryan's cowshed, on the dusty remains of last year's hay crop. Very much alive, though his clothes were damp and smelly and his belly growled with morning hunger. He had just drifted out of sleep and the memories of last night were flooding back, a confused jumble of images wrestling each other for his attention. He shook his head, as if to shut them all up.

He *had* almost drowned. That memory bludgeoned the others out of its way. The cold dark current hurtling him along, arms thrashing to no avail and he gasping for air, swallowing water, vaguely aware that this might be his last moment on earth, too shocked to feel fear. He had been flying along towards home on his sleek cycling machine, mentally reeling from the awful sin he had just committed: proposing marriage to the homeliest girl in the parish. And, what was worse, being accepted by her. How could he have done such an appalling act?

It was the distraction of this mental self-flagellation that had prevented him from spotting Barney Murphy's ass on the bridge till it was too late. He clamped the brakes and tried to swerve and struck the donkey and flew through the air. Hitting the water knocked the wind out of him. After that, all he could remember was gasping for breath, struggling for equilibrium, believing he was done for. Then, somehow, he was on the surface, swimming as he well knew how, forcing himself over to the bank despite the strong current that kept pulling him to the middle. It was the narrowness of the river that saved him: although it was deep and fast-flowing, it wasn't more than fifteen or twenty yards wide along that particular section.

He lay for a long time on the grassy bank, snorting and wheezing, looking up at the stars, waiting for the strength to come back to his shock-exhausted body. Eventually he got to his feet, still weak. And disoriented. Where was he? How long had he been in the river? How far was he from the bridge? His bike – his beloved bike – was it damaged? Shite! Curse of God on Austin Glynn and his bloody money.

He started walking, away from the river. His night vision improved, enhanced by the glow on the horizon that presaged the rising of the moon. He climbed over walls, not knowing where he was going, hoping to come across a house or a road. His soaking clothes irritated him, so he took them off, squeezed out as much water as he could, and put them back on again. A bit later, the silhouette of a building up ahead caught his eye. He walked towards it and came on a shed, in front of which stood a house. A dog barked at him, its chain rattling. Too late now to wake anyone up. He opened the door of the shed. In the dim light he saw or sensed a pile of hay, and dropped onto it. Dusty and crunchy, it was comforting to his tired, damp body.

His morning recollections were disturbed by the creak of the shed door opening. Sunlight streamed in, blinding him. He sat up. A shadowy figure crossed the threshold.

'Jesus Christ Almighty!' the figure exploded.

That voice was familiar, especially the tone of the ejaculation. 'Josie? Is that you, Josie?'

The figure backed out in great haste. The door slammed after another 'Jesus Christ Almighty!'

Martin got off the hay and followed him out. At the other end of the yard, the dog on the chain barked furiously. Josie Ryan was halfway to the back door of his house, running.

'Josie!' Martin called out again.

At the door, Josie turned. 'You're dead, Martin, you can't be here.' He bolted inside and slammed the door.

Martin, his shoes squeaking from river water, followed him and knocked on the door. 'Josie, it's me, Martin. I'm not dead, for Christ's sake. Let me in. I'm soaking wet.'

No sound from inside. He glanced at the window on the left. Josie's nose and hands were pressed against the glass, a look of terror on his face. Martin waved. 'Please, Josie. It's only me. Martin. I'm not dead, wherever you got that daft idea.' The face vanished. Martin waited.

The back door opened. Josie's head appeared. 'Is that really you, Martin?'

'Of course it's me, you eejit.'

Josie stepped out then, gingerly, as if ready to bolt again at the slightest provocation. 'Jesus Christ Almighty, Martin! I was at first mass this morning – it's the men's sodality, you know – and they said you were dead.'

'Who said I was dead?'

'The priest asked for prayers for the repose of your soul.' Josie squinted at him. 'Are you sure you're alive? You're not codding me? You always were a great codder, you know.'

'I'm as fooking alive as you are.'

'Cripes! You must be.' Josie relaxed. 'They'd never let you say *fook* if you were in Heaven, would they? Unless you were – Jesus Christ Almighty! You're not. . . ?'

'Josie, will you cop on. If I was dead how could I be here?'

'The priest said from the altar that you got drowned in the river last night. They found your bike all smashed up at the bridge.'

'Shite!' He had been afraid of that. 'How badly smashed up was it?'

'Damned if I know. They didn't say.' Josie took a step forward. 'But you're really really alive, Martin? Can I touch you?'

Martin raised his fist. 'You can touch your jaw with this in a minute if you don't cut out the *seafoid*. For God's sake, Josie, I'm wet and I'm famished. Can't you give a fellow a cup of tea at least?'

Josie let him in then, boiled the kettle and an egg, and put bread and butter on the table, all the while throwing suspicious glances at him, as if trying to decide whether he was real or a ghost. 'Mammy and Julia just left for second mass. Otherwise they'd be able to tell the priest that you're alive. Jesus Christ Almighty! Won't everyone be shocked to hell when they hear you're still with us?' Josie stretched out his hand and touched Martin's arm for reassurance.

An idea that the tea and bread had sprouted in Martin's brain came to the surface. 'So the whole parish thinks I'm dead, do they?'

'Why wouldn't they? Didn't the priest himself say it from the altar. And he had everyone praying for your eternal rest, the Lord have mercy on you.'

'Josie, do you know what?'

'What?'

'I'm thinking maybe I'm going to stay dead.'

'But you just told me you were alive.' Josie jumped up from his chair and backed away to the fireplace.

'Josie! For God's sake. I *am* alive.' He topped the egg with a spoon, scooped out the contents of the top and put it in his mouth. 'Can a fooking ghost eat a boiled egg?'

Josie came forward slowly and sat at the table again. 'I suppose not.'

'What I was just thinking was that if everyone thinks I'm dead – especially Aideen Glynn – then I'd like them to keep on thinking that.'

'Cripes, Martin, you haven't been riding Aideen, have you?' Josie chortled. 'Jesus Christ Almighty! You got her in trouble, didn't you?'

'Shut up, Josie, for a minute, will you, and listen. I've done worse than ride her: I got engaged to her last night.'

Josie's mouth sagged open. 'You didn't?'

'I did, God help me.'

'You got engaged to fat ugly Aideen?'

' 'Twas for the money that comes with her, of course.'

'Jesus, Martin, no amount of money. . . .' Then came that cunning expression that Josie could never conceal. 'How much?'

'Two thousand quid.'

'That's a power of money all right.' Trying to feign nonchalance.

'It would have got me my old man's farm.'

'Yeah, and got you married to Aideen Glynn.' Josie sniggered. 'That's what would have put me off.' But Josie's face told Martin he'd have leaped at the opportunity.

'However, since I'm dead now I can't marry her, can I?'

'Fooking right. But you won't get your two thousand quid either.'

'I'm better off this way, Josie. Marriage is a mug's game.'

'You wouldn't catch me doing it. But how are you going to stay dead?'

'I'll go to Dublin.'

'They'll be searching the river for your body today. The priest asked for volunteers from the altar. He said the gardai want the river and the riverbank searched all the way to the lake. And then if they have to they'll start searching the lake itself.'

'Even when they don't find me they'll still think I'm dead. I remember hearing of a fellow being drowned in the river years ago and they never found his body. The lake is fierce deep in spots. And they say that otters eat corpses.'

'Cripes! What a way to go? But how are you going to get to Dublin?'

'With your help, Josie. With the help of God and my friend Josie Ryan.' Martin put his elbows on the table, his head in his hands, and did some thinking. 'What I'll do is hide here till tomorrow morning. Then you'll take me to town in the cart; I'll lie down under a couple of sacks so no one will see me. At the station you'll buy me a ticket to Dublin. Then when the coast is clear I'll sneak into the train.'

'You have money on you?' Suspicion in Josie's eyes.

Martin put his hand in a damp pocket. His wallet was gone. 'Shite! It must have come out in the river.'

'So how are you going to pay for your ticket?'

Martin glared at him. 'We're talking matters of life and death here, Josie, and you're worrying about money? My friend Josie Ryan is going to lend me the price of a ticket, of course. As well as another ten pounds that I'll need till I get on my feet in Dublin.'

Josie's cry of pain startled the cat that sat purring by the fire; after glancing apprehensively at him, it jumped up and ran out the half-open back door. 'For Christ's sakes, Martin, where would I get that kind of money?'

'Josie, you know and I know and the whole parish knows that you still have the first penny was ever given you. That you have mattresses stuffed with moola. Anyway, didn't I lend you money lots of times?'

'Twice you lent me a pound. And you bloody hounded me day and night till you got it back each time, so you did.'

'There you are then; you can hound me till I pay you back.'

'How can I hound a dead man? Besides, you'll be in Dublin and I'll be here.'

'Listen, Josie: I have friends in Dublin. I'm going to make a lot of money there. And when I do I won't forget the friend who helped me.' Martin raised his right hand as if taking an oath. 'I'm promising you right now, on my solemn oath, that within six months I'll send you a cheque for a hundred pounds.' Fooking hell he would, but Josie was such a gullible gobshite when it came to money that he'd believe him. He did.

'You promise me a hundred quid?' Josie's eyes were wide with cupidinous wonder.

'I do. As long as you give me ten pounds and a train ticket to Dublin. And another thing: I need a change of clothes. These things I have on me are still damp. And they stink to high heaven from the river.'

'Ah now, I don't know if I have any clothes I could give you.' Josie's eyes were wary. Then they brightened. 'Wait a minute. There's some stuff under my bed that used to belong to my father, the Lord have mercy on him. He was about your size, wasn't he? Wait there a minute.' He hurried out of the kitchen and returned carrying a small trunk that he placed on the table and opened.

'Here's a shirt and a pair of trousers. And a jacket, by God. And his old caubeen, God rest him. His glasses, too. Cripes, Martin, if you put these on they'll think you're Michael Ryan come back from the dead.'

'They'll do.' Martin finished eating, stripped to the buff – to Josie's mortal embarrassment – and put on the deceased Michael Ryan's clothes. After he donned the caubeen and spectacles, he turned to Josie. 'What do you think?'

'By Christ, your own father wouldn't know you in them things, Martin.'

'Great!' He was getting excited about this new prospect. From total disaster he was going to reap success. 'Listen to me now: wash up all those breakfast things so your mother and Julia won't have any suspicions. And I'm going to hide out in your cowshed until tomorrow morning, so you'll need to keep them out of it.'

'There's no fear; we only milk the cows there in the winter.' Josie pointed to Martin's wet clothes. 'What are you going to do with those things?'

'Hang them up in the shed to dry. I'll be taking them with me. And another thing: I'll need something to eat later on.'

'I'll sneak a plate to you when I give the dog his dinner.'

'Don't fooking give me the dog's dinner.'

'Listen, Martin.' Josie put on his worried look, a sure sign he had encountered a thought. 'It's all very well to pretend you're dead to fool Aideen Glynn, but what about your own family? Is it fair to them?'

The same thought had been hovering on the edge of Martin's consciousness – along with some other less worthy notions about extracting money from his father.

'Let me tell you, Josie: neither my father nor my brother will miss me. And that's a fact: they don't give a damn about me. The only one that'll miss me is Rosaleen. And I'll miss her. Tell you what I'll do: as soon as I'm settled in Dublin I'll write to her and let her know I'm alive.'

'Jesus! What if Kieran picks up the letter? He'll recognize your scrawl, won't he?' Triumph in Josie's expression at having caught Martin out.

'He's not going to see it because I'll put it in an envelope addressed to you, and you'll give it to Rosie.'

'And you'll put the hundred quid in the same envelope? For Josie Ryan.'

'You can count on it, Josie. On my solemn oath.'

'Jesus Christ Almighty, Martin! You really scared the shite out of me when I saw you in the shed a while ago.'

13

Father Donovan came to the McDermott house on Sunday evening to present his condolences. On the way he meditated, *sub specie aeternitatis*, on the sad end that had befallen this young man. Just engaged to Aideen Glynn, the girl's mother told him after first mass. The ways of God were surely mysterious. Two families bereaved, another family cut off before it even got started. There was a lesson here for them all, wasn't there? A point to be made in his sermon to the young men of the parish when they came to his triduum tomorrow evening. He'd have to determine what exactly the message would be, but there certainly was one.

The mourners in the front hall and parlour were standing around with drinks in their hands when he walked in the door. Conversation, conducted in the hushed tones usually reserved for wakes and serious gossip, was quickly abandoned at his entry.

'Did you hear anything, Father?' Tom McDermott came forward to shake hands. 'Have they found. . . ?'

'I talked to one of the gardai at the bridge on the way over.' Father Donovan stared at the ground.

'They found him?'

The priest shook his head. 'No. But they found his wallet. About a mile downstream, the garda said. It was washed up on a small outcrop of rock. His name was on it, and there was money in it.'

Tom McDermott turned away to hide his emotion. Until this minute he had harboured just the faintest lingering hope that Martin might be alive. That the smashed cycle did not mean he had fallen into the river. That perhaps he had walked away from the crash, stunned, and was still wandering around in a daze. He even speculated, after hearing his son had got himself engaged to Aideen Glynn, that he might have staged the crash in a panic at what he had done and had run away: Martin was a tricky lad, capable of all kinds of stunts. But one thing that he was not capable of was throwing his wallet with money in it into the river. Tom turned and faced the priest.

'That's it so.'

'They'll search the lake next. But they have to wait for a diver and equipment to come down from Dublin to do that.'

'That damn bike!' Tom blew his nose into a large handkerchief. 'I should never have bought it for him.'

'His time had come, Tom,' Nora O'Brien said. 'If it wasn't the bike it would have been some other way. Isn't that right, Father? When your time has come you have to go.'

'God's ways are mysterious indeed,' the priest said.

In the hall, Barney Murphy was sympathizing with the bereaved brother. 'He was a grand lad, the Lord have mercy on him. You're going to miss him.'

'I am.' Kieran felt the tears coming on, so he said no more.

'Why wouldn't you? Ye were like twins, the two of you.'

'We were, I suppose,' Less than twenty-four hours since he arrived home to hear that his brother was dead, he was in too much shock to say they weren't a bit alike at all.

' 'Tis a terrible thing for a lad to die so young.'

How could he be dead who could never for a minute stand still? The epitome of life and motion. And fun and mischief. And every kind of devilment.

Josie Ryan walked in, his expression even more hangdog than usual. 'Sorry for your trouble, Kieran.' They shook hands. 'Me and Martin were great friends.'

'You were.' Kieran didn't particularly like Josie, or indeed any of his brother's friends, but this wasn't the time to show antipathy. 'He liked you a lot.'

'I don't know what we'll do without him. Glynn's will never be the same again.'

'It won't, I suppose.' Mentally, Kieran was screaming, *Josie, go away.* So he was relieved when Brideen came up behind and said he was wanted in the kitchen. He followed her through the crowd of mourners.

'I'm the one who wanted you in the kitchen.' She kept going, out the scullery door into the yard. 'I thought you might need to be rescued from Josie.'

'He may be Liam's future brother-in-law, but I have a hard time liking him.'

'At the rate things are going, it'll be a long time before he's Liam's

brother-in-law. Sorry.' She squeezed his arm. 'This isn't the time to talk about such matters.'

'All the same, things will be different now.' He choked, and the tears came. Strange: he and Martin never got along, so why was he devastated by his death?

She linked his arm and they walked towards the road. They were almost at the front gate when the Glynns' motor car turned in.

'Kieran.' Austin shook his hand with the solicitude of a grief-stricken father. 'We're destroyed to the world to hear what happened. And to think we only said goodbye to him a short time before. And he happy as Larry and looking forward to a great future. May the Lord have mercy on his soul.'

'My deepest sympathy.' Christine Glynn offered a soft limp hand.

Aideen burst into tears and buried her face in her mother's shoulder. 'She's taking it terrible bad,' her father told Kieran. 'They had just got engaged, you know.'

'Let's go in, sweetheart, and pay our respects to Mr McDermott.' Christine took her daughter by the arm and led her towards the door.

It took a moment for the information to infiltrate Kieran's brain. Then his 'What!' sounded like a cry of pain.

'Yes indeed.' Austin Glynn sounded smugly sad. 'He intended to surprise his family with the good news when he got home last night. Anyway, we'll talk some more later.' He followed his wife and daughter into the house.

'Do you believe that?' Brideen asked, as they walked out the road.

'No way. Martin would never have gone for Aideen. Didn't he tell me himself more than once that she was the homeliest girl he had ever set eyes on.'

'She'd come with plenty of Daddy's money, of course. Unlike some other girls.'

Kieran stopped dead. 'Jesus God!' He didn't know whether to laugh or to cry. 'So that was it. The bloody bugger.'

'Shush! One shouldn't speak ill of the dead.'

'But it would have worked, wouldn't it? And then where would we be?'

Brideen put out her arms and he held her tight.

Aideen Glynn and Rosaleen McDermott were good friends. They had been in the same class in the National School and had stayed close over the years. So when she was considering Martin's proposal, Aideen had to suppress a concern that her moving into the McDermott home might cause a rift in the friendship. Now, after she offered her condolences to

Tom McDermott, she found Martin's sister standing beside her.

'Let's go upstairs.' Rosaleen took her by the arm and led her up to her room.

'Here I'm doing the crying and it's your brother is dead.' Aideen tried to smile through her tears.

'I didn't know you were fond of Martin.' Rosaleen perched on the narrow bed.

Aideen sat next to her. She realized then that she was sobbing over a marriage undone rather than over a lover lost. 'We had just got engaged.'

Imperturbable Rosaleen leaped off the bed. 'You what?'

'He asked me to marry him yesterday evening and I said yes.' So simple to say, so momentous a commitment. But gone now, like last year's snow. She began to cry again.

'You're not serious?'

Would that she were lying; at least then there'd be no reason to grieve. If Martin had died yesterday morning how deeply would she mourn? 'On my solemn oath, Rosie.'

'He actually said, will you marry me?'

'He went down on his knees and said it.' In spite of her misery she had to smile at the recollection.

'Martin swore to me a hundred times that he'd never get married.'

'Between you and me, I think he did it for the money.' Dry-eyed now, feeling calm, relieved to be able to say what she thought.

Rosaleen sat on the bed again and stared at the ceiling. 'The bloody bugger. Daddy told himself and Kieran that whoever came up with two thousand pounds first would get this place.'

The energy drained from Aideen, even the strength to cry. Despite her conviction of his mercenary motive, up till this moment she had retained a fraction of a belief that at least a dram of romance had driven him. 'So that's what it cost Daddy to get rid of me?'

Rosaleen's arm was around her. 'I'll tell you this much about Martin: if he had married you I guarantee he'd have been the best of husbands. Some people didn't like him because they thought he was never serious about anything. But I knew him better than anyone else in the world.' She removed her arm and began to cry softly. 'I'd have run away from here a long time ago if it weren't for him. Daddy can be terribly cross at times, but whenever he'd start giving out to me Martin would always take my side. Kieran wouldn't: he's too much afraid of getting on the wrong side of Daddy. But Martin didn't give a hoot.' She covered her face with her hands. 'Oh God! I'm going to miss him!'

★

'They just got engaged,' Austin Glynn told Tom McDermott.

'Who got engaged?' Tom's tone was sharp. He didn't much like Austin Glynn.

'Martin, the Lord have mercy on him, and our Aideen.'

'Is that a fact?' Tom McDermott grasped the logic of Martin's deed immediately, so his reaction was annoyance with his deceased son for failing once again. Annoyance at Martin seemed to be his chief emotion ever since he had heard of his drowning last night. So much promise, so little fulfilment. And now he was gone forever.

'Poor Aideen, needless to say, is fierce distraught altogether.'

'She would be, the creature.'

' 'Tis a terrible blow to yourself, of course. Losing your right-hand man like that.'

'Come on down to the kitchen and I'll get you a drink.'

Ned Canavan was helping himself to whiskey from a bottle on the kitchen table.

'I'll have a Tullamore,' Glynn said. Tom poured whiskey into two short glasses.

'Eternal rest, grant to him, O Lord.' Ned Canavan raised his drink in a toast.

'And let perpetual light shine upon him,' the publican responded.

'He was a fine lad. May he rest in peace, the Lord have mercy on him.'

'He was. We won't see his like again.' There was an awkward silence then. Austin Glynn tasted his drink. 'Mind you, there's nothing like the Tullamore.'

'I prefer the Powers myself,' said Ned. 'It has more of a sting to it. But the Tullamore's not half bad either.'

'Martin was a great man for the Jameson. He always liked his half one after a couple of pints.'

'He did. A great footballer he was, too. He'll be sorely missed by the Coshlawn Crann team.'

'Indeed he will. He was a son any father could be proud of.'

'Ah, he was. And a lad any father would be proud to have his daughter marry.'

'But his preference was always for the Guinness. You could put the whole world of drinks on the counter in front of Martin and his hand would reach out for the Roman collar every time.'

'The racing bike was his favourite, I'd say. He was never more at home than with his head down and his tail in the air and the legs flailing like a thresher and he going like the wind.'

'He was. Will you ever forget him at the Coshlawn Crann sports the year before last? And he up against the Castlebar fellow that had won every prize in the county. Faith, he was no match for Martin that day, let me tell you. Two lengths he beat him by. And the first prize of two pounds.'

'He did. But sure it wasn't the money he was after at all. 'Twas the thrill of competing, of proving he was the better man. Martin was never a man for the money, I'll say that for him.'

'He wasn't indeed. Not a bit. He was the most generous man you could meet.'

'I better go back to the parlour; they'll be looking for me.' Tom McDermott was suffocating.

It was late, most of the mourners had left, and Tom McDermott was bone weary. He was looking forward to bed when Packy O'Brien came up to him. 'There's something you should know,' the lad said, in a tone just above a whisper.

'There is? And what would that be?' He liked Packy, a sensible hard-working young man.

Packy looked around, as though to see if anyone else could hear. 'When I found Martin's bike lying on the road last night, Barney Murphy's ass was lying beside it. I had to prod him to make him get up. And when he walked away he was limping something fierce.'

'Was he indeed?. Why do you think that was?'

'It's my belief that Martin didn't see the ass on the bridge and ran into him.'

Tom McDermott was silent for a bit. 'Listen to me now, Packy: we'll keep that bit of information to ourselves, you and me. You understand? Not a word about it to anyone. We can't bring Martin back, so we can't, and there's no point in getting poor old Barney into trouble over it.'

'I was thinking the same myself. That's why I mentioned it only to you.'

14

Sunday was interminable for Martin. A cramped, hungry, thirsty, miserable, uncomfortable day. Confined to the cowshed, he sat, stood, paced, griped, peered through a crack in the door, listened for sounds of approaching footsteps. Josie came by in the early afternoon.

'Where's the plate? Where's my dinner?'

'Christ, Martin, how do you expect me to fill a plate for you with those two women there?'

'You want to starve me to death?'

'I'll bring you the dog's dinner if you want – Julia is getting it ready now.'

'You're a hell of a friend.'

Josie put his hand in his jacket pocket and pulled out two spuds. 'That's the best I could do.'

'And you expect a hundred quid for this?' But Martin's disgust was overpowered by hunger, so he peeled the spuds with his fingers and ate them. As Josie was leaving, he said, 'I have a terrible thirst; do you think you could get us a bottle of Guinness?'

Josie came back with a saucepan of water. 'There's your Guinness for you. It was meant for the dogeen.'

He came again in the evening with a hunk of bread, and the expression of a worried man. 'I don't know what I'm going to do about getting you out of here.'

'What's the matter?' Martin tore into the dry bread.

'The ma wants me to cut the hay in the long meadow in the morning, and I can't think of any bloody excuse for going to town in the cart.'

'You could go to the bog, couldn't you?' He knew the Ryans cut their turf on the other side of Lahvauce, in a bog owned by Josie's uncle.

The look of relief on Josie's face was comical. 'Jaysus, Martin, you're a bloody genius. I never thought of that.'

'I need to get the noon train. So don't be late.'

'Be over in the hayshed before anyone gets up,' Josie told him. 'Hide under the tarp in the cart. I'll be out as early as I can.'

'Don't forget my ten pounds. And bring me some breakfast, for God's sake.'

The sun was low in the eastern sky when, still dressed in Michael Ryan's clothes, including caubeen and glasses, he tiptoed across the yard to the hayshed. He had bundled his own clothes into a sack he found draped over a stall. The dog barked at him a couple of times, but stopped on being petted. Martin stretched out under the tarp beside the horse cart and went to asleep again. He was awakened by the hens; several minced into the shed, cocking their heads and clucking huffily. He stayed still so as not to annoy them: frenzied fowl could bring the women out to see if there was a fox on the prowl.

Shortly after, he heard footsteps crossing the yard: not Josie's heavy clump but the light brisk steps of a young woman. Julia no doubt, and heading in his direction. He pulled the tarp over his head again.

'So where are you hiding your eggs this time, missy?' He heard her poking around the shed, then her cry of triumph. 'There they are! Three, no less. See! You can't hide them on your Aunt Julia.'

She passed so close that he heard the crunch of her shoe on the edge of the tarp. He peeked out after her. Nice ankles. Not beef to the heels like so many country girls. Pretty, too. And fierce stuck-up – he had never been able to entice her for a date. But plenty of women in Dublin: they said half the girls of the country were up there and that there weren't enough men to go around. Jesus!

Still contemplating this delightful future, he heard the clack of horse's hoofs. He slid out from under the tarp. Josie led his brown garron into the shed. From a bucket he was carrying he took slices of buttered bread, a hard-boiled egg, and a bottle of water.

'That should keep the hunger off you for a while.'

'Where's the ten quid?'

Josie pulled two five-pound notes out of his pocket. 'You're not going to forget my hundred, are you?'

Martin grabbed the notes. 'Don't worry, you'll get your money.'

While Josie harnessed the horse he downed his breakfast. Then he stretched out in the cart and Josie covered him with the tarp. They set off for Lahvauce.

'I went to your wake last night,' Josie told him, as they lumbered along the road. 'It was great wick altogether.'

Martin stuck his head out. 'How could they wake me without me?'

'All the people that were searching the river for your corpse came by. They had lashings of booze. Ned Canavan got drunk praying for the repose of your soul. Aideen Glynn was crying her eyes out, telling everyone she had just got engaged to you.'

'I didn't die a minute too soon, did I?'

'Be Jaysus, Martin, you scare the shite out of me every time you talk about being dead. 'Twas bad enough at the wake, listening to everyone saying what a grand lad you were, the Lord have mercy on you.'

'I'd love to have been there to hear that.'

'You wouldn't know yourself. Austin Glynn and Jack Kelly making out to your father that you were almost a fooking saint. Of course they had a power of Tom McDermott's booze in them at the time.'

'I was just thinking last night what a wonderful thing it is to be dead. I mean, you look at the world in a different way.'

'But you're not dead, Martin. Dead men don't need breakfast. Or ten quid. And they don't complain about what they get for dinner.'

'All the sins of my past life are gone. Just like that.' Martin snapped his fingers.

'You don't have to go to the bloody bog either so you can put them on the train for Dublin.'

'And I'm not in Hell. And I'm not in purgatory. Cripes, Josie! Maybe I'm in Heaven. Do you think I'm in Heaven?'

'You're in my bloody cart so you are, on your way to Lahvauce. And then you're going to Dublin. And out of my life for good. Fookit, I hate to see you go. Do you know that? Who else is there round here that's good for a decent bit of blackguarding.'

'When I get to Dublin, Josie, I'm going to be a man without a past. Nobody will know me, or where I came from. I—'

'Hey! I thought you said you had friends in Dublin who were going to help you make a power of money? Where the fooking hell is my hundred quid coming from?'

'Well, of course, my one good friend in Dublin is going to help me make a lot of money, including a hundred pounds for my friend, Josie Ryan. But I can trust him to keep his mouth shut.'

'You can trust Josie Ryan, too. As long as I get that hundred – Jesus Christ Almighty, Martin! Get your bloody head back under the tarp. Nora O'Brien is up ahead on her way to town, and sure as shooting she'll be asking for a lift.'

'Just wave to her, and keep going.'

Nora, however, had other ideas. She stood in the middle of the road until the horse stopped. 'Well, if it isn't yourself, Josie. I was just beginning to lose hope of ever getting a lift. There's nobody at all on the road this morning.' She hauled herself up on the opposite side of the cart from Josie, with her legs dangling. 'Is it going to town you are?'

'Ah no, Mrs O'Brien. What would I be going to town for on a Monday morning? I'm going to the bog to foot some turf, as long as the weather is fine.'

'You'll be passing through town anyway. So you can drop me off at Walsh's grocery.'

'I will to be sure.'

Without so much as a pause the woman continued, 'Well, wasn't it terrible sad altogether about poor Martin McDermott? The Lord have mercy on him. What an awful thing to happen to him.'

'It was indeed. Martin and me were good friends.' Josie raised his voice. 'The nicest lad in the world. I'll say that for him.'

'He was, I suppose.' Nora coughed gently. 'But between you and me, now, Josie, and I know he was your friend and all that, and it isn't right to say anything bad about the dead, they say, but all the same now, just between the two of us, Martin was a bit of a scamp, wasn't he?'

Josie coughed, too. 'He was maybe a biteen wild, I suppose. Mind you, I had no part meself in any of his blackguardism. Josie Ryan sticks to the straight and narrow, as the priest says.'

'Why wouldn't you? Everyone says what a decent lad you are. My own Packy has often said it to me. But sure 'twas chasing the girls was the ruin of poor Martin, wasn't it? That's what they say, anyway. He couldn't keep away from them, you see. Or keep his hands off them, from what I've heard.'

'That's what they say, all right, ma'am.'

'And the drink. Mother of God! They say he'd drink the Lahvauce river dry if it was made of Guinness.'

'Ah now, he wasn't too bad at all in that respect. He liked his pint all right, but then, don't we all?' Josie let out a stupid screech of a laugh that set Martin's teeth on edge.

'Packy is a Pioneer. I made sure of that the minute he turned fourteen. Not a drop of drink ever passed his lips. And won't either, he says, if he lives to be a hundred.'

'Ah, sure the odd pint never did a man any harm.'

The conversation dragged on, from the merits and demerits of drink, to the possible present whereabouts of Martin McDermott's corpse, and soul, to the chances of the fine weather holding up till the hay was saved, to the possible effectiveness of Father Donovan's prayer crusade to get the young people of the parish married.

'You'll be going to the altar yourself one of these days, I suppose,' Nora said.'

'Is it me?' Josie emitted his frightful screech again. 'What the – what would *I* want to get married for? I couldn't, anyway, until I get Julia out of the house.'

'You couldn't, I suppose. Our Packy is in the same fix: we won't let him bring a girl into the house until Teresa gets married out.'

Martin barely restrained himself from sitting up and scaring the shite out of the old windbag. His body was aching from his cramped position and the jolting of the cart. At last they stopped, and he heard the hag say, 'Thanks a lot, Josie.'

A few minutes later, Josie dropped him off at the station.

It was after six when the train pulled into Westland Row. Starving, he went into a restaurant nearby and spent three and sixpence on a feed of rashers and eggs. He had of course lied to Josie about having a friend in Dublin who would make him rich. The only person in the city whose address he knew was his cousin Clare, a writing assistant in the civil service. She had a flat on Dargle Road in Drumcondra. He made enquiries of a garda at a street corner and got directions.

'It's only a couple of miles if you want to save on bus fare,' the guardian of the law told him. Martin walked. It was a long couple of miles. Before he knocked at the door of the small one-storey row house he removed caubeen and glasses.

The pretty young woman who answered wasn't his cousin.

'I'm looking for Clare McDermott.'

'And who are you?' She was tiny, with an accent that wasn't from Mayo.

'I'm Clare's cousin, Martin.'

The girl's eyes opened wide. 'You must be a ghost then. Didn't Clare just get word that her cousin Martin was drowned last Saturday night.'

'Would you ask Clare to come out. Please,' he added when she seemed reluctant.

'Clare! There's a fellow out here says he's your cousin Martin.'

Clare appeared in a jiffy. When she saw him her hand went to her mouth. 'Oh my God, Martin! Aren't you supposed to be dead?'

'I'll explain if we can go somewhere and talk.'

The women looked at each other. 'Come in.' Clare led the way into a tiny parlour that had books and papers and shoes scattered about.

'Sit down.' The sofa had seen better days. His cousin sat on a wooden chair. The other woman had disappeared. 'So what's going on?' Clare would have been a great-looking girl if her nose wasn't a tad too long.

'It's complicated.' It took him some time to tell the story, with all the questions she asked. When he finished, she laughed so hard that the pipsqueak, and a third woman – a tall skinny girl with yellow hair – appeared in the doorway to see what was going on. Clare gave them a summary of his story. The girls thought it was awfully funny, too, though their laughter was polite.

'So what brings you here, Cousin ghost?' Clare asked eventually.

'I need a place to stay till I find a job and get on my feet.'

'Well, you're not going to stay here.' Clare stood. 'Girls, you're looking at the biggest rake ever to come out of County Mayo. Alive or dead.'

'I won't give you a bit of trouble. Honest.'

'You won't because you won't be here.'

'But you can't throw him out on the street, Clare,' the tiny one said. 'Anyway, not at this time of night. After all, he is your cousin.'

'Yeah,' the skinny one chimed in. 'Let him stay. We'll make sure he behaves.' She brandished a bony fist. 'See those knuckles? They've put many a lady-killer in his place, let me tell you.'

So Martin was allowed to sleep on the parlour floor, but only till he found a job and digs – which, Clare said, had better be soon. And on condition that he didn't so much as look crooked at any of them.

'You take one step out of line,' his cousin threatened, 'and everyone in the parish of Coshlawn Crann will know you're alive.'

15

Father Donovan and his teachers had done their promotion work well. The church was more than half full on Monday evening when the priest, preceded by his servers, processed onto the altar, clad in festive white cope and carrying the monstrance. After exposing the Blessed Sacrament and paying It due homage with clouds of incense, he began the rosary.

Kieran McDermott's mind wandered as he uttered the rote responses. How he'd survive without Brideen when he went to England, he couldn't imagine: it was their weekend trysts that gave him the patience to endure the indefinite postponement of marriage. He'd give anything not to have to go, but what was the alternative? He didn't share Brideen's hope that Martin's death might change the old man's mind. There was no softness in his father, no claim of love or pity that would be likely to move him. He had been hard on his sons growing up, more demanding still on Rosaleen. Work and responsibility were all he ever understood: there was never time for play or the gentler emotions. 'It's a hard world,' he used to say, 'and you have to be hard to survive in it.' Which was why he had turned against Martin when his eldest leaned towards pleasure rather than work.

It was inconceivable that Martin could suddenly have vanished as if he never had been. Never again to be seen speeding back the road on his racing bike, pedalling furiously, jacket streaming. Or wandering in at night just after they'd finished the rosary, expressing tongue-in-cheek regret that he had missed it. He was gone forever. But where did he go? Was the real Martin somewhere at this moment? Was he conscious? And if he was, how did he feel now about those taunting jibes he loved to throw at his younger brother?

You've got to get what you can out of life because if you don't, no one else will get it for you. Or, *I don't believe in Hell,* which he had said more than once when Kieran was on his way to Sodality night confession. Was it possible that he was in Hell himself this minute? Or was he right when he said, *I can't believe that a good God would make me burn forever just for cuddling a girl.* His brother's way of thinking had shaken Kieran's own faith, so that he had got out of the habit of monthly confession. But now in this atmosphere of faith and devotion, the fear of damnation swept him anew.

'Last Thursday evening I spoke to a young man named Martin McDermott about our crusade of prayer,' Father Donovan began his sermon. ' "Will we be seeing you at the triduum on Monday evening?" I asked him. "I wouldn't miss it for the world, Father", he told me.' The priest paused. 'Martin McDermott intended to get married; he told me so himself. Almighty God, in His wisdom, did not see fit to give him the opportunity. But He has given that chance to you young unmarried men here tonight. Avail yourselves. . . .'

'Cripes, but isn't talk mighty cheap?' Liam Conway said afterwards outside the church. 'The way your man was spouting in there you'd swear to God that all we had to do was get off our arses and walk down the aisle and we'd all live happy ever after.'

'He means well, I suppose.'

'But totally clueless, the poor eejit, about the world the rest of us have to put up with. Look at the mess you and I are in, for Christ's sake! *You* can't marry Brideen because you don't have money, and *I* can't marry Julia until you two get married.'

'I'll try my father again. Though I don't have much hope.'

'Tell me,' Liam said in a very low tone – they were standing at the church gate – 'is it true that Martin was going to marry Aideen Glynn?'

'It appears so. Martin, as you know, would do anything for the bit of money.'

'They say the fellow that marries her will be in clover, all right.'

'That may be, but would *you* marry her?'

'By hell no. Apart from her looks, that girl has a temper that'd set the house on fire. God only knows what Martin would have done with her after he spent the money.'

Kieran looked quizzically at his brother-in-law to be. 'Didn't Brideen tell you? We figured he was going to give Aideen's money to the old man so he'd get the place.'

'Bloody hell! Of course. By God, you two would be in a right pickle then.'

'So I was just thinking: if you'd marry Aideen now, and give her money to Brideen, our troubles would be over.'

'And I'd be joining Martin, God rest him. Julia Ryan would throw me into the river.'

'That might be another solution.' Kieran was feeling giddy. 'You tell Julia you're going to marry the wan. She drowns you, and Brideen and I get your place.'

Brideen stewed on their predicament. Damn De Valera's government and its backward policies that kept them poor. Father Donovan, God bless him, was sadly mistaken in thinking Dev's dream was what the country needed. How could we say we were free while we were still going hat in hand to the old enemy looking for work? Thinking of Father Donovan, however, gave her an idea. She went to his house after school.

'He's in,' Cait told her, 'but I think he might be saying his breviary. And he doesn't like to be disturbed when he's at his prayers.' She padded off and came back in a few seconds. 'He's at the breviary all right, but he said he'll see you anyway.' She smirked. 'You must be an important person.'

'Brideen!' Father Donovan greeted her as if she were the archbishop himself. 'Come in, have a seat. You did a great job with the visitation; almost every man from your quarter of the parish attended.'

'Thanks, Father. But listen: I told you Kieran and myself are planning to get married.'

'You did indeed. A fine young man, Kieran.'

'We were hoping the father would hand over the place to him.'

'And are your hopes being fulfilled?' The eyebrows went up in what seemed happy anticipation.

'Unfortunately not. Tom McDermott is the biggest skinflint this side of Hell.'

'I haven't talked to the man yet, other than a few words at what they called the wake.' Father Donovan's expression switched to utmost solemn. 'No success in the search for the body, I suppose?'

'Not that I've heard of. Anyway, Father, the only person Tom McDermott cares about is Tom McDermott. His one surviving son could starve for all it matters to him as long as he gets what he wants. He'd let you die on the side of—'

The priest put a finger to his lips. 'It behooves us not to judge our fellow men too harshly.'

'Sorry, Father. But he wants Kieran to give him two thousand pounds before he'll hand over the farm.'

'Does he indeed? And where would Kieran get that kind of money?'

'He'd have to go slave in England for at least five years. Maybe longer.'

The priest shook his head. 'You know how I feel about people going to England.'

'Me, too, Father. So I was wondering if maybe you'd have a word with Tom. He might listen to you.'

Father Donovan hesitated before he said, 'I'll be happy to do that.'

'You're a brick, Father. I knew I could count on you.'

The priest grimaced, as if swallowing something distasteful. 'So what do you think is the best approach? An appeal to his better nature?'

'That man doesn't have a better nature. Give him your hell and damnation sermon.'

After Brideen left, the buzzing in Father Donovan's head became a cacophony.

Of course you'll talk to Tom McDermott, Reason stated stoutly.

You're asking me to make the supreme sacrifice, Lovelorn wailed.

You're jealous, you bloody bugger, aren't you? Could there be anything more pathetic in the whole world than a jealous celibate?

I just don't want her to marry Kieran.

Well, you certainly can't marry her yourself, you miserable eunuch.

But at least if he goes to England, Kieran will be out of the way.

Out of whose way?

Mine. If I can't have her, nobody else should either; she should join me in holy celibacy, rather than unite with Kieran in carnal marriage.

Listen, you selfish oaf: if you don't persuade Tom McDermott to hand over the farm, you'll be sending another Irishman to England. You'll be preventing another marriage from taking place. You'll be failing Ireland and De Valera. Not to mention Almighty God who needs more souls to people Heaven.

But if. . . .

No buts or ifs. You have to genuinely try to persuade Tom McDermott to hand over the farm to his son.

He dragged himself there late that evening. The farmer answered the door. They sat in the parlour and discussed the weather. Then Tom went to the sideboard. 'You'll have a drop, Father?'

He knew he shouldn't but, reading the challenge in the eye of his host, he said, 'Just a little.' A teetotaler in the seminary, during post-ordination celebrations he'd been introduced to alcohol and discovered an immediate, possibly dangerous, affinity for the stuff. 'Terribly sad about poor Martin.'

'Foolish lad.' His host offered him a generous glass of whiskey and raised his own in a toast. 'May he rest in peace.'

'Amen.' The smell, the taste, the burning sensation: a magic potion indeed. 'Any news about. . . ? I mean they haven't found. . . ?'

'No. Sergeant Kelly came around today. He said there isn't much hope now. The lake is very deep where the river flows into it.'

Father Donovan murmured sympathy and sipped his whiskey to bridge the silence. 'You're fortunate to have such a fine son as Kieran.'

'He's a good farmer; I'll say that for him.'

'A grand lad. I had a long chat with him when I was here last week.'

'I was out myself that night. I go down to give Barney Murphy a hand most evenings; the poor man doesn't get around too well any more. We have a duty to help our neighbours, the Man Above tells us.'

'Speaking of which, Kieran tells me he's planning to get married.'

'He's talking about it.'

'His fiancée told me they're ready to go to the altar as soon as you sign over the place to Kieran.'

Tom McDermott smiled. 'I'm afraid they'll have a wait for that. I have my own needs to take care of. A man's first duty is to himself. Isn't that right, Father?'

Father Donovan put down his glass; it was time to deliver his prepared sermon. 'I'm reminded, Tom, of the story in the Gospel about the rich man and Lazarus. And the Lord's admonition: *what does it profit a man if he gain the whole world and suffer the loss of his own soul?*'

Tom McDermott smiled again. 'And I'm reminded, Father, of the story about the king who gave away his kingdom to his daughter, thinking she'd take care of him in his old age. She didn't. She was terribly nice to him until she got what she wanted, but she didn't give a damn about him after that. Let me tell you, Father, that's not going to happen to me. I told Kieran he can have this place – farm and house and livestock – as soon as he provides me with what I need for my old age. I think that's a fair bargain.'

'From what I've seen of Kieran and Brideen, I'd be quite sure you can trust them to take care of you in your old age. Just as you're taking care of Barney Murphy.'

Tom McDermott finished his whiskey and reached for the bottle. 'Have another drop, Father. The *Farmers' Almanac* said it would be a wet summer and I'm afraid they're right. 'Twill be a sorry year for the crops.'

On his weekly visit to the school, Father Donovan told Brideen about his visit to Tom McDermott. 'I'm afraid your assessment was all too accurate.

Asking him to accommodate you was like appealing to the good nature of a stone wall.'

There were tears in Brideen's eyes. 'I won't be able to stop Kieran from going to England, then.'

Father Donovan repressed an unworthy buzz of elation at that prospect.

16

Most Saturday afternoons Brideen Conway and Julia Ryan, good friends since their earliest schooldays, went grocery shopping together in Lahvauce. Brideen would cycle over to Julia's house and they'd ride in together. Those outings were opportunities for discussing recent events and neighbours' antics, and for venting frustrations about the shortcomings of their nearest and dearest. Brideen's principal cross was her invalid mother, who demanded more time and attention than her daughter could afford to give, and who scowled and banged her cane on the floor when she didn't get immediate service. Julia's mother was an easy-going woman, but her brother Josie was, Julia said frequently, a royal pain in the arse. Nothing she ever did would please him: her cooking was terrible; his clothes weren't washed properly, she never did what he told her. He made no attempt to hide the fact that he couldn't stand the living sight of her. 'I wish to God you'd get married and get the hell out of here,' was his favourite chant. Worst of all, the mother never scolded him for ill-treating his sister: he was her favourite child and Julia was the odd third.

'God help the woman he'll get,' Brideen said, the Saturday after Martin drowned, when she heard her friend's latest complaints.

'Arrah, who in God's name would marry that amadhan?'

'Some poor eejit of a girl might have him. Won't he come into the place after you get out?'

'Sooner if he gets married, according to Daddy's will. Mammy has been telling him this for years but he won't do anything about it.'

'Doesn't he like girls? I'm told there are lads who don't.'

'He likes them all right, only he's afraid of making a fool of himself with them.'

'I don't know why: he's a good-looking amadhan.'

'He's a— Never mind.' Julia suddenly pedalled ahead so furiously that Brideen had trouble catching up with her.

'What's the matter?'

Julia slowed. 'The bugger tried to practise on me when we were younger.'

'Jesus, Mary and Joseph!' Brideen almost swerved into the bank. 'Julia! You can't be serious?'

'Why do you think he can't stand the sight of me?'

'You never told me.' Accusation in her tone: they weren't supposed to keep secrets from each other.

'To tell you the truth I was ashamed. And, of course, I was dead afraid to tell Mammy: you know how thick that pair are?'

'I knew a girl in Dublin it happened to, only it was her father. Can you imagine?'

'Josie didn't actually *do* anything. Though it wasn't for want of trying. The first time he went after my knickers I managed to get away – I could always run faster than him. The second time he pushed me up against a wall in a field and said "I'm going to do you now". So I gave him a knee in the balls. He never tried again.'

'This girl said she never got over it. And that she'd never get married.'

'Anyway, it's no fun living with Josie.'

Brideen couldn't think of anything positive to say to that, so they rode the rest of the way without further talk. The silence gave her time to think about her own marriage problems. Which was how it came about that as they were getting off their bikes at Walsh's grocery shop an idea struck her, so outlandish that she decided not to tell Julia about it for the time being. They ordered their groceries and chatted with other shoppers while Timmy Walsh, a silent man who breathed heavily through his moustache, parcelled their purchases.

Afterwards, as they pedalled up Main Street past the church, Julia said, 'No confessions today?' She knew Brideen had begun confessing to Canon McCarthy.

'Once a month is enough. I'm tired telling all about my wicked life.'

At the Cornmarket, they went into Mary Forde's tea shop. 'The usual?' the proprietress asked, and brought them tea, scones, butter, and strawberry jam.

'I'm desperate to get married,' Brideen said, as Julia put sugar and milk in a cup. It came out more as a blurt than the calm statement of fact she intended.

'Me, too.' Julia poured for Brideen.

'Are you and Liam. . . ?'

Julia put sugar and milk in her own cup and poured. 'Are we what?'

'You know. I mean do you. . . ?'

Julia looked at her. 'You mean do we engage in the unmentionable?'

'Yes.'

'No, we don't.' Julia cocked an eyebrow. 'Do you and Kieran?'

Brideen blushed. 'Sort of.'

'What do you mean sort of? You do or you don't.'

'Sort of we do some things, but not the thing that could get me into trouble.'

'Do you take your clothes off?' But Julia immediately raised her hand. 'No, don't tell me; I don't want to know.'

'So what do you and Liam *do*, if you don't mind my asking?'

'A lot of kissing and cuddling. With our clothes *on*.'

'Don't you find it hard not to go any further? I mean, you've been going out for a couple of years now.'

Julia put down her tea and folded her arms. 'Honest to God, Brideen, there are times when I could scream with the frustration of it all.'

'I know what you mean. Which is why. . . . As well be hung for a sheep as a lamb, I tell myself.'

'Me, too. I'd strip to the buff any time. Only Liam is afraid.'

'Do what we do: everything except what would get you into trouble.'

'Liam is afraid of hell fire, not of getting me pregnant.'

'So am I, but some things are worth the risk.'

'Not to your pious brother they're not.'

'Anyway, we have to get married. All of us.' Brideen banged on the table with her spoon.

'But how?' A trace of sob in Julia's tone.

'Listen. I had this ridiculous idea when we were going into Walsh's a while ago. I don't know if it would work.'

'I'll try anything.'

'You heard about Martin McDermott getting engaged to Aideen Glynn?'

'Liam told me.'

'Did you hear about the dowry her father was giving them?'

'Yes. And I heard, too, about Kieran suggesting that Liam marry Aideen and give the money to you pair. Hah hah!'

'That's what gave me the brilliant idea. Listen to this: supposing Josie were to marry Aideen? And give you her dowry to get you out of the house. Then you could marry Liam and give your dowry to me to get me out of the house. And Kieran and I could get married and give the dowry to blasted Tom McDermott and get him out of the way.' She smiled in triumph. 'What do you think of that?'

Julia chortled. 'You're funny.' She bit into a scone.

'Well, what's wrong with it?'

'Oh, it's a brilliant idea all right. But it wouldn't work. Josie won't marry anyone, not to mind Aideen Glynn.'

'He might if he had enough incentive.'

'He likes the money sure enough, but I don't think he'd want it badly enough to go for Aideen.'

'On the other hand, he hates the living sight of you, so maybe he'd do it to get you out of the house. What if you were to dangle in front of his nose the promise that you'd leave if he gave you Aideen's dowry?'

Julia sipped her tea, then put down her cup. 'Do you think, maybe?'

'It's worth suggesting to him.'

'Arrah he'd never go for it.'

'You won't know unless you try.'

'I do know that Josie Ryan is the thickest mule the world has ever seen. The minute he realizes that this is something I want he'll say no.'

'Even if it means he has to put up with you for the rest of his life? You could put it to him that way.'

'Our Josie is so spiteful he'd cut his balls off if he thought it would bother me.'

Brideen ate a scone without speaking. Then she said, 'Supposing the idea came from your mother? Supposing she said she was tired of listening to the two of you fighting, and she wanted you out of the house so she could have some peace?'

'That might work. One of the excuses he gave her for not wanting to get married was that he didn't want to bring in a woman with me still in the house.'

'There you are, then.'

'I can try. I'd do anything to get out of there.' Julia was silent for a bit, thinking. 'But even if Mammy got Josie to agree to the idea, there's still the job of getting him together with Aideen. You've no idea how much afraid of the girls our brave Josie is.'

'I think maybe we can manage that.' Brideen arched a conspiratorial eyebrow. 'You get your mother to do her bit and I'll get Kieran and Packy to work on Josie. Those two jokers are geniuses at getting people to do what they don't want to do. Except for Tom McDermott,' she added ruefully.

When Kieran came to see her that evening he looked so woebegone that she decided not to broach the subject till another day. However, after Mammy went to bed and he held her tightly for the longest time and said could they just sit and talk because he didn't feel up to doing anything else tonight – 'because of Martin, you know' – she curbed the lust that had been building within her all day and told him about her plan.

'It has definite merit,' he said. 'And, what's more, they deserve each other.'

'Mrs Ryan is going to try to talk Josie into it.'

'She'll need all her powers of persuasion: that lad is as thick as the wall.'

'But Julia is afraid that even if he does agree he won't have the courage to propose to Aideen. He's terrified of girls, she said.'

Kieran grinned. 'Ah yes, the bugger is a bit shy in that department all right.'

'She says he wasn't that way when he was younger.'

'She didn't tell you the story then?' He looked quizzically at her. 'Maybe she never heard it; I don't suppose anybody would want to tell her.'

'What story? Tell her what?'

'It happened about five years ago, while you were at school in Dublin. Martin himself told me the story. Josie was about eighteen or nineteen at the time and he had never been able to talk any girl into going out with him. So he asked my brother if he'd find him a girl since Martin was so good at picking them up himself. Martin said sure, and he took Josie to a dance in Lahvauce one Sunday night. The bold Martin, as usual, picked up a nice-looking girl for himself, and offered to take her home. She was willing – they always were, with him – only she had come with her girlfriend, she said, and she didn't want to leave her to go home on her own. So Martin got Josie to give the girlfriend a ride home on the crossbar of his bike; she lived about a mile on the far side of Lahvauce. Which Josie did. A couple of days later when Martin met Josie he asked him how he got on.

' "I told you I'd find you a nice girl, didn't I?" ' he said to Josie.

' "Be Jaysus", Josie said, and he all worked up, "you damn near got me killed, that's what you did".

' "What happened? Did you fall off the bike?" ' Martin asked him.

' "I did no such thing", said Josie. "I took the girl home, like you asked me to. And then I went for the kiss and squeeze before I let her off the crossbar, like you said you always did. Jesus Christ Almighty, Martin! That girl let a screech out of her that'd waken the dead. The next thing, before I had barely time to let her off the crossbar, this old fellow comes charging out the gate with a pitchfork, yelling at the top of his voice and coming straight at me".'

' "Did he get you?" ' Martin asked.

' "Damn near did", Josie said. "I pedalled down that boreen faster than you ever did, Martin, and this fellow chasing me with his pitchfork and yelling like a stuck pig".'

'Ever since that episode,' Kieran told Brideen, 'Josie has been afraid to ask a girl out.'

'Well, it's high time he got over it. And that's where you and Packy come in. The two of you, if you put your minds to it, should be able to get him bulling enough to propose to Aideen.'

'Not quite the right way to put it, a stor. It's the heifer that goes bulling, not the bull.'

She slapped his hand. 'You know what I mean. Anyway, I'm sure the two of you will figure out a way to get our shy Josie panting after Aideen.'

'God! Wouldn't that be a sight to see.' Kieran McDermott laughed out loud, for the first time since he heard his brother had drowned.

17

As he vested for the first night of the ladies' triduum, Father Donovan admitted to himself that he was going to enjoy preaching to the women. There was always a positive response from their side of the church when he expounded the word of God: the look on the faces, the posture of the bodies, as he laid down the moral law or exhorted to penance and prayer, indicated they were absorbing his message. So different from the men, who hardly ever gave a sign of being moved by his oratory. Perhaps it was their male sense of superiority that made them resist acknowledging his admonitions. Or simply their male embarrassment at displaying religious feeling: an attitude he himself had learned as a boy – any outward show of fervour was girlish. Anyway, he had been left with a dry sense of frustration last week after preaching to the men of Coshlawn Crann; it was as if his voice were being sucked into an endless cavern from which no echo returned.

At the altar this evening, as he meditated on the mysteries of the Rosary, he found images of Brideen Conway intruding between him and the Blessed Virgin. Brideen, also, was a virgin. Perhaps the Mother of God looked a bit like her at the very time she was approached by the angel Gabriel. Maybe Brideen, too, would remain a virgin, even become a nun. *For God's sake, will you get that notion out of your head, Ger: such an outcome would be contrary to everything you're trying to accomplish with the triduum.*

He preached well that night, if he said so himself. Beginning with the divine command to increase and multiply, he moved forward to Mary and Joseph in the scene at Bethlehem, from whence he progressed to the holy house of Nazareth, then on to the wedding feast at Cana, to St Paul's exhortation that it was better to marry than to burn, and finally to the great apostle's likening the union of spouses to that of Christ and His Church. He used the sacred texts to expound the special role of woman in fulfilling God's plan for the human race.

'You are the chosen handmaidens of the Lord,' he thundered. 'To you is given the high honour and privilege of bringing into the world the future citizens of Heaven.'

He could feel their attention in the silence of his dramatic pauses, in the rapt faces his glance bounced off as the word of God poured forth from his heart and lips. After he finished and turned to the altar to begin Benediction, it was very many seconds before the first harsh cough broke the reverent stillness of the house of prayer. The best sermon he had ever preached, he reflected, as he spooned incense into the thurible and offered its sweet fragrant smoke in homage to his God in the Monstrance.

Father Donovan struggled daily to attain the peculiar type of sanctity proper to his priestly state. It involved not only striving for intimacy with his God and a continuing effort to root out his faults, it also demanded a deep concern for the spiritual welfare of his fellow human beings. At the same time it required a deliberate shunning of intimacy with the opposite sex and a profound detachment from the goods and glories of the world. So when he examined his conscience at bedtime a glaring flaw in the work of his day protruded like a new-sprung pimple on the nose. Wasn't it Brideen Conway who had inspired him to such heights of oratory tonight? The knowledge that hers was among those faces, the hope that she was observing him with admiration, had been in the shadow of his mind as he spoke, vitiating what ought to have been done for the glory of God with the conceit of earthly praise. He must correct that fault, expunge Brideen Conway from his heart where she had taken up residence like a swallow building a nest in the eaves of his house.

The fervour of prayerful resolution, however, proved no match for the demon of darkness that assailed him later in his solitary bed. In the shadowy state between sleeping and waking, when will is weakened and libido refreshed, Brideen, his angel of purity, became the seductress in his lustful cravings. Her form, her face, her lovely green eyes, tormented him, while her remembered laugh – girlish, bewitching – reverberated in the quiet of his twilit room. He dozed off in her amorous embrace and dreamed he was chasing her over hills of sand that impeded his steps as she, fleet-footed, fled from his sight.

At mass next morning he begged his Lord for the grace to do what was right in the matter of Brideen Conway. What was right was to avoid her presence in thought and in person to the extent that his ministry of souls would allow. Yet he couldn't put that simple straightforward need into a simple straightforward prayer. Instead, he asked his Lord for guidance to deal prudently with this delicate situation, for light to remain on the path of virtue, for strength to oppose the wiles of the Wicked One. And that He might have compassion for this young virgin who wanted to marry but could not. He went to breakfast feeling humbled but buoyant: though he had fallen prey to mankind's *bête noir*, the lure of the flesh, he had promptly recognized the temptation and with the grace of God had put it away. His sense of recovery was strengthened throughout the morning as he recited the divine office and prepared his evening sermon. Yes, he decided, as he sat down to his one o'clock dinner, he could deal with Brideen Conway once again as a good priest should: with pastoral concern and personal detachment.

Which confidence was tested at a quarter past three when she came to see him.

'You preached a lovely sermon last night, Father.'

'It's one of the central themes of the Christian life. It would be hard to preach a bad sermon on it.'

'Ah now, you're being very modest.' Her smile sent wavelets of pleasure down his middle.

'I don't imagine, however, that you came to talk about my sermon.'

'True for you. Remember I told you that Kieran was going to have to go to England so he could earn the money we need to get married?'

'He has changed his mind?' *Stop that sinking feeling, Ger.*

'I came up with an idea that might get us the money we need.'

'Wonderful.' He listened while she explained her scheme. 'And do you think it will work?'

'The biggest difficulty will be getting Josie Ryan to approach Aideen.'

'Why is that?' What was it about a lovely woman that could flutter the heart of a celibate priest, despite all his resolutions and prayers?

'You'd have to know Josie, Father; he's terribly timid altogether when it comes to dealing with girls.'

'Well, I wish you luck in talking him into it.'

'I was hoping you might be able to help us.'

He was instantly wary. 'If I can, of course I'll be glad to.'

'It's one thing for his mother to persuade Josie that he ought to get married, but he's going to smell a rat the minute the lads start trying to set him up with Aideen. So I thought that maybe if you were to talk to him, as part of your follow-up from the triduum for example, you might be able to convince him.'

Definitely not! He should refuse immediately: it wasn't appropriate at all for a priest to do such a thing. But how could he refuse his Brideen? Anyway, she might have a point: what she was asking was nothing more than a call to pastoral duty, the kind of thing he *should* be doing as a follow-up to his crusade of prayer. 'So you want me to be a match-maker?'

'You'll be getting three weddings for the price of one.' *Dear God! That smile is bewitching.*

'Even so, it hardly seems appropriate.' Every pastoral instinct shouted that he should not be urging particular mates on members of his flock. What if they married and were desperately unhappy and blamed him for their woes? They might even lose their immortal souls by rejecting their priest and the church he stood for.

'Ah, go on, Father; give it a try. Sure it can't do any harm. And if it works it'll save Kieran from having to go to England. And we can all get married and live happily ever after in Coshlawn Crann.'

Could even a saint resist that lovely face? 'Let me think about it.'

'Thank you very much, Father.' The dimpled smile suggested she knew he had already succumbed, and that the promised thinking was merely pro forma. But after she left he really did think. It *would* save Kieran from going to England. So how could he, who had dedicated his priestly life to the fight against emigration to that godless country, not come to their aid? Sure there was risk of an unhappy marriage. But what he was trying to do was a positive good, and if, unintended, a bad result ensued no moral culpability could be imputed to him by God or man.

By the same reasoning, of course, if he were not to help link Aideen Glynn with Josie Ryan because of a well-founded fear of future evil, then neither would he be culpable in the matter of Kieran McDermott being forced to emigrate.

After mulling the matter sporadically throughout the evening, he went to bed without making a decision. In the days that followed he tried to put it from his thoughts, along with Brideen Conway. But neither was willing to be sent away.

18

It took Martin McDermott two weeks to find a job. Strictly speaking, it shouldn't be said he found it, for that would imply he had performed an active role in moving from the unemployed to the employed state. He hadn't. To put the matter kindly, he had not been diligent in searching. Each morning he was roused from his floor-bed sleep by a gentle poke in the ribs from cousin Clare's pointy-toed shoe, accompanied by her kindly admonition, 'Martin, you lazy loafer, will you get up out of that, for God's sake, and get out and find yourself a job.'

Each morning he'd be locked out of the flat when the girls went to work, and each evening when they reconvened for dinner, Clare would ask, 'Well, Martin, did you get a job today?'

Each evening Martin would give the same reply, 'Not yet, I'm afraid, but I am trying hard to find one.'

He wasn't. There was something about the state of being officially dead that made it impossible for a fellow to look for work. Why this was so, he couldn't explain, but he was quite sure that it was the case. So, day after day, he roamed the streets of Dublin, spent hours in cinemas seeing the same films several times over, visited pubs where he drank pints of plain – the cheapest version of Guinness – and sat on park benches watching the girls go by. Not a bad life really for a dead man. Once, he climbed Nelson's Pillar and surveyed O'Connell Street and surrounding rooftops, and wondered why the living wanted to cram their dwellings so close to each other.

After a week of this, and even though his behaviour in the flat had been irreproachable, his initial grudging welcome from his cousin died of acute impatience.

'You'll have to go now, Martin,' Clare announced on Monday evening.

'But where will the poor fellow go?' Mona Graham, the pipsqueak, objected. She had taken a kind of motherly interest in him, making sure that he got his fair share of whatever dinner was cooked and making up his bed on the parlour floor before retiring for the night herself.

'I have an idea,' said Angela Moloney, the skinny girl with the yellow hair. 'The uncle is a construction foreman. When I was visiting him and the family yesterday he was talking about a couple of hundred houses they're building up beyond Glasnevin. Can you imagine! Good class houses, too.'

'So there should be lots of jobs there.' Clare stared at Martin.

'Well, that's what I was thinking.' Angela smiled at him. 'So, if you like, I'll ask the uncle if he can get you some work.'

The idea didn't appeal at all to Martin: there was something obscene about asking the dead to build houses for the living. On the other hand, from the look in Clare's eye, he could tell he'd be sleeping on the street this very night if he objected. Anyway, he had already spent half of the ten pounds Josie had given him. So he forced a smile and said that would be terrific.

Angela asked her uncle, and the uncle said he'd see, and a couple of evenings later she came home with the news that Martin was to report for work at a building site in Ballymun next Monday morning. A labourer's job was what he had for him, the uncle said when Martin reluctantly turned up. Mixing mortar and carrying it in hods to the plasterers. Backbreaking work for ten hours a day, Monday to Friday, and a half day on Saturday. For which he'd get the sum of five pounds a week, payable each Saturday.

It surely wasn't a brilliant job, and it wasn't at all worthy of the talents and education of Martin McDermott. Or of the money he knew he was worth. The worst part of it was that he'd have to actually work: any shirking, the foreman had said, and he'd be sacked on the spot; there were plenty of lads waiting to take his place. Shite! Shite! And shite again. On the other hand, the job would pay enough to keep body and soul together, with enough left over for a few pints of Guinness every evening.

Clare, eager to be rid of him, found him digs on the North Circular Road: a small room in a big red-brick house not far from the Phoenix Park. For two pounds ten a week the landlady would also give him his breakfast and dinner and a lunch to take to work. The Saturday he got his first wages, Clare brought him up on the bus to his new abode and left him on the doorstep.

'You're on your own now,' she told him. 'Of course you're always welcome to visit us.'

'For God's sake, don't tell anyone I'm alive,' he warned her, for the umpteenth time, as she walked away.

★

The work was hard, the hours were long, the pay was low. After a month of mixing mortar and carrying hods, he knew he'd have to make a better life for himself. So far, however, he had no success in figuring out what that life should be. He found, too, that being officially dead had drawbacks when it came to enjoying himself. Now that he had his own place, Clare was more friendly, and invited him for dinner on Sunday afternoon. The girls talked about the dances they went to on Sunday nights at the National Ballroom and what great fun it was. So Martin bought himself a new suit with the remainder of Josie's money, with the idea of going with them the following Sunday.

However, when he mentioned his plan to Clare, she cautioned him, 'It would be risky, I'd say. All the country girls and boys go to the National, so there's a good chance you'd run into someone from home.'

Shite! His only other pleasure was the time he spent in Hanlon's Pub. A lively place, on Hanlon's Corner, near the cattle market. Especially on Thursday evenings after the market, when the cattle dealers and jobbers and drovers were there. Martin briefly contemplated looking for work as a drover – he certainly knew how to drive cattle – until he found out that the job paid even less than his own. Anyway, it was sporadic, night work, driving the animals from the railway station at Cabra, through the city streets to the market, and then taking them down the North Circular Road to the docks after they were sold. A tough crowd, too, the same drovers. They'd line the bar just inside the door of Hanlon's, lowering pints of plain as fast as the barmen could fill them. And when they'd be drunk they'd start fighting. The barmen would invite them to 'take it outside' whenever a row brewed, which was fairly often. On the street, they'd beat each other to pulp with bare knuckles, to the cheers of their comrades, and then return to the bar, covered in blood, for more drinks.

Much more interesting to Martin were the cattle dealers and jobbers, well-dressed fellows who congregated at the inside section of the bar, away from the door. He watched them on Thursday evenings as they drank stout and whiskey that they paid for with pound notes from their money wads, while he and his rough companions ordered pints of plain that they paid for with loose change eked out of various pockets. He'd like to join the gentlemen, feeling that he belonged with them, but he was put off by the distinction of dress-bespeaking class. Then, one Thursday evening, about a month after he started work, he changed into his new suit before coming to Hanlon's, and joined the well-groomed fellows in the inner sanctum. They ignored him. Unlike the drovers, who treated anyone in work clothes as one of themselves, the well-dressed crowd were clannish. Martin tried to start conversations a couple of times but was treated to monosyllabic responses each time. He spent almost an hour drinking by himself before a fellow walking in off the street said hello to him.

'You're new here.' He looked at Martin with the speculative eye of a jobber passing judgement on a bullock at a fair.

'I am indeed.' Martin, pleased to be spoken to by anyone at this point, smiled at the man, a short, stout, red-faced fellow, dressed in heavy tweeds though it was summer. 'How did you know that?'

'You haven't the cut of a jobber. And dealers don't come here to drink on their own: they come to drink and do business, which means talking to other dealers.' A young fellow, not much older than himself, Martin guessed.

'Are you a dealer?'

'No, I'm a jobber. If I was a dealer I wouldn't give a stranger like yourself the time of day either.' He grinned at Martin.

'What's the difference between a dealer and a jobber? But first let me buy you a drink.'

The jobber said he'd like a Paddy. Martin ordered.

'The jobber,' the man in the tweed suit said, 'buys at the local fairs around the country and sells at the cattle market. The dealer buys at the market and exports the cattle to England.'

'I'm a farmer's son,' Martin told him. 'And I've often sold cattle to jobbers at the fair in Lahvauce. So you're one of those fellows who come around and look and poke and offer half what a bullock is worth?'

The jobber grinned again. 'In my business we have to buy at the lowest price and sell at the highest. Otherwise we won't last long.'

Despite, or perhaps because of, a significant amount of alcohol in his system, Martin was turning over in his mind an idea that had popped into it while the jobber was talking. 'How does a fellow become a jobber?'

'Money.' The jobber finished his whiskey and called for two more. 'And a sound knowledge of cattle.'

'I was sort of thinking of going into the business myself,' Martin heard himself say.

'It's a rare old job, I can tell you. You're your own boss: nobody tells you what to do. And if you're good at it you can make a lot of money.'

Say no more, Martin said to himself. 'If you don't mind my asking, how did you get into the business?'

'I'm a farmer's son. Like yourself. Down in Westmeath, a bit outside

Athlone. When my father died, the Lord have mercy on him, the place went to the older brother, but the old man left me a hundred cattle. When I was getting ready to sell them, an old farmer I knew told me I'd get a better price if I took them up to Dublin to the cattle market myself and sold them there. So that's what I did. Then I used the money I got to buy more cattle at local fairs and bring them to the market up here, where I made a good profit on them. So that's what I've been doing now for the past four years.'

'Good man yourself. Sad to say, however, *I* don't have any cattle to get me started in the business.'

'Is your father still alive?'

'Indeed he is. And no sign of him kicking off for another forty years.'

'Then don't wait till he dies. Maybe you could talk him into getting you started? That is, if he can afford to.'

'He could afford to, all right, but—' Martin stopped dead. He was about to expound on his father's miserliness when a wild thought came at him, like a voice thrown from a passing bus. He clamped his lips shut.

'Tight with the money, I suppose?'

'He's that, all right.'

'Aren't they all? I make deals with those old farmers every day. God almighty! They'd skin you alive to get an extra pound for a bullock.'

Martin left the pub early that evening. He walked briskly down the North Circular Road as far as Phibsboro to clear his head. By the time he arrived back at his digs, he had devised, revised, and corrected a scheme to get himself the money he needed to go into business as a cattle jobber.

Saturday after work, he took a bus into the city, found a stationery shop, and bought writing paper, envelopes, and a fountain pen. Then he went to the General Post Office and bought a stamp. It was time to write to the old man.

19

Prayers, vigils, purposes of amendment, mortification of the senses, self-imposed penances, had no effect: Brideen Conway looked more bewitching to Father Donovan every time he saw her. And more entrancing every time he thought of her, which was often. Finally, in desperation, after much agonized deliberation and a great deal of conscience nagging, he discussed the problem with Monsignor Burke.

'Let me ask you a delicate question, Paddy,' he said, while his friend uncorked a bottle of wine after their monthly lunch.

'Shoot.' The monsignor filled the glasses.

'Have you ever fallen in love?'

'Ah indeed, Ger; if I had a bottle of wine for every time. . . . Who is she?'

'A woman in the parish.'

'And this is your first time?'

'Ah no, now, Paddy; nothing has happened. I—'

'I mean, have you ever fallen in love before?'

Father Donovan grimaced. 'A few mild infatuations maybe. But nothing like this. Nothing even close.'

'You have it bad, huh, you poor oul devil?'

'Jesus, Paddy, she's in my mind day and night. Every time I see her I go weak at the knees. I can't pray. I'm distracted at mass. I daydream through the divine office. Have you ever had the feeling that you'd risk your immortal soul to get relief from the pain?'

'I know what you're going through, all right.'

'So what do you recommend?'

The monsignor lowered half a glass of wine. 'I can't tell you what to do, Ger. I can only tell you what others have done in your situation.'

The young priest's eyes opened wide. 'You don't mean other *priests*?'

'Believe me, it happens often enough.'

'Do you really think? So it's not that—'

Paddy Burke leaned back in his chair and smiled benevolently. 'I'd say, Ger, that one out of every two priests in the country has run into your problem at least once in his life. And a good number of them have come to me about it.'

'So what do you tell them to do?'

'Nothing. That's why they come to me: they know the law and they don't want to be preached at. I simply tell them what their options are, what others have done. The rest is up to them.'

'All right, so what have others done?'

'Some have gone to a Jesuit house and done the full thirty days of St Ignatius's spiritual exercises. Some have gone on pilgrimage to Lough Derg. One man I know spent three days on top of St Patrick's holy mountain fasting and praying. But then there are others. . . . Ah, but you're too young to be told about *them*.'

'Tell me anyway.'

The monsignor finished his wine. 'I've known more than one priest who took a lady friend to Dublin or Killarney or Bundoran to get her out of his system.'

'You're codding me now, Paddy; you don't mean. . . ?'

'I do indeed.'

'Sweet Jesus.' Ger held out his glass for more. 'You said you had run into the problem yourself; what did *you* do, if you don't mind my asking?'

Paddy refilled their glasses. 'I got this wine from a man who told me he bought a case of it for ten pounds a bottle. Would you believe that?'

They finished that bottle and Paddy opened another. Father Donovan began to feel euphoric. He talked about the triduum. 'The turnout was quite remarkable, especially when you consider that it was right in the middle of the hay-saving season. More than half the men of the parish were there, and three quarters of the women, and practically every child over the age of six.'

'I always say, Ger, there's no better Catholic in the whole of Ireland than the man from Mayo.'

'One of the outstanding results of the triduum has been that a young man who had his mind set on going to England has decided to stay home instead and get married, and settle for frugal comfort the way a good Christian should.'

'And they say the age of miracles is past?'

'And what's more, that same young man's brother committed to marrying a very plain girl that everyone said hadn't a chance in the world of finding a husband.'

'Ah, Ger; the Holy Spirit moves whomsoever He wills.'

'Unfortunately, the young fellow was drowned the very night he proposed to the plain girl.'

'Was he indeed?'

' 'Twas a very sad case.'

'But perhaps, not so sad after all. That proposal he made to the plain girl may very well have been his own ticket to Heaven, you see. *Whatsoever you did to the least of my brethren you did to me.*'

'Exactly what I was thinking myself, Paddy.'

'And brethren in this context undoubtedly includes the fair sex. And the not so fair, too, of course.'

'Especially since the lad was considered a bit of a scamp. Maybe 'twas just as well he died when he did.'

'God's ways are wonderful beyond our understanding.'

'Even our school principal, a man not noted for his religious attachments – quite the contrary, in fact – was persuaded to do his share of canvassing for the triduum.'

'Isn't that amazing? It may very well have been the turning point in that man's life. Unless he, too, was drowned, of course. He wasn't drowned, was he, Ger?'

'No, mind you, he wasn't. Not that some people would have had any regrets if he was, I'm sorry to say. A brute altogether with the children, they tell me.'

'A pity then that he survived. But God's ways are mysterious. It's not for us to question them.'

'And then there was a man with money to burn I tried to talk into helping his son get married, but I might as well have been talking to a stone wall for all the good it did. Money for his own future was all he could think about, and he an old man in his fifties.'

'Oh ye of little faith! His eternal future is what should be on that man's mind.'

'I told him that, too; I did indeed. But some people. . . .'

A short time afterwards they were both nodding off to sleep.

Two weeks later another event occurred that confirmed Father Donovan's faith in the value of storming Heaven with the petitions of the faithful. Pat Sweeney, a 75-year-old farmer, collapsed on a Wednesday afternoon on top of a tramp-cock and was dead before the doctor could be fetched. The event itself was tragic of course, even if the man was old, but it was its consequences that revealed once again to Father Donovan that God knows very well what He is doing, that He draws good from evil, and that His ways are far too profound for mortals to fathom. Saturday afternoon, just a few hours after Pat Sweeney's burial, his son knocked on the priest's door. Father Donovan himself answered.

'How are you, Larry?'

'As good as can be expected, Father.' But beneath his peaked cap Larry had a terribly nervous look in his eye. 'I came to talk to you about something.' A tall thin man of 40, he was the only one of Pat Sweeney's ten children still at home. When he removed the cap the pale upper half of his forehead contrasted starkly with his sunburned face. He was still wearing the shabby suit he had worn to the funeral.

'Certainly, Larry.' Father Donovan led the way into his parlour. 'And how is your poor mother holding up?'

'She's good now, Father; better than you'd expect.' Larry perched on the edge of his chair.

'It must be hard on her, the creature. They were married a long time.'

Larry's face darkened. ' 'Tis a relief for her, that's what it is. He wasn't good to her at all, the Lord have mercy on him. He never was.'

The subject of tyrannical husbands was relatively new to Father Donovan, though it was obviously a common problem: he had heard quite a number of complaints about it in the confessional since his arrival in Coshlawn Crann. So far he hadn't been able to formulate a response that would help to alleviate the sufferers' pain and at the same time satisfy the requirements of Catholic theology. Although he felt instinctively that it was wrong for a man to ill-treat his wife, it could not be gainsaid that the husband was head of the wife as Christ was Head of the Church without rejecting St Paul himself. So his advice to his women penitents waffled from advocating wifely patience to suggesting that she find new ways to mitigate the good man's causes of irritability.

'She'll miss him all the same,' Father Donovan said now to Larry Sweeney.

' "Sorra one bit", she says. "Bad cess to him anyway", she says. "I wish to God he had died years ago", she says. And I feel the same myself. He wasn't good to any of us, so he wasn't.'

Man's anger can best be softened, the priest felt, by reference to the eternal verities. 'Your father is dead, Larry. He has already given an account for his actions to his Maker. So my advice to you and to your mother is to do what St Paul himself tells us: *let not the sun go down upon your anger.*'

'Sorry, Father. It wasn't to complain I came.'

'I'm sure it wasn't.'

'I was at the triduum. I came every single night.'

'Good man yourself.'

'I've been wanting to get married these past fifteen years.'

'Indeed. And what was stopping you?'

'*He* was. He wouldn't hear of me bringing a woman into the house. "Time enough for you to get married when herself and myself are gone", he used to say.'

'Did he? I'm sorry to hear that.'

'Well, he's gone now, and my mother says I can get married whenever I want. And that's what I'm going to do, Father.'

'I'm delighted to hear it. And you have a girl all ready and waiting, I expect?'

'Arrah, I do not. I don't know if any girl would have me now, but I was hoping that you might be able to help me find someone.'

Father Donovan hadn't yet been able to make up his mind what to do *vis-à-vis* Aideen Glynn and Josie Ryan, so it was understandable that he didn't have an immediate response to Larry Sweeney's expressed hope. 'There are quite a number of single girls in the parish; I'm sure you'll be able to find a suitable wife from among them.'

'The way it is, Father, I do never get a chance to meet any of them. I'm too old to go to the dances, and where else would I be running into them?'

'I see. Is there any particular girl you have a preference for?'

'There's one or two, mind you. But I'd need to talk to them first, wouldn't I, before I'd make up my mind?' Larry allowed himself a brief flash of sly grin.

'You would, I suppose.' He stood to indicate the session was over. 'I'll give the matter some thought and see if I can devise a way for you to meet those young ladies.'

'Right you be, Father.' After the priest escorted him to the door and they shook hands, Larry added, 'I'll be hearing from you so.'

20

Father Donovan failed to keep his mind on the psalms as he paced the path between house and sacristy. What on earth was he to do about finding a wife for Larry Sweeney? And what about Brideen's request regarding Josie Ryan? Surely, it was hardly the priest's place to. . . . On the other hand, if twice in a week he had been asked to arrange such partnerships, just after he had galvanized his parish to plead with Heaven for more marriages, should he not take that as a sign of God's will? What else could it be? Then he mustn't shirk his duty. He finished the Little Hours and Vespers, and hurried into the house to find Cait.

'Is it a matchmaker you want to be?' the housekeeper demanded, when he explained the problem, without mentioning names, of course.

'No. But a matchmaker is what we need, isn't it?'

'There was an old lad in Kilmorrin by the name of Seaneen Joyce used to make matches. He died some years ago. But the way it is now, Father, people prefer to make their own arrangements.'

'But they aren't making them, Cait; that's the problem. And we have to do something about it.'

'Would you like me to give it some thought, Father?' The gleam of the creative thinker shone from Cait's eyes.

'I'd be very grateful indeed for any ideas you may have on the subject.'

'Right so. But I have to make your tea first.'

The matter slipped his mind for the remainder of the day, what with confessions and preparing tomorrow's sermon. But it returned after last mass on Sunday the minute he sat down to a late breakfast. 'Did you come up with anything?' he asked the housekeeper as she placed the bacon and eggs in front of him.

'I did.'

'So tell me about it.'

'Wouldn't you rather finish your breakfast first?'

'That's all right. You talk and I'll eat.'

'Right so. What you need is some place where the older ones – those over-thirty – can meet and talk to each other. The young ones are all right: they meet at the dances.'

'Unfortunately, we don't have a parish hall. One of these years, maybe?'

'What about the school? The teachers could organize a ceilidh dance.' She gave him her sly smile. 'Them that have most to gain should be the ones to help.'

'You're a genius, Cait. We could hold one every Sunday evening after Benediction.'

He reflected on Cait's brainchild throughout the week. And the more he thought about it the better he liked it. Thursday he decided: he was going to do it. He discussed it with Brideen and Maura Prendergast on his school visit; the two women thought it was a sound idea and committed to help. Maura suggested leaving out the dance part: the older lads and girls would be intimidated by the thought of having to get out on the floor; a social evening with tea and cake would be better, she said. Alphonsus Finnerty expressed no opinion: he was in a hurry to leave precisely at three o'clock.

'I'll announce it on Sunday so,' Father Donovan told the teachers.

Many stories were woven around Austin Glynn's wealth and business dealings. A besotted customer once claimed to have seen a flour-sack of American dollars behind the bar mirror, the one with *Paddy's Irish Whiskey* written across it. Another knew for a fact that Glynn owned more than twenty guest houses up in Salthill, out of which he made a mint of money every summer from the visitors to that holiday resort. Then there was the fellow who heard from a cousin in the Civil Service in Dublin that the gardai down in Dingle in County Kerry were hot on the trail of a band of smugglers who had been bringing in tea for the black market during the war and since, and were so clever that they had never been caught with the goods; their boss, it was suspected by the gardai, was a Mayo man by the name of Aibhistin MacGloin, which everyone knew was the Irish for Austin Glynn. The most common story about Austin's supposed great wealth, however, was that he had made a power of money making bootleg whiskey when he was living in America during the Prohibition.

Austin himself smiled a good imitation of Mona Lisa whenever reference was made to the extent of his wealth. Or he'd laugh out loud if someone in his cups alleged that he must be filthy rich, and plaintively ask his listeners if any one of them would be so stupid as to tolerate his job if he could afford to be elsewhere. Ah but, the diehards insisted behind his back, the pub was a cloak of respectability for his other nefarious activities. Not that they thought any less of the man for that. There was actually a kind of pride in the way they spoke to men from other parishes at fair days in Lahvauce when they'd be describing the supposed shady dealings of their returned Yank pub owner. He was a man out of the ordinary, the like of whom other parishes were lacking; a man to boast about.

Glynn was quite aware of his special standing in the community: he was a man of wealth and a man of mystery. And he intended to remain so. His happiness, he felt, would be complete if only he didn't lack what mattered to him most: grandchildren. Hence his obsession with finding a husband for his daughter. Himself the only son in a family of six, and the only one to marry – three sisters had entered convents, the other two remained spinsters at home – he felt it incumbent on him to carry on the proud Glynn bloodline. Christine's inability to bear any more children after Aideen was a source of bitter regret to him, and he was determined that this one daughter should propagate his blood to future generations. But the years were going by and Aideen had failed to attract a husband, and his hopes for a grandchild were beginning to fade when Martin McDermott came along. Sadly, that hope had vanished as quickly as it came. So he was electrified when, standing just inside the church door at last mass on Sunday, he heard Father Donovan propose a social evening to get spinsters and bachelors together with a view to marriage.

'By God we'll find a husband for you yet,' he told Aideen over the Sunday dinner. 'There are some great lads out there that never come in for a drink, you see, and now you'll have a chance to meet them.'

'Will you leave the girl alone,' her mother remonstrated. 'Maybe she'd be better off without a husband.'

'I don't want to meet them anyway,' Aideen said. 'I hate all lads, so I do.'

'So you hate your poor old father?' Austin put on a pout.

'I don't hate *you*, Daddy. You're a man, not a lad.'

'But, my little cherub, what are you going to do when big Daddy kicks the bucket and is taken up to Heaven? Then you're going to need a man to take care of you.'

'Oh, for God's sake, Austin.' Christine stood. 'Is everyone finished?'

'You'll go anyway, Aideen, just to please me.' He stood at the kitchen door watching the women wash and dry the dishes.

'Daddy, I know exactly what would happen if I went: I'd be standing there like a cow at the fair waiting for a jobber to come along and buy me. They'd probably squeeze my backside to see how plump I was.' She giggled at that.

'Aideen, don't be vulgar,' her mother said.

'Ah now, that's not the way it's going to be at all, a stor. What you'll have at this event – and it run by the priest himself – will be nice sensible lads with good manners who don't get drunk, lads who had education beaten into them by the Christian Brothers, lads who read books and newspapers. And they'll talk politely, let me tell you; them are the boyos who'll be able to carry on the kind of intelligent conversation you like, not the sort of *seafoid* that goes on around the bar.'

Aideen frowned. 'Maybe I'll think about it. But' – and she wagged a finger at him – 'just maybe.' And though he and his daughter were very close, that was all the assurance she'd give him for now.

After brooding on the matter all that evening, he decided to visit the priest – which was not a decision he reached lightly: the hostility of many priests and bishops to the fight for Irish freedom had left him with powerful anti-clerical feelings that time had not dissipated. So, although he had no personal animosity towards Father Donovan, he was antipathetic to the church the man represented. Besides, Austin Glynn by his own admission was not a religious man. True, he only occasionally missed Sunday mass, but mass-going was simply the outward sign of conformity that was necessary to maintain his good standing with the community in general and with his patrons in particular. He had his own doubts about the efficacy of religious practices to affect his eternal welfare. In fact, he had concluded that Heaven and Hell were very likely mere priestly myths, and that the only form of eternity a man could attain was in passing his blood to future generations.

As he walked in the gate to the priest's house late next morning Father Donovan came out the door and headed for his motor car. Austin swung around immediately, happy to postpone what he feared might be a difficult visit. But the young priest had already spotted him. 'Did you want to see me, Austin?' he called out.

'I'll come back another time, Father.'

'Not at all. I'm not in a hurry anywhere. Come on in.'

'Are you sure you have the time now? My business can keep till another day.'

'I always have time for my parishioners. And especially for a man like yourself.'

The bigger the sinner the more time, I suppose. 'If you have a couple of minutes, then, I'd like to have a few words.'

'By all means. We'll go inside. I think it's going to rain.' Father Donovan led the way into his parlour. 'Take the weight off your feet now.' He removed his biretta and waited till Austin was seated before sitting himself. 'I've been meaning to drop in on you one of these days: we haven't had a chance to talk since I came to the parish.'

The breezy tone, to put me at my ease. 'I'm sure you're a busy man, Father.'

'I don't suppose I can offer you a drink?'

'Ah no, not at all. Much too early in the day for that. I came over to talk about the social evening you mentioned from the altar yesterday. It's a grand idea.'

'I'm delighted you think so.'

He could almost see the priest relax; maybe he, too, had been worrying about what was going to be said. 'I've always felt we have far too many bachelors and spinsters in the parish. In the whole country for that matter.'

'We have indeed. 'Tis a great pity.'

'And it's well time somebody was doing something about it.'

'We all have to do our bit.'

'And who better than the clergy to take the lead. There's nothing like good example from the top, I always say.'

'We do our best. But we'll need a lot of co-operation from the laity, of course.'

'You will. And let me tell you right now, Father, in this matter I'm behind you a hundred per cent.'

'That's grand, Austin. Your support will be very much appreciated.'

'I was trying to think how I could help you out with the social, and it struck me that a half barrel might come in useful.'

The priest sat back abruptly, as if pushed by a keg of Guinness. 'Do you think so?'

'To loosen the lads' tongues, you see. Some of them are terribly shy altogether around the girls. But give them a couple of jars and they'd talk to the Pope himself.'

'You might have a point there. Anyway, it's something to think about.'

The priest scratched his nose. 'Well, all right so, if it will help matters. I imagine there'd be no harm in it. We'd have to see to it that there would be no inebriation, of course.'

'You can leave that to me, Father. I'll be in charge of the half barrel and there will be a two-pint limit, strictly imposed on all.'

'And, of course, we'll have tea for the girls. Cait is arranging that. And currant cake and maybe jam rolls as well, Cait says.'

'How about a little cider for the girls? They're likely to be a bit on the bashful side, too, aren't they?'

'I expect most of the girls are Pioneers, so they won't be interested in the alcohol.'

'Mind you, I never do like to see a woman drinking myself. It demeans them. Don't you think so, Father.'

'It does to be sure.'

There was a brief silence then till the publican said, 'I was wondering, Father, if I could ask a small favour of you?'

'Certainly, Austin. If there's anything I can do?'

'As you know, I have an unmarried daughter myself.'

'Aideen is a very fine girl. Isn't she at Communion every Sunday?'

'I'd like to see her married.'

'You would of course. Why wouldn't you?'

'Soon.'

The priest gave him a startled look. 'I see.' His hitherto affable tone turned suddenly formal.

'Ah no, Father, nothing like that at all. When I said soon I meant because she's getting on. She was twenty-five last birthday.'

'Yes, of course. Though twenty-five is hardly old, I should think.'

'It is for her, Father. You see, she's not what might be called a raving beauty. Mind you, she's the nicest girl in the world, but the lads do tend to look at the outside only and they miss the real Aideen. So I'm worried that she'll wind up on the shelf.'

'We're hoping the social evening will remedy that for her. And for a lot of other girls as well.'

'I was wondering, Father, if you might take a special interest in her. Maybe you'll come across some good lad who would be just right for her. A lad with the right breeding and education who can see below the surface and recognize the true gold that's in the girl.'

'I'll be most happy to look out for her, Austin. There are sure to be some fine lads at the social that might suit her, and I'll make it my business to see that they talk to her.'

'Thanks very much, Father. I'd do it myself only she'd be suspicious of any suggestions I might make. Girls are funny that way with their fathers, you see.'

At that moment Cait stuck her head in the door. 'Have you forgotten, Father, about your meeting with Canon McCarthy?'

'Oh my goodness, yes.' Father Donovan jumped to his feet and grabbed his biretta. 'I have to meet with my parish priest and I'm late already.'

It had been a frustrating week for Kieran and Packy in the matter of Josie Ryan and Aideen. When they failed to find Josie in Glynn's on three successive evenings – such a long absence was unusual, the publican said – they went to his house.

'He's spending all his spare time with the granduncle,' Julia told them. That 95-year-old relative, who lived alone on the far side of Lahvauce, was in extremely poor health and wasn't expected to last much longer. 'Between ourselves, I think Josie's taking care of him more with the expectation of getting the place than out of any milk of human kindness. Not that there's much to get,' she added. 'A thatched cottage and about fifteen acres.'

Kieran was growing pessimistic about the whole scheme. 'I might as well go to England. That old codger could last for years.'

'Let's give him a few weeks anyway,' Packy pleaded.

'It's just putting off the inevitable.'

It was with relief then that they heard from Julia on Sunday morning as they were coming out of mass that the granduncle had just died. 'But I'd wait till after the funeral before talking to Josie about Aideen,' she cautioned.

'We'll give him a week,' Kieran said.

As the two of them were strolling down the village street wheeling their bicycles Packy said, 'What do you think of this social evening the priest was talking about?'

'I'd like to be able to peek in the school window and see what's going on. It should be great wick.'

Packy stopped suddenly. 'What if Aideen is there and someone the like of Larry Sweeney snaps her up? I hear Larry's on the prowl for a wife, now that his old fellow has kicked the bucket.'

'Cripes almighty!'

'We better light a fire under Josie before the social, or it might be too late.'

'If we can find the bastard.'

'I'll tell you where we'll get him for sure – at the sports meeting in Lahvauce next Sunday.' Josie, with his pretensions to be a champion weight-thrower, was sure to be there.

21

Canon McCarthy heard confessions every Saturday afternoon from four to six in Lahvauce parish church. The hours were popular with the women who cycled into town to shop for the week's groceries: it saved them coming in again later in the evening. As a result, the canon and Father Daly, his Lahvauce curate, were usually kept busy for the entire two hours. So when, on the Saturday prior to the Coshlawn Crann social evening, the portly parish priest tripped on the hem of his alb coming down the altar steps at the end of his morning mass and had to be carted off to hospital with a fracture of the tibia, Father Daly, a young man just a year ordained, sent a panic message to his fellow curate in Coshlawn Crann asking if he might be so kind as to help him with the afternoon confessions. Father Donovan assented: his own confession hours were from seven to nine. He arrived in time to have a cup of tea with Father Daly before taking his place in the canon's confessional. And lest any penitent should think she was confessing to the canon, he placed the FATHER VISITOR card over the parish priest's name.

With a steady stream of penitents, almost all women, the time moved quickly. Though some of his priestly colleagues found confessions tedious, Father Donovan enjoyed this function of his sacred ministry. The confessor got to peer into the undraped souls of his penitents and to apply the salve of grace to their wounded spirits. He admonished the sinner and forgave the sin. He was confidant of secrets and dispenser of advice. And Father Donovan performed all those deeds in the confessional in Lahvauce parish church that Saturday afternoon, while he gloried in the privilege that God had granted him to accomplish such wonders. When eventually the box on his left was empty he looked at his watch: it was already five minutes to six. He peeked out through the curtain: nobody was waiting. He pushed back the right grille cover one last time.

'Bless me, Father, for I have sinned. It's been a month since my last confession. I confess to Almighty God. . . .' But instead of the usual mumbling of the confession prayer at breakneck speed, this woman recited it slowly, pronounced every syllable, stressed and accented the words with a fervour that impressed him. There was something familiar about her whispered voice: probably a woman from Coshlawn Crann who had come into town to shop. She went on to recite the usual litany of minor sins – impatience with her invalid mother, anger at her brother, a lie, impure thoughts – the faults of a good person. Then she stopped, and he thought she was finished. But before he could take over she resumed.

'I deliberately wished a certain person would drop dead, because he's getting in the way of several people's happiness, including my own.'

'We must not wish evil on others, no matter how deserving they may seem of it.'

'Yes, Father.'

'Is that all?'

'No, Father; I've been doing bad things, too.'

'What kinds of bad things?' Routine question. Canon law required the penitent to be specific: a vague acknowledgment of evil did not suffice for the sacrament to have effect.

She hesitated. 'I engaged in sexual touching.'

The category of carnal sin, though her description was not yet specific enough, since all carnal sins were materially mortal. So he asked the further question, 'With yourself or with another?'

'With my fiancé, Father.'

His moral theology courses had familiarized him with a variety of sinful acts under the heading of sexual touching between persons. The same courses taught him that the confessor must find out exactly which of those acts had been committed. So important was this last requirement, the moral *periti* cautioned, that he must elicit the information even should it result in involuntary sexual titillation to himself. So Father Donovan pressed heroically on with his questioning.

'Were you touching each other's private parts?'

'Yes, Father.'

Although Father Donovan was already feeling that involuntary titillation – not only from what she was telling him but also because she was an attractively-voiced woman whose mouth was just an inch or two from his right ear – he persisted with his interrogation.

'How often?' The code demanded that the number of instances in which the sin had been committed must be confessed.

'Lots of times.' She paused. Her lips were so close that he heard the faint plash of her sibilants. 'I don't know how often.' A touch of impatience in her tone. 'In the heat of passion one doesn't exactly keep count.'

Father Donovan swallowed and tried not to squirm.

'Did you achieve full carnal pleasure?'

Again the wet sound of opening lips. 'I think so, Father.'

Now for the final question that would pinpoint the precise species of carnal sin his penitent had perpetrated.

'Did you commit fornication?'

'No, Father.'

No need then for further questioning. He gave her a homily on the importance of chastity, even as his own body struggled to be chaste. He asked her when she was planning to marry; when she said she didn't know, he urged her to do so as soon as possible, and in the meantime to avoid the occasions of sin. To which she uttered an unintelligible murmur that he understood to be assent. While he pronounced the words of absolution she recited the act of contrition, again praying slowly and in accents clear. He was struck once more by the familiarity of that voice, and when she left the box, unable to restrain his curiosity, he peeped through the curtain.

The penitent walking away was Brideen Conway.

He remained where he was till she left the church, then shuffled to the altar rails and knelt. A shattered man. It couldn't be, yet so it was. Hadn't he heard her with his own two ears and seen her with his own two eyes? The woman he had so chastely loved, the virgin he had idolized as the epitome of her sex, was just a common sinner. Almost a fornicator, for God's sake. Another thought struck him: why had she come to Lahvauce to confession? Wasn't it obvious? So she wouldn't have to reveal to her rightful confessor the lascivious life she was leading behind her mask of piety. *God help me, I can't bear it.* He had surrounded her with virtue, entrusted to her keeping his own celibate heart, secure in the knowledge that with her it would be safe.

'Come in for a bite of supper, Ger, when you're ready,' Father Daly whispered.

'Ah no, Joe, I have to be back in Coshlawn Crann for confessions at seven.' He got to his feet, genuflected, shook his fellow curate's hand, and shambled head-bent from the church. As he drove home sorrow gave way to bitterness. How dare she perpetrate such an outrage on him: posturing in his presence as Thérèse of Lisieux when all the while she was Mata Hari: pleading for his help so she could chastely marry, even as she usurped the pleasures of the sacred bed. Pretending to endure the pains of abstinence while she gorged in the trough of carnal delights. Over and over he contrasted her outward piety with her hidden shame, and condemned her for the clanging dissonance. It was the deceit that stung, he assured himself. She had led him to believe she was pure: wasn't it her purity he had fallen in love with? And now her sin was his shame, too. There had been a kind of chaste marriage between them: he had cherished and protected her, and she was to be his special friend. Who had stood up for her against Alphonsus Finnerty? Who had pleaded her cause to Tom McDermott? Between whom was there a pact to promote the triduum for the glory of God and the populating of her school? Who had begged him to make a match between Josie Ryan and Aideen Glynn? Those events had committed them to each other. He had been faithful but she had cheated. So the bond between them was broken, irrevocably sundered like the veil of the temple.

He took a quick supper before heading to the church and another two hours in the confessional. Tomorrow was the women's Sodality, so the penitents were mostly women. His temper was short, though he made heroic efforts at restraint. And succeeded, except in the case of the young woman who confessed fornication. She admitted to doing the deed but once, yet in Father Donovan's mind she was Brideen Conway, and he roundly flailed her for her sin. The injustice of that reprimand sobered him, and for the rest of the session he was kindness incarnate to his penitent flock.

That night at his bedside, when he acknowledged his own faults of the day and asked his God for forgiveness, he was reminded that as he expected to be pardoned so he, too, must pardon. And that meant forgiving Brideen Conway for whatever it was that he thought she had done to him. Calmer now, a bit more objective, he admitted that he had no right at all to treat the sins she had committed against her crucified Lord as offences against himself. On the contrary, he also had sinned by becoming infatuated with her, against all the strictures of his vow of celibacy. Her sins were hers, his sins were his, and they each must pray that the same loving God would forgive them both.

And yet, as he settled for sleep, he sensed within him a residue of bitterness. He might forgive her with his will, but his craw was something else again.

22

After reading the gospel at first mass on Sunday, Father Donovan made the weekly announcements, the first of which was a reminder to all the unmarried men and women to come to the social in the school that evening after Benediction.

'You may meet your future husband or wife there,' he remarked with a smile.

That geniality vanished when he began his sermon.

'By their fruits you shall know them,' he thundered, quoting Christ's admonition from the gospel of the day's mass. Brideen Conway, near the front on the women's side, settled back in her seat: she liked a good sermon, and Father Donovan preached well.

'Those words of the Lord, my dear brethren, are timeless and timely; they warn us against mere lip-service and hypocrisy, traits that are all too common among human beings. Not excluding Christians. Or devout Catholics, for that matter.' He paused for effect. 'And not entirely unknown even here in Coshlawn Crann.'

Good man yourself, Father, said Brideen to herself.

'They come to you in the clothing of sheep, but inwardly they are ravening wolves, said the Lord. These are the people who pretend to be good, who would like everyone to think they are kind and charitable and chaste and honest, but who behind closed doors where no one can see them flout and ignore the commandments of God.'

I hope you're listening, Tom McDermott. You who boast about how you help your neighbour Barney Murphy, yet don't give a fig for the welfare of your own son.

'But before we cast about in our minds for neighbours to castigate, let us examine our own souls and see what secret offenses we have committed against Almighty God, the uncovering of which to our neighbours would be for us a cause of everlasting shame.'

Well, Brideen Conway? Are you so holy you can afford to throw stones? If the neighbours only knew what she and Kieran did on Saturday nights – though not last night, after going to confession – what would they think of her?

'Be warned. God will not be mocked. Though He loves the sinner, He hates all sin. And He has a special hatred for the piety that masks evil deeds. "Ye are like unto whited sepulchres", Jesus said about the hypocrites of his time, "which appear beautiful on the outside, but within are full of dead men's bones." And there may be those among us in church this morning who would have us believe they are good and worthy followers of Christ, but whose deeds in secret mock and crucify their Lord and Saviour.'

She felt herself blush. Dear God, let no one see the guilt in my cheeks.

'I say to such people, stop being two-faced: showing a pious front to the world while the filth of your sins affronts your God.'

Well anyway, she had gone to confession yesterday. And kept her clothes on last night in the presence of Kieran. Which hadn't been easy: he had recovered remarkably from Martin's death, laughing and joking for the first time since the drowning. And he wanted to make love to her in the worst way. Despite her state of grace and firm resolution of sinning no more, her body cried out for his touch.

Dear God, what is this awful love-lust that has taken over my being like a red-hot fever? And why did You inflict it on me only to deny me its fulfilment? And why does it draw me to Kieran McDermott in particular? I had lots of boyfriends in Dublin, some even better-looking and one or two who excited lust, but none of them ever affected me like he does. I feel as if I'll die if I can't have him. Now. Always. Even at the risk of eternal damnation.

After mass she waited outside the sacristy door for the priest, to discuss the social with him.

'Good morning, Father.' She greeted him with her usual smile. 'I think we're all ready for the big event this evening.'

'Good. I'm sure it will all go well.' But he didn't even look at her, and without stopping, as he always did, to talk to her, he set off in the direction of his house.

'There are just a couple of things, Father.' She followed him.

'Can they wait till this evening? I'm in a bit of a hurry now.' Without so much as looking back at her.

'I need to get into the school in the afternoon. We're setting up for the tea, and Austin Glynn is bringing over his half barrel.' She was almost running to keep up with him. 'And I don't have a key to the school door.

And I don't know where to find Mr Finnerty.'

'So how are you going to get in?' He turned on reaching his front door.

'Maura said you have a spare key.'

'I didn't know that.' His tone was curt.

'She said Cait would know.'

'Well, ask her then.' He strode through the door and shouted, 'Cait!'

Brideen waited outside: she hadn't been asked in, and the asperity of Father Donovan's attitude made her feel unwelcome. Whatever was wrong with him this morning? Cait appeared.

'Good morning, Brideen. He said you were looking for something.'

'I need the spare key to the school.'

'I'll get it for you.' She turned to go, then turned back again. 'I don't know why he didn't ask you in. Would you like a cup of tea?' Brideen and Cait had become quite friendly over their support for Father Donovan's marriage projects.

'No thanks.' She lowered her voice to a whisper. 'What's wrong with him this morning? He acts as if he got out the wrong side of the bed.'

'You noticed it, too? Well, I don't have the foggiest notion what the problem is.' Cait rolled her eyes to Heaven as if pleading for enlightenment. 'It's very unlike him I must say, but he's been that way since yesterday. He went in to Lahvauce to hear confessions in the afternoon and he's been cranky ever since. Anyway, let me get you the key.'

Brideen felt her legs losing strength, as if the blood had been drained from them. Her cheeks flushed; her forehead turned sweaty, her breathing felt impeded, her stomach punched. Jesus, Mary and Joseph! What had she done? *You realize it could even be Father Donovan,* she had teased herself yesterday as she waited her turn and saw the FATHER VISITOR sign. But of course it couldn't be: visiting confessors were always priests home from the Missions, men you'd never seen before and most likely would never see again. In the confessional, she never once looked at the priest behind the grille. But *he* must have recognized *her.* Hence his sermon against hypocrisy: she was the wolf in sheep's clothing, the whited sepulchre.

'I was just thinking,' Cait said, returning with the key, 'maybe you should come in for a bit and have a chat with him. He's always more cheerful after he talks with you.' She smiled at Brideen, who at that moment wished the ground would open and swallow her.

'I can't now, Cait, I'm afraid; I have to get home in a hurry to take care of Mammy.'

'I don't know what's got into him at all.' Cait shrugged.

Brideen almost ran from the door. She'd die of humiliation, so she would. She could never face Father Donovan again. Knowing that he knew her shame, that he was angry with her, was more than she could bear. However, she couldn't walk away from the social this evening: he was depending on her. She got on her bike and pedalled miserably home.

That afternoon, Josie Ryan went to the sports meeting in Lahvauce, an annual event at which the youth of the area demonstrated its prowess in running, jumping, cycling, and weight-throwing. The latter contest was Josie's specialty. Big and strong – 'even his head is solid muscle,' Packy O'Brien once cracked when Josie's athletic abilities were being discussed – he could hurl the fifty-six pound weight further than any of the lads from Lahvauce or Coshlawn Crann. He was extremely proud of his reputation as local champion, so, when he read in the *Connaught Telegraph* that a fellow from Castlebar was considered the best weight thrower in the county and that he'd be competing at Lahvauce, Josie said to himself that he'd see about that. He went early to get in a bit of practice.

The day was fine, the meeting was popular and a big crowd was expected. People were streaming in when he arrived. The large flat meadow on the outskirts of the town had been recently mowed and an oval track marked in its centre with generous lines of whitewash. Josie paid his shilling admission, grumbling under his breath that a great athlete like himself should be welcomed with open arms and not be asked to pay. But by God, he was going to show them today who was the best weight-thrower in Mayo.

He spotted the fifty-six pound weight – borrowed from a shopkeeper's scales – on the carrier of an organizer's bike, got permission to take it, hauled it to the wall at the far end of the field, removed his jacket and loosened his tie, rolled up his sleeves, spat on his hands, and grabbed the weight by its chain. The leather handgrip fitted snugly into his palm. He bent, spread his legs, swung the weight between them a half dozen times, then let go. The iron flew through the air and dug deep into the soft green sod. Josie straightened, placed one large shoe at the spot from which he had thrown, placed the other shoe in front of it. 'One, two,' he counted, then placed the first shoe in front again. 'Three.' He measured to the point where the weight hit the ground. Almost twenty feet, he estimated. Not bad for a first throw. He'd improve with practice, and before the day was out he'd show the Castlebar bugger how it was done.

The first event of the afternoon, the three-mile bicycle race, was announced over the loudspeaker. Martin's race: if he was here today, by

God he'd be rearing to go. Which reminded Josie that the fecker still hadn't sent him the hundred quid he'd promised. Josie picked up the weight and threw again, a mighty heave, as if to relieve the frustration of not getting his money. Just as he let go, a voice behind him shouted, 'You've a powerful arm there, Josie. Them Lahvauce lads won't stand a chance with you.'

Fecking O'Brien. And Martin's brother Kieran. He didn't like either of them. Always making fun of him. Well, this afternoon he'd show them what Josie Ryan was made of. 'I'm only doing fair to middling today.' He wouldn't say more: they could never accuse Josie Ryan of boasting.

'What's the furthest you've thrown it?' Kieran asked.

'Twenty-one seven last year. I don't know if I'll ever do better than that.' Just being modest of course: one of these days he'd throw it twenty-three or twenty-four.

'Why wouldn't you? Sure you'll beat out Ned Tobin himself in another year or two.' Ned Tobin was all-Ireland champion at throwing the fifty-six pound weight.

'You're pulling my leg now.' But he was pleased all the same at the compliment. 'I'll do one more and then give the arm a rest.' He picked up the weight again, swung it a half dozen times and let go.

'Begob, there'll be no stopping you today,' Kieran said.

It seemed to Josie there was genuine admiration in the fellow's tone. He let down his sleeves and retrieved his jacket from the wall. They walked to the edge of the track to watch the cyclists make their final sprint for the tape.

'The girls will be killed admiring your muscles at the social tonight,' Packy said.

'By hell, you won't find me there.' He scowled, knowing O'Brien was teasing him. Part of him would like to go to the social: he'd love to meet a nice girl. But he always either choked up or made a fool of himself whenever he had to *talk* to a girl, especially a pretty one. However, since Martin's escapade with Aideen Glynn he had been wondering if he might work up the courage to court that particular girl himself. Especially since the Mammy was pushing him again to get married: only last week she said it was high time for him to settle down. So maybe he should go after Aideen. He knew her well enough, so he wouldn't be afraid of making a fool of himself. And her £2,000 dowry was a hell of a lot of money. *Give her a try, Josie, even if she is so God-awful ugly.* Besides, if he brought her home as his wife, bloody Julia would have to get out, and by God he'd like that. With Aideen's money he could even give his sister a few hundred quid to speed her on her way.

'Fecker from Claremorris wins,' Packy groaned, as a lad on a sleek racing bike puffed by well ahead of the rest, all of whom were riding upright Raleighs and Humbers. 'I hate that joker.'

'If Martin was here, he'd be a bloody poor second,' Josie averred.

'He might,' Packy admitted. 'Though he beat Martin last year.'

'That was only because Martin had too much porter the night before. Next time they met he was going to leave the fooker a mile behind him, Martin told me after. Too bad there won't be a next time.' He said this last in a tone of sorrow: he had to be careful not to let the cat out of the bag about Martin.

'Why would you want to go to the bleddy social, anyway?' Kieran asked. 'The fellows that'll be there this evening will be looking for money, not girls. 'Tis the dowries they'll be after; the women will just be thrown in for good measure.'

'All the same now,' Packy said, 'don't knock the bit of money. What good is a girleen if you can't afford to marry her?'

'The next race is the under-eleven boys hundred yards,' the loud-speaker announced. 'Competitors line up under the goal-posts.'

'Who fecking needs to get married?' These two jokers were only trying to get him to go to the social so they could laugh at him when he made a fool of himself with some girl.

'Me for one,' Packy retorted. 'I'd like a nice cuddly girl in the bed with me on a cold winter night.'

Kieran laughed. 'Who'd have the like of you, with your big nose and your hair half gone?'

'Aideen Glynn would have me.' O'Brien puffed out his chest and straightened his lapels. 'She told me that herself the night I took her to the dance. And that's the girl that'd make a great squeeze, let me tell you. Not to mind her dowry. Holy Christ! A man could do a lot of things with that kind of money.'

Was the fecker trying to compete with him for Aideen? Josie said, 'I could have Aideen any time, if I wanted her.'

'Go on out of that.' Kieran looked at him in disbelief.

'Not a bloody chance,' Packy shouted. 'She wouldn't look twice at a yob like you.'

Hah! The fecker seemed upset at the idea of competition. 'Like hell she wouldn't. Wasn't I there the night Martin decided to go after her? He knew damn well she had her eye on me, so he asked me first if *I* was going to marry her.' Telling a few fibs of his own to get a rise out of those jokers.

'He only proposed to her after I told him I wasn't interested.'

'You're skinning lies now, Josie.' O'Brien went red in the face. 'I'll bet you a pound note she won't give you the time of day at the social this evening.'

'She won't because I won't be there.' Josie grinned at Kieran, then turned to stare at three young women who passed behind them. 'Now if that heifer in the middle with the legs was there I might be tempted to go.' That was the kind of thing Martin would say.

'Arrah, you're all talk, man,' O'Brien said. 'Any eejit can boast as long as he doesn't put himself to the test.'

'On my oath, Aideen was making eyes at me the night Martin set his cap at her.'

O'Brien pulled a crumpled note from his pocket. 'This quid here says you won't get more than a feck-off from her this evening. I'm not even saying you'd have a chance with her, because you wouldn't. All I'm saying is that if you walk up to her she won't as much as say *how are you, Josie*?'

'She won't because she won't see me there.' No way were those feckers going to lure him into that bloody social.

The starter's gun set the boys' race in motion. Kieran tapped Josie on the shoulder. 'If I were you, I'd take that quid off him.'

'Wouldn't trust the bugger. He'd make out she didn't say it even if she did.'

'Tell you what, Packy,' Kieran said. 'I'll be the referee. If Aideen Glynn says *how are you, Josie*? to your man here, he and I get to split the quid.' He grinned at Josie. 'How's that? We both win if she as much as says hello to you.'

Josie ran a hand through his hair. A quid was a quid, and it would be added pleasure to take it off fecking O'Brien. 'All that has to happen is for Aideen to say *how are you, Josie*? to me, and I get the quid?'

'Half of it – ten bob. I get the other ten for keeping your man here honest.' Kieran grinned again. 'It'll be the easiest ten bob we'll ever earn.'

'You're on,' Josie told O'Brien. All he'd have to do was walk into the school, say hello to Aideen, wait till she said *how are you, Josie*?, collect his quid and leave.

'I'll take that quid now.' Kieran grabbed the note from O'Brien.

'Just so there's no argument later,' Josie said, not trusting the pair one bit, 'I don't have to stay another minute after she says *how are you, Josie*?'

'You don't, but you might want to for the free booze: Austin Glynn is bringing over a half barrel.' Kieran winked at him. 'Why do you think I'm going and I already engaged?'

'So the little squireen is really selling her off, isn't he?' By hell, maybe he *would* set his cap at her. Two thousand quid. Jesus Christ Almighty!

23

She put the fry in front of him. 'Was it something *I* said, Father?'

He reached for knife and fork, his mind on the rashers, ravenous after fasting since midnight. 'Sorry. What was that?'

The housekeeper folded her arms, a sure sign she had something unpleasant to say. 'You've been going round with a long face since yesterday evening. And this morning you were rude to Brideen Conway, leaving her standing that way at the door. Even Brideen wanted to know what had got into you. So I thought maybe 'twas I had said something out of turn, or that maybe you didn't like the dinner yesterday.'

He waved his knife at her. 'Not at all.' She was telling him off, wasn't she? He wished she'd let him get on with his breakfast. 'The dinner was lovely. As always.'

The arms uncrossed. 'Right so. If you need more toast, call me.'

But after she left he was forced to come to grips with his foul humour. Of course it had to do with Brideen. Even though he had promised his Lord that he'd bear her no resentment, still his bile had spilled all over his behaviour this morning: his preaching at both masses reflected it, and his treatment of the young teacher was unpardonable. The fasting might be partly responsible: it was a long time to be without food, though you'd think he'd be used to it by now. Significantly, after he devoured his rashers and eggs and toast and three cups of tea he felt more mellow towards the world. And towards Brideen Conway.

On to the social then. And the vision of Eamon De Valera: he had read the text again while saying his communion thanksgiving. This evening could be a significant step towards achieving that vision in Coshlawn Crann. God willing, the lads and lassies would come and meet and form the bonds that would lead to marriage and beyond. The Larry Sweeneys and the Aideen Glynns. He had yet to resolve that question, hadn't he? Two people desperately wanting to get married. And though he wasn't a matchmaker, yet as shepherd of his flock how could he reject their cries for help? *So help them!* What could be simpler than to introduce those two souls to each other and watch the fires of love take hold?

There was a snag, of course, in this simple solution: Brideen Conway's plea for Josie Ryan. Had Heaven placed this woman in his path just to tempt him? Maybe that was how he should view her? On the other hand, her confession yesterday had dampened the fire of his longing, perhaps even put it out. How could he ever again look on her as he had before – his own sweet Brideen, innocent and pure. A serpent in the grass, more like, tempting him with her guileless smile while she wickedly sinned. His special relationship with her was now over. Furthermore, he resolved, swept up by a sudden passion for retribution, he'd repay her deceit by getting *Larry Sweeney* together with Aideen Glynn.

Ah, but that would be revenge, wouldn't it? Maybe. But *revenge is mine,* said the Lord. On the other hand, it wasn't unreasonable to match Larry with Aideen: they might make a wonderful couple. And the match would likely please Austin Glynn. So what more rationale did he need? If it made Brideen unhappy that couldn't be helped. Still, he *would* be getting back at her, wouldn't he? Despite the rightness of the act his motive must be suspect. Of course, he only promised her he'd *think* about introducing Josie to Aideen: he hadn't actually said he'd do it. Nevertheless, if she saw him getting Larry and Aideen together, what would she conclude? Especially in the light of his recent frosty behaviour towards herself. It would also be letting information he had acquired in confession affect his behaviour outside the box, an act that would place him perilously close to breaking the confessional seal.

So it had to be Josie Ryan and Aideen Glynn; he'd have to find another girl for Larry. He picked up his breviary and went outside. Sunshine and breeze completed the dissipation of his morning peeve. He began to recite the divine office, walking briskly up and down. It was just as he was finishing the third psalm of Sext that the thought hit him. Where it came from he had no idea – he had been focusing to the best of his ability on the sacred text – it simply arrived with the suddenness of summer thunder and stopped him in mid-stride, mid-phrase, mid-way between church and house. He stood perfectly still for several minutes, nodding his head and tapping his toe; then he strode through the front door with resolute step, deposited his breviary on the table, marched forth again, out the gate, down the street, and knocked on Austin Glynn's front door.

'Come in, Father,' Christine said. 'Did you have your dinner?'

'I had breakfast a short time ago. Thanks all the same.'

'We just finished eating; there's half a chicken left, and some colcan-non.' Eyebrows raised in teasing challenge. American Christine was always friendly towards him, though he had heard from others that she was inclined to be standoffish.

'I better not. Cait will be cooking for me later, and we wouldn't want to interfere with her schedule, now would we?'

They both smiled: the priest's housekeeper and Christine were friends, so the latter knew all about Cait's obsession with punctual meals. 'Come in and sit down anyway. Can I get you a cup of tea?'

'Maybe later. I'd like to talk with Austin first, if he's around.'

'He's in the house somewhere; I'll find him for you.' She returned in a minute with her husband. 'I caught the rascal just in time: he was about to take his afternoon nap.'

'I can come back another time.'

'Arrah not at all,' Austin said. 'We always have time for the man of the cloth.'

'I'll leave you to it then.' Christine pulled the door shut.

'I thought maybe we could take a walk back the fields while we talk.'

Austin stretched and yawned. 'Right. I need a bit of exercise after that dinner.' They went through a gate at the back of the house and picked their way through a field sprinkled with thistles and cow dung. The priest was still trying to formulate a suitable opening when the publican said, 'So what's on your mind, Father?'

'It has to do with Aideen.'

'You've got a sound man lined up for her?' Glynn's eyes brightened like a wick turned suddenly up. 'I knew I could count on you.' He hopped over a cow plop, as if dancing with delight.

They stepped through a gap in the wall into a field where cattle were grazing. 'As a matter of fact, I do have a good man in mind for her.'

'Good man yourself.'

'They tell me your daughter will bring a dowry of two thousand pounds with her.'

'Well, on my word!' Austin Glynn halted. 'Isn't Coshlawn Crann a great place for the gossip? Now where did you hear the like of that tall story?'

'Ah sure a lot of talk comes to my ears, Austin. I don't pass it on, of course, but I can't help hearing it.'

'You can't, I suppose. It's in the air, everywhere. Like this bloody this-tledown.' He kicked the head off a thorny weed, sending its pappi wafting in all directions.

'The question is, is the story true?'

'Ah now, Father, wouldn't that be telling?' The publican resumed his slow pace and they walked in silence for a bit. 'Of course now, if it has a bearing on the matter of finding a husband for Aideen, I suppose you'd need to know, wouldn't you?'

'That would seem logical.'

'Well, let's say then for the sake of argument that some of what you heard is true. I'm not saying *any* of it is true, mind you, but for the moment let's assume that it is. Except that the amount of money in question is one thousand, not two.'

'All right.'

'What then?'

'In that case we'll suppose as well that you already have the money in the bank, earmarked for Aideen. Though we won't ask how it was acquired.' Father Donovan had heard the tale of the illicit booze.

' 'Tis nobody's business how I got it.' Austin Glynn glowered. 'But I'll tell you this: I worked hard for every penny of it.'

'I have no doubt about that, Austin; no doubt at all.'

'Hard-earned money, Father. The sweat of an honest brow.'

'And you'd like it to be well spent, too, I'm sure. I mean, you would-n't want your hard earned money to be squandered.

'And it won't either, by God, because only a sound man will get to marry Austin Glynn's daughter. You can count on that, Father.'

'I wouldn't recommend any other kind to you, Austin.'

'There would be no need, of course, to let on to the sound man exactly how much he might expect to get. That'll be something to strike a bargain on, you see, when the time comes.'

'I understand you perfectly.'

They retraced their steps towards the house. After they had crossed half a field, Father Donovan said, 'Something just occurred to me, Austin. Suppose I were to find a sound man for Aideen who didn't need all of the dowry, maybe we could put the remainder to some worthwhile use?'

Austin Glynn stopped dead, looked suspiciously at him, then marched on in silence. When they were near the house he stopped again. 'By hell, but you're the cute lad, Father; this is what you came about, isn't it?'

'The thought I had was that there are a lot of young men and women in this parish who'd get married tomorrow if they had a little bit of money to help them get started.'

'And you think Austin Glynn has money to burn? That I can give away a thousand pounds without blinking an eyelid?'

'Well now, they say Austin Glynn made a power of money when he was over in the United States of America.'

'The people of this parish talk an awful lot of *seafoid*. But I can tell you this: Austin Glynn is not a rich man. So what on God's earth makes you think I'd be willing to give away the hard-earned money I've saved for my daughter's dowry?'

'I'd say you might do it because you're a good Christian man; because you believe it's a good thing to help those in need. And I'd say you'd do it all the more for your conscience's sake if you had any moral doubts about the way you might have accumulated some of that money.'

'Now what exactly do you mean by that?'

'No offence meant, Austin. It's just that, when a man is in business for himself, it's terribly hard for him to be always scrupulously honest in the way he makes his money. Or in the way he observes the law of the land, especially when he judges that law to be foolish. So a generous gift to a charitable cause might be the best way to clean the slate, as it were, with the Almighty.'

Glynn walked off again, not in the direction of the house but back towards the gap in the wall; Father Donovan followed in silence. When they were halfway into the next field he stopped. 'So, Father, supposing you found Aideen a rich man who didn't need all of my dowry, and supposing – and I'm just supposing, mind you – I were to give you the remainder, what exactly would you do with it?'

'I'll tell you. I've been asking myself why are there so few marriages in Coshlawn Crann? There are a lot of reasons of course, but among them I've heard of cases where a father won't let a son marry into the house until a daughter has a dowry first to marry out. So it struck me that if the bride coming in had a dowry that could be given to the bride going out you'd solve that problem. And, to carry the idea further, if you could set up the right chain of brides coming in and going out, a single dowry could be passed from one to another and make possible a whole series of marriages. Do you know what I mean?'

'It sounds like the three card trick to me.' Austin Glynn turned and walked back in the direction of the house. 'Who, might I ask, gets to *spend* the money?'

'Every father gets to spend it: doesn't he have a dowry to give his daughter that he wouldn't otherwise have? And whoever is at the end of the chain gets to spend it any way he likes.'

'So you want my money to set up your chain?'

'You'd be a great benefactor to the parish.'

' 'Tis a good thing to be charitable, I suppose.' Then Austin Glynn was silent till they reached the house. As he opened the door he said, 'Come in, Father, and we'll drink to your great idea.'

24

It would be unfair to say that Father Donovan skimped Benediction that Sunday evening. Though his mind *was* partly elsewhere, he strove to perform the rite with his customary reverence and devotion. Nevertheless, at least two members of his congregation did note the presto tempo of the proceedings.

'He looked like a man chasing sheep without a dog, he was going up and down the altar so fast,' Nellie Ruane remarked to Nora O'Brien on the way out of the church.

'In a hurry to get over to his social thing he is.' And indeed they were barely outside the gate when the man whizzed by them at a rate of knots unseemly for a priest, heading down the street in the direction of the school. 'What did I tell you?'

'Well there'll be great wick over there tonight. Are your own girls going?'

'Not a one of them. Teresa doesn't need to, of course: she's doing a strong line and I'd say she'll be getting engaged soon. But I told the two young ones that maybe they'd pick up husbands if they went. Sure they only laughed at me: there'd be only old codgers there, they said, meaning fellows over thirty; the kind, they said, they wouldn't be found dead talking to. I don't know what's got into young girls nowadays; nobody is good enough for them, it seems.'

'I'd like to be a *ciarog* in the corner tonight, watching them lads eyeing the girls that do go. There'll be fierce craic altogether.'

'Packy says he'll be there, but since he's going steady with the McDermott girl I'm thinking it's because he's up to some devilment.'

'They'll be like jobbers at the fair looking at heifers. I'm wondering if they'll be carrying sticks to prod them with?'

'Himself and Kieran McDermott are scheming something for Josie Ryan. They're an awful pair of blackguards them two lads when they get together, the Lord save us from all harm. Up to all kinds of *rí-rá* they do be.'

'And it won't be just the young pucks that'll be there either, I'll bet. Didn't I hear Cait's brother John say the other night that he was thinking of going. And the man near sixty years of age.'

'Tricking Josie into making eyes at some unfortunate girl is what they're up to.'

'Sure if a man isn't married by forty-five 'tis as well for him to stay that way. He's not a bit of use to a girl after that.'

'But for God's sake what girl in her right mind would want to marry Josie? Wouldn't he drive her cracked in no time at all?'

'Marriage is for the young and innocent before they get to know any better. What would the like of John Burke want with a wife anyway?'

'But I wouldn't put it past those two devils to find someone for him all the same. There's no stopping them when they get an idea into their heads.'

'I'd say this whole thing is nothing more or less than a scheme concocted by Austin Glynn to get Aideen off his hands. They say he promised to put a new stained-glass window in the church the day she gets married.'

'Well, you don't say, Nellie? And the man hardly even a Catholic.'

Their discussion of Austin Glynn carried them all the way home to Kilmorrin.

There were only fifteen people in Maura Prendergast's classroom when the priest arrived. Maura herself and Brideen were fussing around the table with the refreshments. Over in the corner a half barrel of porter and glasses were laid on the teacher's desk; Austin Glynn stood nearby chatting with his daughter. In front of the fireplace the flame from a small paraffin oil stove licked the bottom of a black kettle. Half-a-dozen women stood in a circle by the window chatting, feigning complete indifference to all others in the room. Five men of varying ages lounged near the door, drinking Austin Glynn's Guinness.

'Where's everybody?' Father Donovan asked Maura, averting his eyes from Brideen.

'God knows.' Maura was placing cups right side up in saucers. 'They're hardly in the pub anyway, because the booze here is free and Austin said his missus promised not to serve any unmarried man this evening.'

'They'll be along eventually,' Brideen said. 'Nobody ever comes on time to anything in this place.' There was a sad quality in her tone, in contrast to her usual ebullience, that forced the priest to look at her.

'They will, I suppose.' Such sorrow was in her eyes that he had to ask, 'are you all right?'

'As good as can be expected.'

'Aren't you well, Brideen?' Maura the solicitous mother. 'What's the matter?'

'I'm fine, thanks, Maura.' But the ever so slight crack in the voice betrayed Brideen's agitation. 'I think maybe I'm getting a cold.'

'A cup of tea will do you a world of good.' Maura walked over to the stove and felt the side of the kettle with her hand. 'If this thing ever comes to a boil.'

The sound of voices in the hall presaged the entry of seven men through the door, single file, each in turn glancing around the room, each letting his eyes rest briefly on the women by the window.

'Welcome,' Father Donovan said.

'Good evening, Father.' The chorus was cheerful, a good sign indeed.

'There's Guinness on the house over here,' Austin Glynn called out. 'Let ye come on over and get it.'

'Don't be shy.' Aideen's voice was strained as she held out a glass. A short stout man in a tweed suit and peaked cap crossed the room and accepted the pint. The others quickly followed.

More men and women straggled in, and within half an hour the place was quite well filled. The buzz of conversation increased noticeably; soon it was interspersed with laughter, some of it boisterous; the kettle eventually boiled and Maura made the tea; women and men crowded around the table and sampled the cakes and tarts; the Glynns were kept busy pulling pints. Father Donovan was pleased beyond measure: wasn't the room occupied by comely maidens and athletic youths? Weren't they talking, getting to know one another? Wouldn't they soon be establishing serious relationships that would lead them to the sacred bonds of matrimony? Indeed, weren't they already on their way to realizing De Valera's dream?

'Good evening to you, Father.' Larry Sweeney standing before him, cap in hand, red in face.

'Larry! I'm delighted you could come.' The priest shook his hand. 'You're looking very swanky, I must say.' And indeed the man looked dapper in a blue serge suit, a white shirt that had been ironed, and a maroon tie. His thinning hair was slicked back and his ruddy face was freshly shaved.

'You have to put the best foot forward at a time like this.' Larry unleashed his crooked grin. 'The mother made me buy a new suit,' he said, caressing his lapel with thumb and forefinger.

'Very elegant indeed, Larry. It suits you well.'

'It cost the price of a fat sheep, mind you, but she said it was worth it if it would get me a wife.'

'Why wouldn't you get a wife? I'm sure all the girls will find you most attractive. And there's one in particular that I'd like you to meet.' After giving the matter more prayerful consideration, and after asking Cait what people thought of both Larry Sweeney and Josie Ryan, he had concluded that not only was Larry the more suitable match for Aideen, he was also far more likely to fit in with the brilliant plan Father Donovan had concocted with her father.

'So if you'll come with me,' he said to Larry now, and turned towards Glynn and his daughter.

'How are you, Larry,' Brideen said from behind.

'How are you, Brideen.'

Father Donovan swung around, irritated at the untimely intrusion. 'Ah now, Larry, don't go making eyes at Brideen here; she's already spoken for.'

'I promised your mother,' Brideen said, her hand on Larry's arm, 'when I met her in Harney's the other day, that I'd introduce you to a very nice girl. And that's what I'm going to do right now.' And before the priest could interfere she was leading him to the window where most of the women were congregated. Oh dear God! If she got Larry fixed up with another girl, as she seemed bent on doing, his whole clever scheme could fall apart. Damn, blast, and bother! She already had him shaking hands with the Dolan woman from Carrigdubh. Kathleen was her name; he'd met her when he was canvassing the triduum. Good-looking, in her early thirties; she'd make a fine wife for any man.

Kieran McDermott and Packy O'Brien trooped in just then, grinning and greeting, and trailed in the door by wary Josie Ryan. Not a bad-looking fellow at all, the same Josie: tall and straight with powerful shoulders, a decent looking mug, and a fine head of jet black hair. Pity he was such a gom, everybody said; meaning, as Cait explained, that he had all the *plamas* of a pig in a parlour. The priest watched the trio and wondered how he might counteract Brideen's preemptive strike. He understood why she did it, of course, and in spite of his chagrin had to admire her brilliant reaction.

A push in the back from Packy sent Josie stepping across the room, cautiously, like a rabbit deciding his next fearful move. He stopped behind Aideen, who was leaning over the desk pulling a pint from the half barrel.

'How are you, Aideen,' he said, loudly, as if for all in the room to hear. The publican's daughter, intent on the slowly filling glass, didn't respond to the greeting.

'How are you, Aideen,' Josie said again, this time half shouting. But the young woman still didn't acknowledge him.

'Hey!' he bellowed, and all conversation in the room ceased for a moment. At the same time he reached out and patted her rump.

Aideen whirled, spilling some of the drink. 'Well, blast you anyway, Josie Ryan. What the hell do you think you're doing?'

'Sorry. I only wanted to say how are you.'

'Well, go feck off.' She grabbed a towel from the top of the barrel and wiped her hand and the dripping glass.

'Ah now, Aideen, don't be too hard on the lad.' Austin Glynn came up behind Josie and patted him on the back. 'Here, let me get you a pint.' He placed a glass under the spigot and poured.

Father Donovan, watching the little drama, felt relieved. Everyone had seen Josie's behaviour and Aideen's reaction, so Brideen could hardly blame him now for not trying to set them up. He stepped over to where she was standing at the makeshift table, teapot in hand. 'It's going well, isn't it?'

'Josie made a right eejit of himself.'

'He did.'

'You can always count on that lad to make a hames of anything he sets out to do.' She poured tea for a not-so-young woman who was holding out a cup.

'Is that a fact?'

'But anyway, Larry Sweeney seems to be getting on well.' Was there a note of triumph in her tone?

'He is.' The fellow was carrying on an animated conversation with Kathleen Dolan. ' 'Tis a pity, though. He'd make a good match for Aideen.'

'Arrah he would not, Father! I've known Larry for years. He'd be a lot better off with Kathleen.'

'Why do you say that?'

'She's more his type. Would you like some tea, Father?'

'No thanks. All the same. . . .' He paused a moment. 'I had a plan worked out for you and Kieran that involved Larry Sweeney and Aideen.'

'What kind of a plan was that, Father?'

'A plan that would have got you the money you need to get married.'

'Sugar!' He felt sorry for her then, such was her woebegone expression. 'I didn't know. Why didn't you tell me?'

'Can I have a word with you, Father?' Austin Glynn was at his side and, if his expression was any indication, he wasn't happy either.

'Certainly, Austin.'

'Could we step outside for a minute?'

'I'll talk with you later, Brideen.' Father Donovan followed Austin Glynn into the hallway.

'Listen.' The man's heavy breathing suggested he was close to anger. 'I thought we had an understanding, the two of us, that you had found a suitable man for Aideen?'

'We do, Austin. And I have a suitable man for her. And I'm going to introduce him to her.' Though how he was going to accomplish that mission now he had no idea.

'Well, we've been here an hour already. I've poured almost a barrel of porter into half the lads of the parish. And not a single one of them has shown the slightest interest in my daughter. Except of course, for that yahoo Josie Ryan who I wouldn't let within an ass's roar of her.'

Father Donovan, facing the outside door, was scrambling desperately for a reply to the publican's just complaint when that door opened and in stepped Alphonsus Finnerty. 'I was waiting for my man to come, Austin, the man I had in mind for your daughter. And that man has just arrived.' The priest could never after explain where the inspiration came from, for the words just seemed to tumble out of his mouth of their own accord. 'How are you, Mr Finnerty?'

'Well, good evening to you, Father Donovan.' The glitter in Finnerty's eye and the jollity in his tone and the wobbly spring in his step said he was well fortified with booze.

'You're just in time, Mr Finnerty. There's a grand young woman in here who's dying to meet you.'

The principal stuck out his hand and shook cordially. 'Call me Fonsie, Father.'

'I will indeed. You know Austin Glynn, of course? Fonsie.'

'Why wouldn't I?' Finnerty shook the publican's hand with equal good nature. 'Though as a matter of principle I never enter your establishment, sir. No offence intended, mind you.' He bowed to Austin. 'It's just that I wouldn't want to give any bad example to my scholars, you see. I mean, what would they think of Mr Finnerty if they saw that he, too, of Jove's nectar sometimes sipped?'

'You have a point there,' Father Donovan said. 'One can't be too careful in the matter of scandal.'

'That's exactly what I always say.' Alphonsus Finnerty shook himself, as if to clear his head. 'Precisely.'

The man was one drink short of being maggoty mouldy, the priest estimated, recognizing that his own judgement in the matter was clouded by his wish that the principal should be at least minimally sober. 'You're here to meet the ladies, I presume?'

'Why wouldn't I? Haven't they all come here to my own school just to meet me?'

'They have indeed.' Austin Glynn's tone left no doubt as to how *he* felt about Father Donovan's choice. 'And if you'll come inside with me now, Fonsie, I'll introduce you to a grand young woman. You are interested in meeting an attractive lady?'

'Oh by Jove I certainly am.' Finnerty's grin was all leer. 'Isn't that what I came here for, to the heifer fair. I may be no two-year old myself any more, but I'll have you know I'm as fine a bull as you'll find anywhere.' He straightened his back and fingered his tie. 'Amn't I, Father?'

'You're a fine-looking man indeed, Fonsie. The women will all be chasing after you, now that they know you're available.'

'Why wouldn't I be available? Haven't I been available for years, only no one gave a tinker's curse?' He stared at the priest with glassy-eyed despair. 'This, I'll have you know, is my very last hope. If I don't get a woman here tonight it's all over bar the shouting for poor old Fonsie.'

'You just leave it to me, Fonsie.' Austin Glynn took him by the arm. 'I'm going to fix you up right now with the finest woman in the parish.' He opened the classroom door and ushered in the Principal Teacher of Coshlawn Crann National School.

Father Donovan took a deep breath and headed out the front door.

25

Alphonsus Finnerty was a weekend drinker. Monday morning to Friday afternoon he abstained from booze; to prove, he told himself, that he wasn't a slave to the stuff. Then on Friday after school he'd bee-line to the Lahvauce Country Club and, after a round of golf with Dick Fogarty, settle in to an evening of steady drinking, initially with his friend, then alone after Dick would abandon him for the comforts of home and family.

On the Friday evening before Father Donovan's social, as the pair were working on their first pints, Fogarty remarked, 'Someone told me today that your favourite priest is holding a big hooley on Sunday to get everyone in his parish married.'

'Bloody fool. He should leave people alone.'

'Well now, Fonsie, you're the man who's always lamenting that you don't have a wife. Maybe you should take advantage of the opportunity. Who knows what *cailín álainn* you might meet.'

'Do you have any idea what kind of streels will be there? The leftovers who hadn't the spunk to emigrate. An ignorant bunch of farmers' daughters, with cow-shite up to the fuzz, who never take a bath, and can't spell a word with more than two syllables. No thanks, Dick. Bad as my present state is, it's better than being hitched to one of them.'

'You're right, of course. My advice to any man who's not married is to stay that way. Women are a terrible curse once they get their hooks into you.'

Finnerty nodded and let the subject drop. But after Fogarty went home and he was boozing alone the notion entered his sodden brain that maybe he *should* go to the bloody priest's social, *should* make a last-ditch effort at finding a wife. All very well for Fogarty to say a man was better off single. Though it might well be true in the bank manager's case – he had a real bitch of a missus – the solitary life was sad and lonely, and a mediocre wife would be better than none at all. That thought stayed with him as he made his way home. It was strengthened when he burned the eggs for his late-night supper. And it returned in force next morning after he soberly surveyed the disaster that was his kitchen. 'It's either a wife or a house-keeper,' he intoned out his dirty parlour window.

Although he publicly professed to have given up on the idea of marry-ing, deep in his craw he yearned for a woman in his bed. His was what might be considered a normal preoccupation with sex, which he sort of satisfied with self-gratification and occasional forays against Galway City ladies of the night. A woman who would satisfy his lust, keep a clean house, cook his meals, wash his clothes, be able to converse halfway intel-ligently, would be worth whatever aggravation she'd cause with tongue or deed. But could he find such a woman in backwater Coshlawn Crann? Middle-aged women gone to fat? Good-looking young girls, he knew from sad experience, wouldn't offer him a second glance. So he'd only be humiliating himself by going to the school on Sunday evening. He wasn't going to go.

However, another evening of drinking followed by the usual Sunday morning misery forced him to reconsider. So maybe he wouldn't meet anyone suitable; maybe he would be humiliated. But would he be any worse off than he was now? And there was always the chance, however slight, that he might meet someone. He'd better go.

Then the questions invaded. What effect might a wife, if he found one, have on his writing? Would she laugh at him for being Laura Devon? Or would she nag him to death with things to do and places to go till he had no time left for the consuming passion of his life? One thing was certain: he'd test any prospective wife beforehand to ensure she would-n't interfere with his art. If it came to a choice between wife and writing, Laura Devon must come first.

So Alphonsus Finnerty, having fortified himself with distillery courage, went to Father Donovan's social. His first reaction on being introduced to Aideen Glynn was *what an ugly young woman*, with her short round figure and uneven proboscis; not being a resident of Coshlawn Crann or a patron of Austin Glynn's pub or a member of Father Donovan's congregation, he had never before seen the girl close up. But the second thing he noticed was that she had attractive eyes: warm, sparkling, friendly, even inviting. Which, coupled with her voice that had been refined of its Mayo brogue by five years of boarding-school nuns, prevented him from making a speedy getaway after Austin Glynn made the introductions and left them alone. The girl might be worth investigating. Good looks, after all, weren't everything: he had been rejected by too many beauties to have a high opinion of their sort. Maybe better a plain woman who valued him than a gorgeous one who'd be forever on the lookout for someone else.

'Where did you go to school?' His romantic heroes always used questions about home or school or work as introductions to more intimate queries.

'Kiltimagh; the St Louis nuns.'

'A fine school, I hear.' It was well known that the cream of the county – the rich and thick, the joke went – sent their daughters there to be prepared for suitable marriages.

'I hated it; the nuns were terribly strict.'

And rightly so, he almost said, before his recovering brain shouted *don't*. 'They would be, I suppose. Didn't let you smoke or drink? That sort of thing?' He smiled; gain her confidence so he could probe her mind.

'Rules, rules, it was nothing but rules.'

'I had the same experience at school myself.' *Sympathy is the gateway to the heart* a Laura Devon character once remarked.

Her expression, hitherto guarded, became animated. 'Go to bed when the bell rings; get up when the bell rings; blow your nose when the bell rings; go to the toilet when the bell rings.' She blushed and giggled. 'But do you know the thing that annoyed me most? The library. I love to read, but their library had nothing except stuffy old books that were a hundred years old and that nobody would ever want to read any more. And they wouldn't let us read romantic novels, even if we brought them with us from home. I love romantic novels.'

'One of the things I disliked about teacher training college, too, was that we were restricted in what we could read. History, biography, and *serious* novels only.' His head was beginning to clear. 'So who's your favourite romantic author?'

She rattled off a slew of names, none of them his Laura. 'But I've almost never read a romantic novel I didn't like.'

'Have you ever heard of Laura Devon?'

'Ooooo!' It came out as a squeal of delight. 'Didn't I mention her? She's one of my favourite favourites. I've read her *Sundered Sweethearts* five times.' She giggled again. 'That's silly of me, isn't it?'

'Not at all. A good book is worth reading many times.' And a young woman who read *Sundered Sweethearts* five times must be a serious contender for becoming Alphonsus Finnerty's wife. So he chatted her up for the next hour, and when leaving suggested he'd see her soon again. She offered him a handshake and said she'd be delighted to talk to him any time.

★

When her father asked her that night over a bite of late supper if she had enjoyed the social, Aideen said, 'I didn't meet young Lochinvar if that's what you mean. If it wasn't for Alphonsus Finnerty talking to me it would have been a terrible evening altogether.'

'That awful man,' her mother said. 'What was he talking about? How he beats the children?'

'He was very nice, Mammy. An educated man who can converse intelligently. Not like the yobs that come into the bar and can talk only about the size of turnips or the price of sheep.'

'So you liked him then?' The faint touch of eagerness in her father's tone raised a question that Alphonsus Finnerty's conversation had not.

'Were you putting him on to me, Daddy?' He *had* made a point of bringing Mr Finnerty over to her and then left them alone. Which hadn't aroused any suspicion in her mind at the time because of the man's age; he was after all at least fifteen years older than her. Hadn't he started teaching in Coshlawn Crann just after she went to convent school?

'Oh God, not at all.' But though she recognized Daddy's denial as patently fake she didn't make an issue of it. Alphonsus Finnerty had left her with the kind of warm feeling that she hadn't quite experienced before and, although she had failed to link it to romance at the time, it now struck her that perhaps it was so connected.

So she thought about him as she prepared for bed. He was, of course, a *confirmed* bachelor – everyone said that: it was a point of conversation more than once in the bar, coupled always with vilification of the man by his former pupils. But he had been so nice to her. And wasn't it amazing that he had read *Sundered Sweethearts* and could talk so intelligently about it, giving a dimension to the characters that even after five readings she herself hadn't fully grasped.

When she got up next morning Daddy said, 'Alphonsus Finnerty was in a while ago on his way to school asking for you.'

'What did he want?'

'He said he had a lovely time talking to you last evening and wanted to say hello again.' Daddy looked around to make sure Mammy hadn't come in from mass. 'Between you and me, Aideen, I think the man is keen on you.'

'Arrah go on out of that.' But she was pleased all the same. And when her mother came home from church and complained about 'that awful man' coming to see her daughter so early in the morning, Aideen resolved to take seriously any interest the principal teacher of Coshlawn Crann National School might show in her.

An opportunity to do just that came shortly after three o'clock. She was sitting in the parlour reading Laura Devon's *Moonlight Kisses* for the third time – since Mr Finnerty was such an expert on *Sundered Sweethearts* perhaps they could converse on *Moonlight Kisses* next time – when the front door knocker was discreetly tapped. It was him.

'I enjoyed our talk so much yesterday that I thought I'd drop by to say hello again.' His embarrassed grin dispelled any thought she might have had of being coy.

'Come in.' She showed him into the parlour, but before she could close the door her mother invaded.

'Hello, Mr Finnerty,' in the friendly but chilling tone that was the Mammy's specialty for the truly unwelcome.

'Mrs Glynn.' The teacher beamed and stretched a hand that the mother couldn't refuse without positive insult. She took it gingerly. 'My pleasure to meet you a second time in the one day. We met this morning when I dropped in to say hello,' he explained to Aideen.

'That was so nice of you.' Aideen hoped her warmth would neutral-ize the icy blast of her mother's smile. 'Sit down, please, and take the weight off your feet.'

'I don't mind if I do; I've been standing most of the day.' The teacher sat in an easy chair and looked around. 'Lovely parlour you have here, Mrs Glynn. It's a credit to you.' Aideen was reminded that Martin McDermott, God rest him, had made a similar remark on entering this very room.

'Yes.' Mammy's curt response was glacial.

'Would you like a cup of tea,' Aideen asked her guest. Something had to be done to warm the atmosphere.

'If it's not too much trouble.' Alphonsus Finnerty settled back in his chair as if he felt completely at home. 'But just a cup in the hand.'

Aideen got to her feet, sensing as she did her mother's dilemma: whether to leave her daughter alone with the awful man or be left alone herself with him. The latter fear triumphed; Mammy stood. 'I'll get it, dear; you stay and entertain your guest.'

You had to hand it to the mother: the manners never failed, whatever the crisis. She brought tea and biscuits on a tray, then left them alone, saying, 'I have a few things to attend to.'

'I hope I haven't interrupted you in your work,' the teacher said.

'Not at all. I was reading *Moonlight Kisses* for the third time. It's another

Laura Devon book. Have you read it?'

Alphonsus Finnerty sipped his tea, put down his cup, then picked it up again and sipped some more. He seemed agitated, and she was about to ask him if something was wrong with the tea – had Mammy put poison in it maybe? – when he said, 'There's something I'd like to tell you, but you must promise me you'll keep it absolutely secret.'

She loved secrets. 'Certainly. Your secret will be absolutely safe with me.'

He put down the cup again, folded his arms, and looked intently at her. 'I'm talking about *absolute* secrecy now; not the Coshlawn Crann variety where everybody hears about it within the hour.'

'Honest to God, you can count on me. I'll never ever reveal it to anyone.'

'All right so. It has to do with Laura Devon.'

'Don't tell me you've read *all* her books? I've read four of them, but I haven't been able to find her very first one: *For Love of his Ice-cream Girl.*'

'I've not only read them all, I've written them all.'

The crimson flush spreading over his sallow face told her she was in receipt of a momentous disclosure. 'I don't understand.' Then the import of his statement hit her. 'Oh my God!'

'*I'm* Laura Devon.' The words were too soberly said to be in jest.

'Jesus God!' she jumped up and did a little dance. 'This is just too incredible.'

He put a finger to his lips. 'Remember. It must remain our secret. No one else knows, and I intend to keep it that way.'

'But why would you want to hide it? What a wonderful thing to have written all those great books.'

'Because it would be a terrrible embarrassment to the Principal of Coshlawn Crann National School to be known as Laura Devon, the writer of romantic novels.'

The eyes were averted as he spoke, so she could examine his face more closely. Not a bad-looking mug, though the nose was a bit small and pointy and the lips thin and tightly drawn. Their children's noses should be interesting. 'I suppose,' she agreed, but only for the sake of agreeing: men were such cowards when their masculine image was threatened.

'And you will keep it secret?'

'Oh indeed. I promised you, didn't I?'

The moment's silence that followed was broken by a knock on the door and Daddy stuck his head in. 'How are you, Alphonsus?'

'Very well, thank you, Austin.' Mr Finnerty got to his feet, awkwardly;

he seemed almost in awe of Daddy.

'Don't get up. Not at all. I didn't mean to disturb you.' But then the Dad stepped into the room. 'I just dropped by to ask if maybe you'd like to have dinner with us tomorrow evening?'

'I'd like that very much indeed.' The teacher's smile was almost slavish. And the thought crossed Aideen Glynn's mind that the man who terrified schoolchildren mightn't be so difficult to tame after all.

26

When Father Donovan walked out the classroom door with Austin Glynn the night of the social, he left behind a devastated Brideen Conway. 'A plan that would have got you the money you need to get married,' he had told her. Whatever could that plan have been? And she had destroyed it, he said, by not letting him introduce Larry Sweeney to Aideen Glynn. But how could she have known? Of course she couldn't, but she should have trusted her priest. Which she hadn't: when she saw him turning towards Aideen and beckoning Larry Sweeney to follow, she had concluded that he was still acting out of pique because of her confession. Which maybe he was, and maybe his talk about a plan to get them money was just another form of revenge. Ah no! Father Donovan wouldn't lie to her. He might be angry, and he certainly had been in the morning, but he wouldn't lie.

Which brought up the question that in her embarrassment she hadn't hitherto raised with herself: why was he angry at her because she confessed to him? Was it because of what she told him, or because she had gone to confession in Lahvauce rather than in Coshlawn Crann? It had to be the former, otherwise how explain his vitriolic sermon on hypocrisy? But surely he was accustomed to hearing all sorts of sins, including the kind that she had told? Anyway, a priest should never be angry at the sinner. Unless the sinner offended him personally. Which, of course, she hadn't.

Or had she? No! The new thought that just entered her head was not to be considered. Father Donovan was a holy man. Even if he did show delight at seeing her, and did spend a lot of time in her classroom on his weekly visits – Maura Prendergast had recently remarked on that – his liking could not be *that* kind? He was a priest, and priests didn't . . . or did they? A story came back to her that Nuala Caffrey had told in teacher training about a lad she met at a dance in Dublin and dated and fell in love with and let do unmentionable things to her until she visited her aunt some miles north of the city and went to mass in the local church and there was your man on the altar *saying* the mass.

All this was going through Brideen's head while she was pouring cups of tea and cutting pieces of cake and smiling at people and making banal conversation. So if he had fallen for her was she to blame? Surely not. She was madly in love with Kieran. And she had always been cautious with lads who seemed ready to flirt with her; which used to happen quite a lot when she lived in Dublin. But she had felt no need to be wary of Father Donovan. Why should she? He never acted in any way improperly. Nevertheless, it wasn't impossible, was it, that he might be smitten? Such a nice man. He'd have made a grand husband for someone if he hadn't become a priest.

So what was she to do? Act as if she was unaware of any amorous feelings on his part, while keeping an eye out for signs of them? But for now she needed to focus on what to do about herself and Kieran, since her Josie Ryan scheme had fallen through. She went over to the two lads. 'Josie made a horse's collar of that, didn't he?'

'Feck him,' Kieran said.

'Will you look at this.' Packy pointed across the room. Austin Glynn was beaming at Alphonsus Finnerty who was grinning and shaking hands effusively with Aideen. 'Don't tell me that bloody fecker is having a go at her?'

'Josie is such a yob. You wonder he's able to put his pants on in the morning.'

'Well he won't be taking them off for Aideen, that's for sure.'

'It's the first time I've ever seen a smile on fecking Finnerty's face. I'd like to go over this minute and rub it off with my fist.'

'So I'm off to England.'

Brideen didn't have the heart to say anything to that. Neither could she tell them what Father Donovan had said about her bollixing his plan for their marriage.

Although he had never hitherto considered Alphonsus Finnerty a candidate for matrimony, the minute Father Donovan saw the man come through the school door that evening it was as if a revelation had been granted him. In a flash of extraordinary – and, he felt, supernatural – insight he perceived the cause of the principal's perduring misery that spilled over into daily cruelty to his pupils: the frustration of a man without vocation to celibacy who yet lacked the comfort of woman.

Afterwards, walking home in the bright summer evening it was further revealed to the priest that the teacher's precise moment of arrival was in fulfilment of both their destinies: the termination of Finnerty's single state, and a vital step in the accomplishment of De Valera's dream. Aideen Glynn, bride, eagerly awaited the principal, and since the groom would likely need no dowry, Father Donovan would have the benefit of Austin Glynn's entire thousand pounds to meet the needs of poor but worthy candidates for marriage. Furthermore, wasn't it a perfect match? What more suitable husband for the daughter of genteel *Christine* Glynn than a teacher? Aideen, convent educated and spoiled only child, was not cut out to be a farmer's wife. She'd be miserably unhappy trudging through muck and dirt, feeding hens and ducks, milking cows and boiling pigs' pots, all inevitable chores were she to marry a Larry Sweeney or a Josie Ryan. And what more suitable son-in-law for prosperous *Austin* Glynn than a man who could afford to give his daughter the material comforts her father had hitherto provided?

So he was prepared to be complimented when Christine Glynn came through the sacristy door immediately after mass next morning. 'Good morning, Christine.'

'What in God's name were you up to, Father?' Her eyes were smouldering.

'Sorry. What was that?'

'What were you thinking of, matching up my daughter with that cruel man?'

That particular thought *had* flitted across the priest's mind late last night, but he dismissed it with the consoling reflection that he had known several disciplinarian teachers who seemed to be kind to their wives. 'He may not be as cruel as you think. I believe he's a bit like Goldsmith's village schoolmaster: *If severe in aught, the love he bears to learning is at fault.*'

'He's a sadistic monster and I don't want him anywhere near my Aideen.'

Was it possible, Father Donovan asked himself now, that he had made a mistake, that he had allowed his obsession with De Valera's dream to cloud his judgement? But what else could he have done at the time, with the publican breathing fire and not a suitable man in sight and his share of the dowry about to vanish? Besides, Austin had been highly pleased with his choice. However, he mustn't fight with Christine, one of his very best parishioners. 'Would you like me to tell Austin I made a mistake?'

'Too late. Finnerty came around to see her already this morning.'

'Go on!'

'I came out the door to come up to mass and there he was, hat in hand. "I stopped on my way to school", he said, "to say hello to your daughter".'

'Well, would you believe it?'

'I told him that Aideen was still in bed. And do you know what he said?'

'What did he say?'

'He said "ah, how lovely indeed!" Rolling his eyes to heaven as if he were Prince Charming himself enquiring after Cinderella.'

'Well, isn't that something.'

' "Tell her I'll be round to see her after school", he says, and off he goes, looking pleased as Punch with himself.'

'He's obviously smitten.'

'He's a brute; that's what he is.'

'Not the gentlest of men, I'll grant you that.'

'What are we going to do, Father?'

'What does Aideen think of him?'

'Poor Aideen is flattered by any idiot with trousers who pays attention to her.'

'Austin seemed quite pleased.'

'Austin is a fool when it comes to marrying off his daughter. Worse still, he's a snobbish fool. Or a foolish snob. It's a terrible Irish failing. He always wanted an educated man for her: someone with a bit of class, as he said himself. So he's happy with Finnerty. He doesn't give a hoot that the man's a sadistic savage.'

'Perhaps he's not aware. . . ?'

'Oh he's aware all right. But he himself believes in strict discipline for children. *He* was beaten in school, he says, and is none the worse for it, so why shouldn't every other child be beaten. Ugh!'

'I have a feeling, Christine, that your daughter may soften Mr Finnerty; make him mellow. I believe his brutality is caused by his own unhappiness, and that the influence of a good woman will change him for the better.'

'I'm also told, and on good authority, that he doesn't even believe in God.'

Father Donovan was aware that the principal was not a particularly religious man. But that he was actually an atheist? 'I'll have a talk with him about his religious beliefs. He will, of course, have to go to confession and communion before the wedding.'

'Oh my God! Don't even talk about a wedding between my baby and that wicked man.' And Christine Glynn abruptly fled the sacristy, leaving behind a chastened and perplexed young curate.

27

Tom McDermott usually rested for half an hour after his one o'clock dinner. He'd sit on his throne, close his eyes, and allow his thoughts to wander. On this particular day, as he did every day since Martin died, he thought about the madcap son who had drowned. Two months had not diminished the pain; if the poor lad were here this minute he'd be sitting on the couch smoking a Woodbine and talking nonsense.

He opened his eyes when he heard someone say, 'God bless the work.' The postman walked in through the scullery, where Rosaleen was washing the dishes.

'How are you, Mattie?' Tom said. 'You have something for us?'

'A letter, Tom. From Dublin, by the postmark.' He handed the white envelope to the man of the house, then lingered as if awaiting an invitation to sit.

Tom stood, stretched. 'Thanks, Mattie. I better be getting back to work. The oats is ready for cutting.' He didn't open the letter.

'I'd say it is, all right.' Mattie took the hint and left. After he passed the window again Tom sat, ripped open the envelope, pulled out the three-page letter. Good notepaper, he noticed before beginning to read.

Dear Daddy
I know this will come as a great shock to you, but, I hope, a pleasant one.
I am alive.

What? Great God Almighty! Whose bad joke was this? He turned the pages over – written on both sides – and searched in agitation till he found the signature on the back of the last page.

> *Your fond son,*
> *Martin*

It looked like his writing for sure. Could it be possible? Was the son he was mourning alive? For a day or two after the reported drowning he had hoped and hoped against despair that Martin might still turn up. But when nothing happened he reconciled himself to the reality of his death. Now this! Was he dreaming? Or hallucinating? He took a deep breath and read on.

I didn't really drown that Saturday night, though I almost did. I managed to swim out of the river and stumbled across the fields to Josie Ryan's and spent the night in his shed. It was only when Josie found me there in the morning and told me the priest had announced at mass that I was dead that I decided to stay that way. As you've probably heard, I had just got myself engaged to Aideen Glynn and was horrified at what I'd done. No reflection on Aideen, but I couldn't possibly marry her. So I decided to escape to Dublin and let people go on thinking I was dead. I hope you won't be mad at me for not letting you know sooner, but there wasn't any way I could.

No. He wasn't mad at his son yet, but he had a growing feeling that as soon as he got over the shock he would be. Two months had passed. Two long sad months. Unnecessary sadness, it turned out now. Why hadn't the blackguard written before this?

Anyway, I intend to stay dead, so please don't tell anyone I'm alive, other than Kieran and Rosaleen of course. I've got a job here in Dublin that will keep me going for the time being. However, it's not a good job and I have a better one in mind. I've been talking to the fellows who buy and sell at the cattle market here, and I've found the perfect career for me – cattle jobber. There's an awful lot of money in it – you should see the wads of notes those lads flash, and the way they dress – and it's just the kind of work I'm cut out to do.

The only problem is, I need money to get started. A jobber I met told me his father set him up in the business with a thousand pound loan, which he was able to pay back in a couple of years. So I'm writing to ask you if you'd loan me a thousand quid to get started? You have my absolute guarantee that you'll get your money back in two years. With interest, too. Please, Dad, it's all I'll ever ask of you. And when I get rich, as I surely will in a very short time, I'll take care of Kieran and Rosaleen for you so you can keep all your hard-earned money for yourself, and live the good life in Lahvauce, as I know you'd like to. And giving me the money to get started will keep me from ever returning to Coshlawn Crann, which I'm sure you'll be glad of: it would be a terrible embarrassment to you all if I turned up there alive – can you imagine all the sniggering that would go on back at Glynn's?

You can reach me here, c/o Clare Joyce, 37 Dargle Road, Drumcondra, Dublin.

With renewed apologies for not writing to you sooner and hoping to hear from you soon, I remain,

Your fond son,

Martin

He sat there, staring at the letter, his body not moving, his thoughts screeching like crows at a circling hawk. The sheer inconsiderateness! The casual revelation that he was still alive, as if he were announcing his safe arrival from a trip. The colossal nerve of the bodach, writing only because he wanted money! The anger began to flow inside Tom McDermott.

'Rosie! Come here quick.' His voice a croak of urgent anguish.

A collision of pot in sink before Rosaleen stepped into the kitchen, drying her hands on her apron. 'What is it, Daddy? Are you all right?'

'No, I'm not all right.' He waved the letter at her, his mouth forming words but no further sound coming out.

'What's the matter? Who is the letter from?'

'Martin. The blackguard is alive.' The words tumbled out.

'What? Daddy! What's the matter with you?' She came right up and made to touch his brow. He waved her hand away.

'Martin is alive, Rosie.'

She stared at him with vast incomprehension. 'Daddy, Martin is dead.' Quietly, as if he were off his head and needed to be corrected with the utmost gentleness.

'Here! Read this.'

She took the letter.

'Mother of God!' She turned the pages to verify the writer's name. 'Martin!' She collapsed onto the sofa and struggled to catch her breath. 'But he's dead, Daddy.' Her eyes were wild, as if she, too, had gone mad. 'Didn't they find his wallet on the river-bank?' She looked at the letter again. 'For God's sake, it is his writing.' She read the whole thing, then closed her eyes, breathed deeply, opened them, slapped herself on the face. 'Help me, sweet Jesus, what am I to believe?'

'The blackguard is alive all right.'

'And to think I cursed God Almighty Himself for taking him, especially so suddenly.' She joined her hands and raised her eyes to the ceiling. 'So sorry, dear Lord, so sorry. Oh me of little faith.' She turned to her father. 'How dare the bloody bugger not let us know he's alive! I for one will never forgive him, so I won't.' At which point the dam burst and Rosaleen dissolved in tears.

Tom sat there in silence. Rosaleen continued her sobbing. Kieran came in from the yard.

'Are you coming, Daddy? We need to get going on the oats.' Then he spotted Rosaleen. 'What's the matter, Rosie?'

'Rosie, give him the letter.'

Without a word she handed it to him. Kieran started to read it standing, then plopped on the sofa beside his sister. 'Is this a joke?' He looked at her. 'If it is, it's in terrible taste.'

'It's no joke,' his father said.

'Holy God!' Kieran continued to read, turning over the pages, till he read it all. 'I don't believe it. Jesus! He's been alive all this time and never bothered to tell us.' He pointed a finger at his father. 'And obviously he only wrote to you now because he wants money. That's Martin for you, all right.'

'I'll never forgive him,' Rosaleen said again. She dried her eyes with her sleeve, got up, went back to the scullery, and continued washing with a vicious banging of dishes and pots.

'He's a terrible bugger,' Kieran said. 'What was he thinking of at all?'

Tom McDermott just sat there, staring out the window.

'Are you going to give him that money?' Kieran asked.

His father glared at him. 'The blackguard will never get another penny from me. Rosie! Come in here.'

The clatter in the scullery stopped. Rosaleen came in. 'What is it?' Crankily.

'Sit down the two of you.' They sat. 'Now listen to me. Martin said one right thing in his letter: we'd all be shamed if the word got out that he's alive. The whole parish would be laughing at us for the next twenty years. So we'll keep it to ourselves and no one will be any the wiser. You're not to tell Brideen or Packy or anyone else, do you hear?'

'But what if he decides to come back?' Rosaleen objected.

'If there's one sure thing, it's that Martin is not about to come back. He'd be ashamed to put his head into Glynn's again after running out on Aideen.'

'You're probably right,' Kieran said.

★

Saturday evening, after an early supper, Tom McDermott got ready to go into town. He went in most Saturday evenings, 'To have a few drinks with the quality,' as Rosaleen liked to put it. Before harnessing the horse to the sidecar he stepped into the cowshed where Kieran was milking. 'Listen to me now.'

'I'm listening.' Kieran went on milking. He didn't like the old man's tone: it had the bark-like quality that usually presaged something unpleasant.

'About your wanting me to hand over the place to you.'

'Yes.' He stopped milking. Despite the tone, maybe the man was softening?

'I have an offer for you if you want to get married.'

'You have?' Right now Kieran would listen to any suggestion. Though he and Brideen were again indulging their lusts on Saturday nights, it wasn't nearly often enough.

'Get married and let Brideen move in here; Rosaleen will be getting married soon so Brideen will have the kitchen to herself.'

Shite! The man was as thick as the wall. 'We've been over this before, Daddy.'

'What's different now is that I'll increase your wages to three pounds a week.'

Kieran thought for a moment. 'It wouldn't work, Daddy. Brideen won't move in as long as you're living in the house.'

The old man walked out, slamming the cowshed door behind him.

When he brought the milk in, Kieran told Rosaleen what their father had said. 'There's nothing left for me and Brideen now but to go to England,' he added.

Just then Packy walked in. 'I've been thinking,' he said, the moment he came in the door.

'God help the world.' Kieran rolled his eyes. 'Packy O'Brien is thinking.'

'Never mind that gom.' Rosaleen kissed her fiancé. 'Tell me about it.'

'I was thinking that the only way you and I will be able to get married is if we go to America.'

'I wouldn't mind that a bit.' Rosaleen smiled at him. 'I was thinking the same thing myself just last week. And now that Kieran says he's going to England, I don't want to stay here on my own with Daddy.'

'What do you think, Kieran?' Packy asked.

Kieran shrugged. 'There's nothing for any of us around here.'

'My sister Teresa is thinking of going, too. She just told us she got engaged.'

'Good on her,' Rosaleen said. 'I'm delighted to hear it.'

'Cripes! Father Donovan is going to love this.' But there was bitterness in Kieran's grin. 'Three weddings coming up and not one of them will be in Coshlawn Crann.' Then he went to his room and dolled himself up and cycled over to make love with Brideen.

28

After Liam went off to court Julia and the mother went to bed, Kieran and Brideen relieved their most pressing discomforts. Afterwards, they sat in Brideen's bed, still naked, and discussed options for their future.

'I'm definitely going to England.' He forced himself to say it with authority, an almost impossible task when he knew she'd disapprove.

She covered her face with her hands. He thought she was going to cry, but her voice was steady – too steady – when she said, 'I thought we had been over this before and agreed you wouldn't go.'

'I know. But I have to find the money to move Daddy out of the way so we can get married.' He caressed her breasts. 'You do want to get married, don't you?'

'That's not the point.' She shivered deliciously beneath his touch. 'But—'

'It'll only be for a year or two. I promise you that.' He raised his right hand. 'I, Kieran McDermott, do most solemnly swear on Brideen Conway's left breast that I will return within two years, bearing two thousand pounds. And then we'll have a big wedding.'

Brideen pulled his hand down and placed it on her right breast again. 'You'd do without this for two years?'

He kissed her neck. 'God help me, I don't want to, but what else can I do. If I'm to have you for life it seems I must do without you for a couple of years.'

'I hate this.' She covered his hands with hers. 'Not this; I hate the idea of your going to England and my being without you for two whole years.'

'You could come with me?' His tone most tentative, knowing what her answer would be.

'I might have to.'

'You will?' Shock and phlegm made his question a croak.

'You know I don't want to. But I can't let you go by yourself either.

Apart from my own needs, I'd be afraid that some English tart might get her hands on you over there. And then where would I be?' She glared at his look of innocence. 'You don't think I'd trust you, now that you've tasted. . . ?'

Wednesday afternoon Father Donovan was called to administer the last rites at the far end of the parish. The moribund was a very old woman: 104, a neighbour told him with a touch of pride, a survivor of the Great Hunger itself. The centenarian looked shrivelled and tiny now in the kitchen wall-bed called the *cailleach*, almost as if she were shrinking herself to return to the womb. She was the parish's last link to those terrible times, her 70-year old daughter noted sadly, and the priest had an undefined sense of loss at that thought. On his way back he mused that while present-day parishioners might be poor, and indeed the majority of them were, they were still an awful lot better off than their forebears had been a hundred years earlier. Such reflections on the past helped to put in perspective the complaints of the Brideen Conways and Kieran McDermotts that they couldn't afford to get married. Frugal living, as Mr De Valera had so wisely advocated, was the only true Christian answer.

On returning to Coshlawn Crann he found Brideen sitting in his parlour. He hadn't talked to her – except in public on his school visits – since their unfinished conversation the evening of the social. And while he should have been still angry with her for preempting his effort to introduce Larry Sweeney to Aideen Glynn, not a twinge of the bilious passion stirred inside him at the sight of her. Such equanimity might have been due to his own adroitness in matching Aideen with Alphonsus Finnerty. On the other hand, while her sin had brought him to his senses and banished his infatuation, he still found pleasure in her presence.

'How are you, Brideen?'

'I've been better.' He sensed she was close to tears.

'Oh dear!' He parked on the sofa opposite her. 'What's the matter?'

'Kieran is off to England on Saturday.'

'I'm sorry to hear that. As you know, I feel strongly about people going to England.'

'And I'm going with him.' Her body shook with sobs.

His 'No!' was an anguished cry from the heart.

'Yes.'

'But you mustn't.'

'We can't wait any longer.' She looked crossly at him. 'Celibacy is for priests and nuns, Father, not for us ordinary sinners. But of course you have never been in love, so you wouldn't understand that.'

Father Donovan felt the red hue of embarrassment suffuse his body. 'We'll find a solution, Brideen. As I told you the night of the social, I have a plan for—'

'Well, whatever your plan was, it's too late now.'

'But *you* can't go. The schoolchildren need you.'

'I have to go with Kieran.'

'I'll talk to his father again.'

'It's no use. He told Kieran again last Saturday that if we want to get married I should move in and keep house for them. Which I never will do as long as he's living there, the tyrant. So what else can we do but go to England? I'm not going to let Kieran go off by himself, so I'm not.'

'But Brideen—'

'And, for your information, Kieran's sister Rosaleen is going to America with her fiancé, Packy O'Brien. And Packy's sister Teresa is going to America with her fiancé.'

'Good God Almighty!' His whole wonderful scheme for marriages and frugal living in Coshlawn Crann was coming unravelled. 'This is awful.'

Brideen glared at him. 'Josie Ryan was our best chance until you butted in with Alphonsus Finnerty.' She stood abruptly. 'So I just came to say goodbye and to tell you that Friday will be my last day at school and I'm sorry things have to end like this.' Then she turned and fled the room.

Father Donovan didn't move. He heard the front door slam. He heard a rattle of dishes from the kitchen. He heard the crunch of cart wheels on the road. But his body wouldn't stir and his mind wouldn't function. It was the entrance of Cait, like the finger-snap of a hypnotist, that released him from his trance. 'Would you like your tea now, Father?'

'What am I going to do, Cait?'

'I can make it later if you like.'

'They can't just go to England and America like that.'

'Who would you be talking about, Father? If you don't mind my asking.'

'Brideen Conway and Kieran McDermott are going to England because Tom McDermott won't let his son have the place to get married. And two other couples are going to America.'

'I like Brideen. She'll be a big loss to the school.'

'She will indeed. We just can't let her go, can we? So how can I persuade Tom McDermott to hand over the farm to his son?'

'I don't know, Father. It won't be easy, I suppose.'

'Maybe you could think about it, Cait? I mean, you came up with that brilliant idea about getting the teachers to help with the triduum. And the social evening was entirely your brainchild.'

'Right so. I'll think about it. Would you like your tea now or later?'

Father Donovan engaged his own brain in deep, and sometimes devious, scheming that evening without coming up with a single worthwhile idea. Having already argued with Tom McDermott, he knew how thick that farmer could be. He toyed with thoughts of trickery: perhaps the likelihood of Kieran committing suicide, indirectly conveyed? Or the threat of a priest's curse if Tom McDermott failed to deliver? But, though this latter notion pleased his growing anger, he obviously couldn't resort to it. He fell asleep searching for a solution and had barely woken in the morning when the mind was off again hunting elusive inspiration. His mass was distracted, his thanksgiving a jumble, and his exasperation quotient was high when he sat down to breakfast.

'I gave the matter a bit of thought, Father.' Cait placed his meal before him.

'So did I. But I'm afraid there's no solution. The trouble is, we're dealing with one of the stubbornest men in the world.'

'Everyone says that about Tom McDermott all right.'

'I don't think the Pope himself would be able to change the man's mind.'

'Well isn't he a holy terror, Father, not to listen even to the Pope. What kind of man is he at all?'

'But thanks anyway for giving the matter thought.'

'You've heard of Father John O'Malley, Father? Sure of course you have.'

'I know a couple of Father John O'Malleys. Which one are we talking about?'

'I was thinking of the man who stood up to the landlords; the priest who invented the word boycott.'

'Ah yes, that Father John.'

'And what I had in mind was maybe you could do the same sort of thing to Tom McDermott.'

Father Donovan stopped short of stuffing a piece of rasher into his mouth. 'You mean boycott him?'

'Exactly.'

'So no one would talk to him?'

'That too.'

'From what I've seen of Tom McDermott, I doubt if he'd care very much.'

'He'd care if no one would work for him.'

'Does he need someone to work for him?'

'He will if Kieran goes to England. He has a big harvest to save.'

'What an interesting idea, Cait. I'll have to give it some thought.'

The proposal was ridiculous of course, but he couldn't hurt his housekeeper's feelings by saying so. However, since he had no other solution himself, he remained at the table after she cleared away the dishes and ruminated. Would farmers refuse to help a neighbour because he wouldn't hand over his farm to his son? Their own sons might be sympathetic all right: many of them might even feel the same way about *their* fathers. But the fathers, of course, would be aware of this and feel threatened by it, and so might be inclined to help Tom McDermott just for that reason. However, they in turn might be stopped by their sons threatening to strike against *them* if they were to offer such help. Which might permit the boycott to go ahead. So it *was* a possibility.

But who would instigate it? Although Father John O'Malley had personally incited his flock to ostracize the notorious Captain Boycott in 1880, and was revered ever since as a hero, this was 1946 and Tom McDermott was no hated English landlord. Were Father Donovan to be the *provocateur* of such an act today he'd be hauled over the coals by the archbishop and sent back to teach Latin at St Fiachra's. So someone else would have to foment the boycott. Perhaps Brideen and Kieran? As Cait might say, them that had most to gain. . . .

Then there was the moral question. Would it be right to do such a thing? He looked up the subject in Prümmer's *Handbook of Moral Theology* – that confessor's guide to separating right from wrong. Harm would undoubtably be done to the man if no one would help him save his harvest. However, that was not the *intent* of the boycott: its object was to bring him to heel by holding out the threat of damage. The man would have the option of redressing the wrong he was doing to his son and thereby getting the help he needed. If he were to sustain the loss of his harvest, the damage would be brought on by his own evil deed. The priest sat up a little straighter: maybe a boycott *would* be admissible.

However, the author noted in a footnote, the Sacred Congregation of the Holy Office had condemned the Irish Land League boycotts back in 1888. So that was it: *Roma locuta est, causa finita est.* Rome had spoken, the case was closed.

29

While Father Donovan was still dealing with the disappointment of finding that a boycott of Tom McDermott would be immoral, a knock on the front door brought Cait padding down the hall. A few moments later she stood before him, stony-faced. 'The pub man wants to talk to you.' Though Cait and Christine Glynn were good friends, there was no love lost between the housekeeper and Christine's husband.

'Austin!' The priest stood and shook hands.

'I've something wonderful to tell you, Father.' The man's excitement was bubbling like water on the boil. 'My Aideen just got engaged to Alphonsus Finnerty.'

'You don't say? Well, well, well! That was fast work indeed. Sit yourself down and tell me all about it.' He was happy for the man, of course, but it was the dowry that was uppermost in his mind.

'Alphonsus has been visiting Aideen every day after school since the social; then last night he stopped in and popped the question.'

'Imagine that.'

'He gave her the ring, too.'

'Marvellous indeed. Our first response to the triduum of prayer, Austin. Thanks be to the good God.'

'You'll celebrate with me, Father, won't you?' Glynn pulled a bottle of Tullamore Dew from under his jacket.

'I will.' He got two glasses from the cabinet in the corner. What he was really going to toast was the dowry.

Austin poured, and raised his glass. 'To a happy marriage for my Aideen.'

'May God grant them a long and happy life together.' The raw burning spirit felt good in his throat.

'And may they be blessed with lots of children. I can hardly wait to see my first grandchild, Father.'

'Here's to grandchildren.'

'Alphonsus has a fine house in Lahvauce, though they say it's gone to rack and ruin inside for want of a woman's touch.' Glynn lowered the remainder of his drink. 'But Aideen will soon take care of that. Have another one for luck, Father.' He held out the bottle.

He really shouldn't. But, at least for the publican, hesitation was assent: he filled the priest's glass to the brim. 'Whoa!' Father Donovan called when the damage was done.

' 'Twon't do you a bit of harm, and we have a lot to celebrate. It isn't every day a man gets a husband for his daughter. Especially a husband the like of Alphonsus Finnerty.' Back went the publican's head and the whiskey drained from his glass.

Father Donovan drank again. He could feel the stuff going to his head already. He mustn't have any more. On the other hand, he couldn't offend the man of a £1,000 dowry. He finished the glass. 'Good whiskey,' he remarked to fill the sudden silence.

'The best.' Austin Glynn refilled his own glass and without permission replenished the priest's. 'There's nothing like the Tullamore, I always say.'

'Did he ask about a dowry?' The words popped out of Father Donovan's mouth without reflection. But what harm? He'd have to ask the question sometime.

'Divil a word. And needless to say I didn't bring up the matter myself.' Glynn drank some more.

'No. Of course not. Why would you, if the man himself didn't ask?'

'Ah sure he has plenty of money. What would he want a dowry for?'

'Better it should go to them that need it.'

'Who needs it most now is Austin Glynn. It'll provide him comfort and whiskey in his old age, so it will.'

Father Donovan bristled: he had been striving for the most refined diplomacy in raising the question of the dowry's disposition, but there was no way he could let that last remark go unchallenged. 'Don't forget we have an agreement about the dowry, Austin, you and me. Whatever part doesn't go with Aideen will come to the church for the benefit of those who have no dowry.' That was the agreement, so it was, and the man would have to abide by it, so he would.

Austin Glynn stopped the glass halfway to his lips. 'Ah now, that was only just in case I got away with giving less than the whole lot. But here we have the case where none of the dowry goes with Aideen. That's a whole different kettle of fish.'

'I'm afraid I don't see any difference, Austin. Not a whit. Not a jot.

Not even a tittle. It's just that we hadn't expected *all* the boodle to be available, that's all.'

'Ah, but that is the difference, Father, don't you see. *All* the dough. I never ever promised you the whole works.'

'Look at it this way.' Father Donovan shook his head to clear it so he could argue properly. 'Before, you wouldn't get back any of the money. So now you don't get any back either.'

Glynn looked puzzled for a moment. Then he drank more whiskey and his face brightened. 'The thing of it is, Father, I never promised you the whole entire cabbage, only the remainder. But now there's no remainder, so there's nothing for you to get.'

It seemed to Father Donovan that he was being cheated by a sleight of words. Another sip might straighten out his thinking. 'Did you, or did you not, promise me the remainder of the dowry?'

The publican refilled both glasses. 'I did, faith. I promised you the remainder. And you'd have got it, too, if there had been a remainder. Austin Glynn is a man of his word.' He raised his glass. 'Here's to Austin Glynn, a man of his word.'

Father Donovan wasn't going to be so ingenuous as to be fooled by that ingenious argument. 'Hold on now. Before we drink to it let's settle what we mean by remainder.'

The publican lowered his glass. 'We will. A remainder is a remainder, and Austin Glynn is a man of his word.' He pointed a finger at the priest. 'If there is a remainder, that is.'

Father Donovan marshalled his unruly thoughts. 'The remainder is what's left after you subtract one number from another. Right?'

Glynn stared at him. 'By God you're a hell of a smart man, Father, I don't mind telling you.'

The priest stared back at him. So far so good, but what came next? He took a quick nip. 'So how much do we subtract? In other words, how much of a dowry did you actually promise Alphonsus Finnerty?'

'Not a brass farthing. Why would I? Sure the man has more money than meself.'

'So we subtract not-a-brass-farthing from a thousand pounds. And what do we get?'

The publican's stare was glassy. 'Ah now, that's a hard sum, so it is.'

'The answer we get is a thousand pounds, Austin. And that's our remainder.'

Glynn stared into his glass for a long time. 'And the priest is always right, isn't he? Whether he is or not.'

'A thousand pounds is the remainder then.' Father Donovan pressed home his advantage. He could smell the money already. 'So that's how much you owe the church.'

'By hell, if that's what I owe the church then that's what I'll pay the church. Austin Glynn is a man of his word.' He splashed whiskey into both glasses again. 'Here's to Austin Glynn, a man of his word. Even if he is being cheated.'

When Cait looked in half an hour later they were both asleep.

30

Rumour, Willie Shakespeare said long ago, is a pipe that's blown by surmises, jealousies, and conjectures. He might have added to his list, had he known about it, the wagging tongue of Father Donovan's housekeeper. Cait was a rumourmonger. And she had lots of tidbits to monger. She hovered around the spiritual power centre of Coshlawn Crann and was privy to information before it was announced to Sunday congregations. She had been able, for example, to whisper abroad the news of the triduums and the Sunday evening social days before the priest proclaimed them from the pulpit. She had no malicious intent, of course: like most busybodies, she just enjoyed being the first with juicy gossip. And, like the butterfly flapping its wings in China, she gave no thought to the ultimate effect of her precipitous pronouncements.

A couple of hours after she proposed a boycott of Tom McDermott, and very shortly after she roused her priest and the wretched publican from their drunken stupor, Cait walked down the street to Harney's Grocer and Victualer to procure a lamb chop for the one o'clock dinner. On the way out of the shop she ran into Nora O'Brien who was on her way in. Her keen eye spotted the dejection that Mrs O'Brien's attempted smile couldn't hide. 'Is something wrong?' she asked, with information-sucking sympathy.

'Things could be better, Cait. Packy just told us he's going off to America one of these days.'

'Is he indeed? I'm sorry to hear that. Packy is such a nice lad.'

'It's that Rosaleen McDermott that's making him go. She can't wait to get away, the puss. They just got engaged, you know.'

'I did hear that, mind you.'

'Did you now? And they only told us on Sunday evening.'

'News travels fast in this parish, Nora.'

'Bad cess to Rosaleen anyway. Packy would never dream of going of his own accord. Why can't she be satisfied here at home?'

'Some people do have the wanderlust in them.'

' 'Tis in the blood, I suppose. Isn't Kieran off to England with Brideen Conway, and they not even married yet. Between you and me, Cait, I don't think that's right.'

'Well as a matter of fact, Nora, just between the two of us, and I wouldn't want it to go any further, I have good reason to believe that pair won't be going after all.'

'Do you think? When they were talking back at the house last night they seemed dead set on taking off. Saturday morning, I heard them telling Packy.'

'Ah yes. But they wouldn't have known then what I know now.'

'And Brideen having a pensionable job and all. I can't understand why they have to go, so I can't.'

'Brideen was back to see Father Donovan yesterday. She was in a terrible state of agitation altogether.'

'Was she indeed? I'm sure the poor girl would rather stay where she is. But the McDermotts again, you see. They're the ones that want to travel.'

'And when she left, himself was in a state of agitation as well.'

'Well was he, the creature? It must have been something she told him then.'

'And he asked me how on God's earth could he get Tom McDermott to hand his farm over to Kieran so they wouldn't have to go to England.'

'Faith, Tom isn't about to step down for a long time yet.'

'I wouldn't be too sure about that, Nora. I put a notion into Father's head that might change Tom McDermott's mind.'

'If you want my opinion, he'd be better off to have Brideen in there as the daughter-in-law. If he doesn't, he'll be on his own after Rosaleen goes to America. And what's he going to do then?'

'Father Donovan thinks it's a great scheme to keep them at home, so he does.'

'Does he indeed? He's fond of Brideen all right, they say. He wouldn't want to lose her in the school.'

'Tom McDermott is going to get the shock of his life, let me tell you.'

'It's hard on the creature, I suppose. Nobody wants to give up the bit of land. Especially when you're getting old and you don't know what the future holds. And he just after losing poor Martin and all.'

'Father Donovan says he's the stubbornest man on the face of the earth. He says he wouldn't even listen to the Pope.'

'Sure Packy would like to get the place from us, too. But what would

Teresa do if he brought Rosaleen into the house while she's still there?'

'So he's going to organize a boycott to make Tom hand over the place.'

'Kieran is? Well isn't he a terrible lad to go against his own father. Better he should go to England than do a thing like that.'

'Not Kieran. Father Donovan.'

'Father Donovan is going to England? Well I never—'

'No, no, Nora. It's Father Donovan who's going to have Tom McDermott boycotted till he hands over the place to Kieran so he can get married to Brideen.'

'Well, is he now? Father Donovan?' Nora stared into her basket as if it might grant her understanding of this strange turn of events. 'I suppose he has his reasons then.'

'But that's just for your own information, Nora. You understand. He wouldn't want anyone to know about it yet.' And after administering this solemn admonition Cait returned to the priest's house to prepare his dinner.

Nora O'Brien couldn't get the news of the boycott out of her mind. She told her husband Mick about it over the dinner, but he just laughed and said don't be daft the landlord days are gone and Cait was only pulling your leg. So in the afternoon she went back to talk it over with Nellie Ruane. Nellie didn't laugh.

'That's a terrible thing to do to a decent man like Tom McDermott.'

'I suppose the priest has his reasons,' Nora said loyally.

'Maybe he has and maybe he hasn't. Mind you, I never did like the man. The minute I set eyes on him I said to myself that young priest is trouble. I think it's the way he parts his hair that bothers me.'

'I'm sure he's doing the best he can, the creature. And he so young and all.'

'He reminds me of a bantam cock looking for a fight.'

'He's a holy priest, Nellie. We mustn't speak badly of him.'

'Him and his triduums and socials. What'll he think of next?'

'He wants the young people to get married. And sure he's right.'

'Why can't he leave people alone, like Father Heskin did?'

'They say he's worried that if the young people don't get married soon, in a few years there won't be any more scholars and then the teachers won't have jobs.'

'Take my word for it, Nora, 'tis the small men with the big ideas that are the ruination of the world. Look at Hitler. And Hirohito. And look what we put up in the Park for a President? Seaneen T., God help us, and he only half the size of his missus. Give me a big man any time.' Her two brothers, with whom she lived, were big thick goms who didn't give anyone trouble.

'I suppose Kieran and Brideen will be glad of the boycott anyway.'

' 'Tis she's the cause of it I'd say, that Brideen. They tell me she's always hanging around the priest's house. Which isn't right, and he shouldn't let her, so he shouldn't.'

Nora liked her priest but hated an argument, so she changed the subject to the recent failure of some of her hens to lay.

Thursday after supper, Brideen, feeling terribly depressed, cycled over to McDermott's to see Kieran. On Saturday the two of them would take the noon Dublin train from Lahvauce and stay overnight with Kieran's aunt in Glasnevin. Sunday morning they'd catch the boat from Dun Laoghaire, then the train from Holyhead, and by Sunday evening they'd be staring at the bombed-out streets of London. Packy had written to his brother Mattie in London: they'd stay with him until they found a place of their own. A place of their own! Well, she knew what that would mean: sharing a bed and all that went with such an arrangement. Though part of her looked forward to it, part of her didn't. She always wanted to do things right, and this wasn't the right way. They'd have to get married as quickly as possible. Tears threatened as she remembered her dream of a wedding in Coshlawn Crann, with the schoolchildren throwing rose petals at herself and Kieran when they walked out the church door as man and wife. A London wedding was certain to be a drab affair, with no family present and no friends or neighbours to share the occasion. And a room in a shattered city for their nuptial night. No, she wasn't looking forward to it. But she loved Kieran too much to let him go alone: it would surely be the end of their relationship if they separated now.

'He's gone over to talk to Packy,' Rosaleen told her when she arrived at Kieran's house. 'I'm going over there myself now, too.' So they rode over together. It was a fine autumn evening and they all sat outside on the cement wall in front of the house.

'Listen to this,' Packy said. 'You won't believe what Mammy told me a while ago.'

On a normal evening he'd have been bombarded with guesses, silly and serious. Now all he got was a polite 'What?' from Rosaleen.

'She says Father Donovan is organizing a boycott against your father.'

'A what?' Kieran scrunched his face as if hit by sudden sunlight.

'A boycott. She heard it from the priest's housekeeper.'

'That's lunacy,' Rosaleen shouted. 'Why would he want to do that?'

'Apparently to make him hand over the farm to you, Kieran.'

'Jesus God! The man is gone daft,' Brideen said.'

'Maybe he's not so daft at all. In fact, I think it might be a great idea.' Kieran was excited. 'It should be worth a try anyway.'

Packy raised his fist. 'Up the rebels! By hell, we'll win yet.'

'You're a right pair of jackasses, the two of you,' Brideen shouted.

'What's the matter with you?' Kieran demanded.

'What's the matter with the two of *you*, is more like it? If you had half a rabbit's brain between you, you'd know it wouldn't work.'

'Why not?'

'Because half the farmers of Ireland are in the same boat as Tom McDermott, with sons at home waiting for them to die so they can get married. Do you think those farmers are going to support you when the same thing could happen to them tomorrow?'

Before the discussion could go any further, they heard the hum of an engine and Father Donovan's Morris Minor turned in the boreen.

'He's coming to tell us about the boycott,' Rosaleen hazarded.

'Well, if he is don't encourage him,' Brideen said.

Packy jumped down off the wall when the car stopped at the gate. Father Donovan got out. Kieran and Rosaleen stood. 'Good evening to you all.' The young priest's voice was hoarse. Brideen, still sitting, thought his face looked flushed.

'Good evening, Father,' the three on the ground chorused.

'Fine evening.' The priest looked up at the sky. 'Good weather for the oats.'

'A few more days and ours will be ripe for cutting.' Packy pulled the bolt on the iron gate that led into the yard. 'Won't you come in, Father?'

'No thanks, Packy. I'd like to have a talk with the four of you, if I may.'

'Certainly, Father.'

'Brideen tells me,' the priest looked at Kieran, 'that you're planning to go to England soon?'

Kieran looked away. 'We're leaving Saturday morning.'

'As you know, I don't like the idea of your going to England. So I made a last ditch effort to keep the two of you at home. And I'm here now to tell you that I've come up with a solution.'

Brideen repressed a snort of derision. So he was going to try that idiotic boycott stunt. 'It would need to be a lot better solution than Larry Sweeney,' she blurted.

'It is.' His smile invited trust. 'But this time you'll have to have faith in me and not thwart my plan.'

She said nothing: the boycott gimmick was bound to fail.

'Give the man a chance, Brideen.' Kieran's tone was stern, totally unlike any way he had ever spoken to her before.

'All right.' At least she had tried to dissuade them.

'So, what's your solution, Father?' Kieran asked.

The priest looked embarrassed. As well he might be, Brideen thought: like a nipper caught stealing apples in a neighbour's orchard. 'I'm not at liberty to tell you that right now, Kieran. It will all come out in due course. First, I need to talk to your father. I believe I have found a way to make him change his mind about signing over the place to you.' He glanced at Rosaleen. 'And to give you a dowry, Rosaleen.'

'You're codding us, Father.' But Kieran's face was glowing with hope.

'Cripes Almighty!' Packy said. 'Now we can stay home, too, Rosie. We can give your dowry to Teresa and get her out of the house.'

'Before we all get too excited, I think you better talk with Tom McDermott,' Brideen told the priest. 'He told Kieran last Saturday evening there was no chance he'd give him the place. Right, Kieran?'

Kieran looked sheepish. 'Right. That's why we decided to go to England.'

'Never mind that. What I have to tell him will change his mind.' Father Donovan smiled again. 'I'll go and see him right now.'

'He won't be home till nine,' Rosaleen said. 'He's back visiting Barney Murphy.'

'Ah yes; I met him on the road and he told me I'd find you here. I'll see him tomorrow then. And I'll let you know what transpires.' Then Father Donovan got into his car and drove away.

'Do you believe him?' Rosaleen asked Brideen.

'I don't have much hope. But I suppose we should wait and see. Even the smallest hope is better than England.'

31

Tom McDermott was indeed visiting his neighbour. The two of them were sitting in front of the kitchen fire smoking their pipes when Barney asked, 'What's all this talk I hear about a boycott?'

'Boycott?' Tom spat into the flames. 'I haven't heard anything about one. Who's being boycotted?'

'God help you.' Barney's spit fell short and hissed on the hearth. ' 'Tisn't for me to tell you if you don't know already.'

'There was nothing about it on the wireless last night. So it couldn't be all that important.'

'It's damned important to you, faith. I'm surprised no one told you about it.'

'Out with it, then.' Tom took the lid off his pipe, tamped the tobacco with his index finger, replaced the lid, puffed again.

'I heard it from a woman who heard it from a woman who heard it from the priest's housekeeper herself.'

Tom gave a short laugh. 'Well, sorra much good it is if it's just old biddies' gossip.'

Barney puffed in silence. 'I wouldn't be too sure,' he said after a bit. 'What I heard was this: the priest is going to read *you* from the altar on Sunday for making Kieran go away to England to get married. And he's going to forbid anyone in the parish to help you with the crops until you hand over the place to your son.' Barney shot a sizzling spit directly into the fire. 'But I'll tell you this, Tom, whatever the bloody priest says, you can count on Barney Murphy when the time comes.'

Tom McDermott sat there for a long time, puffing and spitting and saying nothing. Eventually he put the pipe in his pocket and stood. 'I better go back and have a talk with the priest.' Then he went home. But the anger soaked deep into him, and neither the rosary nor the night prayers by his bedside did anything to blot it. On the contrary, the dark stillness of night caused it to bubble and expand till he felt he would burst asunder with the pressure of it. All he'd worked for all his life they wanted to take from him now by force – the farm that was his by virtue of thirty years' hard labour and sweat and good sound judgement. Was there no justice left in the world at all? Who the hell did Kieran think he was anyway, that he had any right to any part of it other than what his father might freely give to him? Well, he could say goodbye to any chance of getting it now, that was for sure. He'd rather leave it to the tinkers than give it to him after this. And what business was it of the bloody priest to interfere? Boycott indeed. By hell, he had half a mind to go straight to the archbishop and report the fecker. Maybe he'd do just that. Get the bugger unfrocked, was his final thought before sleep took over.

But when he woke in the dead of night he was overcome by pessimism. What if his neighbours did boycott him? You never could tell with those people; they always said he was a bit standoffish, and this could be their chance to get back at him. He hardly ever helped them with their crops, and now, even if he paid lads, they might refuse to help him. And then where would he be?

He was up early, and had Rosaleen boil water so he could shave, a task he normally reserved for Saturday evening. After which he washed face and hands and feet and got into his Sunday clothes.

'Where are you off to?' his daughter asked.

'I have some business to take care of.' He harnessed the horse to the sidecar and drove slowly back to Coshlawn Crann.

Father Donovan was working on his breakfast when Cait announced that Tom McDermott wanted to see him.

'Show him into the parlour and I'll be with him as soon as I finish.' Please God, the man was having a change of heart.

Cait returned a minute later. 'He's in a terrible temper, Father.' She was whispering. 'He mentioned the boycott.'

'Boycott?'

'The one we talked about yesterday.' Still whispering. 'Didn't you tell him?'

'I certainly did not.' He, too, lowered his voice lest Tom McDermott should hear. 'We can't do it, Cait; the church doesn't permit boycotts.'

'But I thought—'

'Oh my God! You talked about it, didn't you?'

'Oh Father, I'm awful sorry.' She bowed her head in repentance. 'It just sort of slipped out. But only to Nora O'Brien.'

He covered his face with his hands. 'How am I going to explain this to Tom McDermott?'

'Blame me, Father.' Then her repentant expression shifted to crafty. 'Though I just had a thought.' Her whisper tingled with excitement.

'No more ideas, Cait, until we get ourselves out of this mess.'

'No, Father. But it just occurred to me that as long as Tom McDermott thinks you're going to have him boycotted you might as well make use of it.'

'What do you mean?'

'What I was thinking was maybe he'll do what you want him to do as long as he thinks you'll boycott him if he doesn't.'

He was about to dismiss her words when their import struck him. He pushed away the remainder of his breakfast. 'Tell him I'll be with him in a couple of minutes.'

'Yes, Father.'

He put his head on the table and meditated. Then he prayed. Then he meditated some more and prayed some more. Eventually he straightened, stood, and strode into the parlour.

'What's all this *raimeis* about boycotting me?' Anger crackled in Tom McDermott's every word.

'It's not a decision that was lightly undertaken, Tom.' Father Donovan seated himself across from the farmer.

'You have no damn right to do this. By God, I'll go to the archbishop and have you unfrocked, so I will.'

'Ah now, Tom, I'm not the force behind it at all. Boycotting is something that I as a priest could never condone. The church forbids it, you see. All the same, I can understand why some people might want to engage in it.'

'And who are those people? By God I'll—'

'*I'm* not at liberty to divulge their names, Tom. They themselves will likely tell you in due course.'

'They have no right. Absolutely not. God gave me my farm, and it's mine, and no one has a right to take it away from me.'

'Unfortunately, life is not as simple as that, Tom. There are other people to be considered as well as yourself. In particular, those you helped bring into the world. You have an obligation to them. Imposed by Almighty God Himself.'

'I have an obligation to take care of myself first. Haven't I my old age to look to?'

'It seems to me you could fulfil that obligation and at the same time be just and fair to your son. It's that lack of justice that's causing this talk of boycott, you see. So when you come to an arrangement with Kieran I'm sure it will be called off immediately.'

'I don't believe a word of it anyway. The people of Coshlawn Crann would never do that to me.'

'If you believe that, Tom, then, of course, nothing more need be said.'

The farmer sat there so long, silent and unmoving, that the priest began to wonder if he might have suffered a stroke. But at length he said, 'What would *I* do if I gave the place to Kieran? Go to the poorhouse?'

'If you sign it over, Tom, I think we can come to a very reasonable arrangement.'

McDermott's glower mingled anger, mistrust, even a dollop of hatred. 'What kind of arrangement?'

'It's my understanding that your ambition is to buy a house in Lahvauce.'

'It could be something I had in mind.'

'Recently, through the extraordinary generosity of a man in this parish, who prefers to stay anonymous, a sum of money has been made available to me to help young women who want to get married but haven't the means. I'm prepared to help you with that money when you sign your farm over to Kieran.'

'I need two thousand pounds.'

'Unfortunately, Tom, I don't have that much for you. But' – he raised a quick hand as McDermott was about to interrupt – 'I can give your daughter Rosaleen a thousand pounds in dowry when she marries.'

'Make it eighteen hundred for me and I'll take care of Rosaleen myself.' Tom McDermott spat on his hand and held it out.

Father Donovan smiled. 'I'm not a jobber, Tom, and we're not selling cattle. A thousand pounds for Rosaleen on her wedding day is the best I can do.'

'Fifteen hundred, and that's my final offer.' Out went the hand again.

The priest put away his smile. 'There's no room for bargaining, Tom.'

McDermott got to his feet and towered over the young priest. 'I'll see you all in Hell first. And I'm going to report you personally to the archbishop for trying to have me boycotted.' He reached for the door-knob.

'Listen to me, Tom. If you refuse this offer you might lose your crops.'

'I'll sell the bloody place and get *more* than two thousand for it.' McDermott opened the door and stepped through.

'No one's going to buy it from you, Tom,' the priest called after him. 'That's part of the boycott.'

'God blast you all to Hell.' But the footsteps stopped. Father Donovan waited. Tom McDermott reappeared in the doorway, haggard and hunched.

'You'll have the pleasure,' Father Donovan said, 'of helping your son get settled so he can raise your grandchildren.'

'Can't you make it fifteen hundred, Father. I could manage with that.'

The priest bowed his head, stared at the floor. 'From what I'm told, Tom, I'd say you could manage without any help at all from me. But I'm willing to give Rosaleen a thousand. Mind you, it's money that could be well spent on other young people who are equally desperate to get married. But I'll give it to her to help you out.'

Tom McDermott stood without moving for more than a minute. Then he said, 'I want a legal document drawn up by a solicitor with your personal signature on it.'

'Certainly, Tom. I'll arrange that. However, the generosity of our benefactor must be kept in complete confidence. If it becomes known he might refuse to give me the money.'

The farmer glared at him for a long moment. 'If I hear another word about boycotting I'm going straight to the archbishop.' Then he turned abruptly and left.

32

Although he accepted Father Donovan's uncompromising offer with angry reluctance, nevertheless, as he drove home and thought about what he had committed to and what he had gained, Tom McDermott's mood gradually changed. True, it was extremely galling to have been threatened with a boycott by a priest young enough to be his son, but on the other hand he was a thousand pounds better off than when he left the house this morning. And, despite the *poor* story he had mouthed to Kieran, he was free to buy a house in town whenever he pleased. As for that threat of boycotting, he didn't really believe it, and he'd certainly have called the bloody priest's bluff were it not for the money the man had been forced to promise him.

By the time he arrived home he was in tolerably good humour. He puttered around the yard and sheds all afternoon, and after supper sat on his throne and read the *Farmers' Journal*. Later, when Kieran came downstairs all dressed up and was heading out the back door, he said, 'Listen to me, the two of you. I've something to tell you.'

'I'm listening.' Rosaleen, on the sofa, put aside her book and took off her shoes.

'I'm in a hurry,' Kieran said from the door. 'Can't it wait?'

'It'll be to your benefit to listen.'

Kieran hesitated, then said, 'Right,' and leaned against the door jamb.

'We used to have a nice happy family here till Martin did what he did. Since then I hear nothing but complaining: people wanting to go to England and America and no one interested in staying home to work and pull together like a good Christian family.'

Neither of his children said anything.

'Well, *I'm* still a good Christian, even if my children don't want to do their Christian duty. So I'm going to do the Christian thing and divide my goods between the two of you. And then I'm going to leave you. I've done all I can for you. As soon as the crops are in I'm going to look for a house in Lahvauce. The day you get married, Rosaleen, there'll be a thousand-pound cheque waiting for you. And the day you get married, Kieran, this place will be yours.'

Rosaleen jumped to her feet. 'Thank you, Daddy.' She leaned over and kissed him on the cheek. He ignored the gesture and resumed reading the paper.

Kieran remained stuck to the door jamb. 'Thanks, Dad,' was the best he could manage. All he could think of at that moment was that he and Brideen wouldn't have to go to England tomorrow.

A week later, Kieran was weeding turnips with a hoe in the field behind the house when Rosaleen came looking for him. 'What time is it?' he asked, hoping it was dinnertime: weeding turnips was the most monotonous job in the world.

'Just a bit after eleven. Daddy wants you to come in and change your clothes straight away; you have to go to town with him, he says.'

'What for?' Other than on fair days he never went to Lahvauce with the old man.

'You know him: he never tells you anything except what he wants you to do.' She made a face. 'I can't wait to get out of here.'

'Bollix him anyway. I have to get these turnips weeded. And he never does a stroke himself any more.'

'I'll come back after dinner and give you a hand,' Rosaleen said.

'What are we going to town for?' The old man was sitting on his throne in his Sunday clothes, the bowler hat resting on his knees.

'You'll find out soon enough when we get there. Just go and put on some clean clothes and hurry up about it.'

By the time Kieran was dressed, his father had the sidecar ready. They drove to Lahvauce in silence, their relationship even more strained since his father's promise to hand over the place. They left the horse in Reilly's yard and walked up Main Street. Just beyond the post office the old man stopped in front of a door with a brass plate that read TADHG MEEHAN, SOLR. Without knocking he walked in. They went down a short hallway to a white door that said TADHG MEEHAN, SOLR in big black letters. The old man knocked.

'Come in.' A small dark-suited man with gleaming black hair and pencil moustache sat behind a vast desk stacked with papers.

'Mister Meehan sir.' The cheerful tone his father used when addressing people he considered important.

'How are you, Tom.' Tadhg Meehan stood and shook hands. It was only then that Kieran noticed Father Donovan sitting in a chair in front of the desk.

'This is the young fellow.' The old man nodded at Kieran. The solicitor offered a soft limp hand.

'Hello, Tom, Kieran.' The priest didn't get up.

'Hello, Father,' Kieran said.

They all sat. The solicitor retrieved a sheaf of papers from a pile. 'I presume we're all here to do some signing.'

'We are,' the priest said. The old man said nothing.

The solicitor picked up a document, leafed through its pages, and positioned it on the desk in front of his father. 'In simple language, Tom, by putting your signature on this deed, you're handing over ownership of your house, farm, and livestock to your son, Kieran, with effect from the date of his marriage. Is that what you want to do?'

Kieran waited for his father's reply. Only after what seemed an eternal silence did Tom McDermott say, 'It is.'

'Sign here then.' Meehan offered a pen. The old man stared for another eternity at the document, then slowly wrote his name.

'And you, young man' – the solicitor placed the same document in front of Kieran – 'by signing here, are accepting ownership of your father's farm and house and livestock with effect from the date of your marriage. Is that what you want?'

'Yes.' Kieran's voice cracked with joy. He forced himself to slow down lest his signature not be perfectly legible.

The solicitor selected another document from the pile, perused it briefly, and placed it in front of the priest. 'You, Father Donovan, by signing this document are making a legal commitment to pay Rosaleen McDermott the sum of one thousand pounds on the day of her wedding. Should you fail to pay that sum as stipulated, the contract just signed by Tom McDermott and Kieran McDermott is *ipso facto* null and void. Is that your understanding?'

'It is.' The priest signed in a quick firm hand.

The old man stood. 'We're done?'

'We are.' The solicitor held out his hand to Kieran. 'Congratulations.'

'Good luck to you now.' His father briefly shook Kieran's hand.

'May God give you health and long life to enjoy it.' Father Donovan pumped Kieran's hand with enthusiasm.

The old man shook Tadhg Meehan's hand. 'Thank you, sir.' Then, ignoring Father Donovan, he turned abruptly and walked out the door.

'Thank you so much, Father,' Kieran said to the priest. So it was he who had worked the miracle. 'I'll talk to you later.' He knew that if he didn't keep up with the old man he'd have to walk home.

Brideen was thrilled beyond words. 'Signed, sealed, and ready to be delivered,' Kieran sang that evening, doing a dance with her on her kitchen floor. Mammy, looking on, was trying to smile, even as a couple of tears rolled down her cheeks.

'And you say it was Father Donovan who swung the deal?'

'No doubt about it. But where he's getting the money from to give Rosie a thousand-quid dowry is beyond me.'

'Anyway, we can now set the wedding date.'

'Let's get married tomorrow.' He whirled her around the floor again.

She stopped, stared at him, then looked at her mother and shook her head. 'Men! They're hopeless.' She tapped her finger on Kieran's chest. 'We'll have to wait at least a month, my good man: a girl has to arrange for her dress to be made, and a few things like that. And the banns have to be read, of course.'

He put on a long face. 'Actually, we can't do it till the harvest is in. Which means not till near the end of October, when the spuds are dug.'

'That'll do fine. I'll go to see Father Donovan tomorrow and set a date for the end of October. He never said anything to you about how he managed to talk your father into it?'

'Not a word.'

Brideen was eaten by curiosity. Next day after class she knocked at Father Donovan's front door. The priest himself answered.

'How are you, Brideen? What can I do for you today?'

His tone was cool, almost distant, but the eyes were not. Here was, she felt, a man hell bent on fending her off, but fighting a losing battle. 'I dropped by to thank you for what you have done for us. Kieran told me you signed the papers yesterday.'

'Thank God, I was able to come up with something that benefited not just you and Kieran but several other couples as well.'

'You were wonderful, Father. You really went out of your way to make our marriage possible.'

'I couldn't have done less for you.'

She smiled. 'And to think I almost ruined your plans, taking Larry Sweeney away when you were about to introduce him to Aideen Glynn.'

'*Felix culpa* – happy fault.'

'Why do you say that?'

'Well, it actually turned out to be for the best.'

'Really?' She smiled again. 'And how did that happen, Father? If you don't mind my asking?'

The priest hesitated. 'I can't really tell you.' In response to her raised eyebrow he added, 'To explain it I'd have to reveal the name of our benefactor. And he wants to remain anonymous.'

'Ah well, you wouldn't want to tell me then. Not at all. It wouldn't do. It's just that I'm dying of curiosity.' She smiled at him again.

'I suppose I can tell you this much.' His eyes were glowing; the man had a bad case. 'In the strictest confidence, of course.'

'Certainly, Father. Nothing you say will ever pass my lips.'

'It all has to do with a dowry.'

'Ah, indeed. So it's fortunate for us that Aideen chose to marry a rich man rather than Larry Sweeney?'

'I can say no more. And I rely on your absolute discretion.'

'Your secret is safe with me, Father. And now, I'd like to set a date for the wedding.'

'When did you have in mind?'

'As soon as possible, of course. However, Kieran says it can't be till the harvest is all in. Which means about the end of October.'

Father Donovan's face registered gloom. 'I was hoping you'd want a May or June wedding. You see, the benefactor's money won't be available until next May.'

'Sugar!' Brideen wanted to scream. Satisfaction of her lusts would have to be deferred still longer.

'Of course, you don't have to wait for the money, since you know you'll be getting your own place next May.'

Brideen shook a resolute head. 'I am not moving in until Tom McDermott moves out. Definitely not. Anyway it wouldn't be fair to Rosaleen: she can't get married and move out till Packy's sister gets married and moves out. So everything depends on the benefactor's money. Sugar!'

33

'My dear brethren, it gives me great pleasure to tell you that, as a direct result of our triduums of prayer and our recent social evening at the school, no less than four weddings are to take place in this parish in the near future. And the happy couples are all staying at home here in Mayo: none of them are emigrating.'

If Father Donovan expected that announcement at first mass on Sunday to electrify his congregation – and he did – he was right. However, no outward demonstration of feeling took place: it was not the custom in Coshlawn Crann to display emotion in church.

'And there will be more weddings to follow,' he proclaimed, as if daring them to remain unmoved. But unmoved they remained until the mass was done and they had filed out the church door, dipping fingers in the holy water font and making the sign of the cross. Only after completing that ritual did they feel free to engage their tongues once more. And engage them they did for the remainder of the day, in endless wonder at what God, and their priest, had wrought.

'Is your Packy one of them?' Nellie Ruane asked Nora O'Brien on the way home.

'Why wouldn't he? Isn't he already engaged.'

'But they're going to America, aren't they, himself and the McDermott girl? And didn't the priest say the couples are all staying at home here? Well, isn't he a terrible man now to be saying things that aren't true.'

'Hold your horses now, Nellie. Packy and Rosaleen are staying at home.'

'But I thought—'

'I'm not at liberty to say any more now.' Which statement caused the remainder of their journey home to be conducted in awkward silence.

'There's more to this than meets the eye,' Nellie told the older brother at dinner.

'Begob if there is I'm sure you'll get to the bottom of it.' The older brother winked at the younger brother.

After washing the dishes Nellie walked across the fields to visit Barney Murphy. 'Did you know the McDermott girl is getting married to Mick O'Brien's son.'

'So they tell me.' Barney added a couple of sods to the fire.

'And where are they going to live?'

'Back at O'Brien's, of course. Isn't Packy the only son living at home?' Barney lifted the kettle from the hob. 'You'll have a cup of tea.'

'But I was told that Packy couldn't bring a girl in there until Teresa was settled?'

Barney limped halfway to the back door with the kettle before turning. 'I better tell you it all, I suppose; you won't leave me in peace until I do.'

Nellie got off her chair. 'Here, let me fill that for you.' She filled the kettle from a bucket outside the door and hung it on the crane over the fire. 'Now tell me everything.'

'I'm told that Tom McDermott is giving Rosaleen a settlement, and after she gets married that settlement will go to Teresa O'Brien so *she* can get married.'

'Well honest to God, Barney! And I suppose we can guess what made Tom so *flaithiul* all of a sudden.'

'He's giving the place to Kieran and going to live in Lahvauce himself.'

'Glory be to the Blessed Trinity! And I after hearing that Kieran and Brideen Conway were going off to England. Without so much as getting married first.'

'Well that's it now, Nellie. That's all I can tell you.' Barney got up and took the teapot off the dresser. Nellie took it from him.

' 'Twas the priest wanted all those weddings and now he's getting them.' She put the teapot on the hob. 'It would make you wonder, wouldn't it?'

'More power to him. It must be all the praying he did.'

'That man did more than pray, I'd say. 'Twas the threat of the boycott that did it. What else would make that miser Tom McDermott sign over his place to the son and give a settlement to the daughter?'

'The kettle is boiling, Nellie; will you stop your blathering and make the tea like a good woman.'

Austin Glynn declared another round of drinks on the house, even though he had already given one on Thursday. 'It's a historic day for the parish,' he declared. 'The turn of the tide in the fortunes of Coshlawn Crann.'

'The scholars say that Finnerty is a new man,' Jack Kelly noted. 'Divil a one of them he has slapped all week, would you believe?'

'He's saving himself for what's to come.' Mick O'Brien winked at his fellow drinkers. 'A newly married man needs all his strength, so he does.'

'Easy now, lads,' Austin Glynn said. 'I don't want any unseemly remarks directed at my daughter or her fiancé.'

'No harm meant,' said Mick. 'When is the wedding?'

'Not till May. Alphonsus would like it a bit earlier, and sure you can't blame the man for that, given the girl he's getting. But I put my foot down. You can't rush a wedding if you want to do it right, any more than you can rush pulling a pint. So May it's going to be, when the weather is fine and the trees are green and the flowers in bloom.'

'And God is in his Heaven and all's right with the world,' Mick O'Brien added.

' 'Twill be a great bash, no doubt,' Jack Kelly said.

'It will be the biggest and best wedding that Coshlawn Crann has ever seen,' Austin Glynn affirmed. 'I can guarantee you that.'

The long wait till Aideen Glynn's nuptials didn't appeal at all to Father Donovan. Three other weddings were being held up, and there was the risk of something going wrong in the meantime. But there wasn't a thing he could do about it. Alphonsus Finnerty came to his door asking if he'd intercede for an earlier date.

'At my age, Father, the less waiting the better.'

'I'll see what I can do, Alphonsus.' The teacher's addressing him by his formal title wasn't lost on the priest: there might be hope yet for the man.

'I asked Aideen if she could speed things up, but she said she had no say at all in the matter; the decision was up to her father.'

'I'll have a word with him,' Father Donovan promised. But Austin Glynn proved to be just as stubborn as Tom McDermott when it came to changing his mind. 'It's the sacrament that counts, Austin,' the priest reasoned, 'not the celebration.'

'But sure the sacrament will be just as fresh in May as in December, won't it?'

'However, there are other people waiting to get married who can't go to the altar until your daughter goes.'

'And aren't they the lucky ones to have Austin Glynn as their benefactor? So the least they can do is humour me for a few months longer.'

'Alphonsus Finnerty himself is a bit impatient, I hear. You wouldn't want to keep a man like that waiting too long.'

Austin Glynn only laughed. 'A man who has waited till he's forty-five to get married is hardly likely to kick over the traces for the sake of a couple of months.'

34

All through the parish of Coshlawn Crann oats, wheat, and barley were cut. Tom McDermott, with the help of Kieran, and without the threat of a boycott, saved a very successful harvest. Three more Sunday evening socials were held in the school, yet Larry Sweeney still lacked a prospective wife. There was early frost. The potatoes were dug. The mellowing of Alphonsus Finnerty – due, it was agreed by those who discussed the matter, to the influence of Aideen Glynn – continued unabated.

'You hardly ever hear the sound of his strap any more,' Brideen Conway reported to Father Donovan. In general, it might be said that the young priest presided over a fairly contented parish.

In Dublin, Martin McDermott was far from being content. Hod carrying was back-breaking, beast-of-burden labour, unworthy of a lad who had hobnobbed in boarding school with the sons of the wealthy and careered around Mayo ever since as if serious work was only for fools. He must, he said, and he would, do something to better his state. The question was what? Daddy hadn't even responded to his request for cattle-jobbing seed money. Jobs in general were scarce, and for what was available pay was poor. He was shocked to discover that Mona, a clerical officer in the civil service, earned even less than himself.

He had done a line with Clare's flat-mate for over a month. An extremely decorous line, regrettably: she went to the pictures with him, and they went dancing at the Crystal ballroom. However, as regards the physical intimacy he lusted after, she gave him nothing more passionate than a goodnight kiss on the cheek. He had stayed with her, however, in hope of more: for the first time in his lust-life he felt deep attachment.

At least he did until Mona pressured him to marry. He was initially tempted to say yes just to gain possession of her diminutive entrancing body. But he was put off when he discovered that on marrying she'd have to resign her job. Mr De Valera, well briefed in the moral teaching of the

Church by the bishops of Ireland, had enshrined in the Constitution the proposition that a married woman's place was in the home. So Martin McDermott, on plighting his troth to Mona Pipsqueak, would be shackled to hod-carrying for the rest of his mortal life in order to support his wife. Not to mention the family that was sure to come and might be large: Mona was only 23.

He wasn't going to do it. No, sir! Not Martin McDermott. When Mona issued her ultimatum – the result of advice from her confessor at Dominic Street church – that he either agree to marriage or she must break off the relationship for the good of her immortal soul, Martin uttered a strangled cry of frustration that was mingled with a sigh of relief. He relinquished the rights he had never attained over her and became once again a free agent. Just as he was about to *cherchez la femme* once more, he received a letter from Rosaleen. After berating him for the agony he had put them all through, she gave him a sprinkling of parish gossip, among which tidbits there leaped out at him the phrase *you will no doubt be tickled to hear that Aideen Glynn just got engaged to Alphonsus Finnerty.*

Bloody hell! He wasn't at all tickled. Roiled, yes; frustrated, indeed; but definitely not tickled. More and more in recent weeks he had been regretting his precipitous flight to Dublin. Thoughts like *what a fecking jackass you were, Martin McDermott, to give up the two thousand quid Austin Glynn was offering as a marriage price* frequently mocked him as he hauled bricks and mortar to build houses for Dublin's working class. Aideen's face might stop a clock, but her dowry would have let him live in comfort for the rest of his life. So, when Mona gave him the bird, his thoughts reverted to what he had cavalierly abandoned, and he wondered more than once if he might not still retrieve what he had so lightly given up. The news, therefore, that Aideen had gotten herself engaged to the wretched Finnerty struck a blow to his gut from which he spent the remainder of the evening recovering, with the aid of dark frothy Guinness pints.

He was on his sixth, and returning from his third trip to the jax, when the thought came to him. Maybe he hadn't really lost Aideen after all, but merely put her in abeyance with his fake death. If he could undo that death maybe he could get her back. Specifically, get back the dowry rightfully his by virtue of Austin Glynn's solemn promise. A solemn promise was a solemn promise, and by hell Austin Glynn would have to keep his. It remained for Martin McDermott to prove to the man that he was alive and well and had never reneged on his commitment to Aideen. The question was, how to do that?

Weeks of deep hard thinking failed to inspire him with a convincing explanation for his behaviour that would allow him to stride into Austin Glynn's pub and continue where he had left off. Then, on a wet Saturday evening, an answer was presented to him at the pictures by that well-known film star, Gregory Peck, in a film called *Spellbound*, which Martin had gone to see because of Ingrid Bergman, with whom he had been in love since he saw her in *Casablanca* at the picture house in Lahvauce. Martin had always loved the pictures, and the pictures now rewarded him for his devotion.

All Souls' Day was solemnly observed by the parishioners of Coshlawn Crann. It was the day during which, as Father Donovan reminded them the previous Sunday, they had the privilege of setting free the souls of their dear departed from the flames of Purgatorial fires. Plenary indulgences, which gave those souls instant passes to Heaven, could be gained by the dozen on that day, simply by reciting certain prayers, or doing the Stations of the Cross.

The patrons of Austin Glynn's public house, though many were second-mass-just-inside-the-door Catholics, did their duty on All Souls' Day as religiously as their more fervent brothers and sisters. Fellows like Ned Canavan and Jack Kelly, and even Austin Glynn himself, could be seen going around the stations rattling their rosaries. And among the souls they prayed for on the 2 November 1946, was that of the late lamented Martin McDermott. A forlorn hope indeed, most of them suspected: what were the chances, they asked themselves, of that wild man, sent to his death without a moment of preparation or the presence of a priest, winding up in so benign a place of punishment as Purgatory? Nevertheless, they prayed for his soul, and when later they congregated in Glynn's to drink the health of their departed ones, the name of Martin McDermott was mentioned with sad reverence more than once.

It would be hard to exaggerate their reactions then, when just before ten o'clock, after many pints had been consumed and patrons were well downstream from the bridge of sobriety, the pub door opened and the ghost of Martin McDermott wafted in, carrying a small suitcase. At least three laden glasses of Guinness crashed to the floor, their contents immediately absorbed by the plentiful sawdust. Several *Jesus Christ Almightys* simultaneously rent the smoke-filled air. Patrons with backs to the door reacted to the consternated expressions of those facing them and swivelled to see the cause. Even Austin Glynn dropped the glass he was polishing, a very rare lapse for that hard-headed, steady-handed man.

Almost alone among that sozzled crowd, Josie Ryan kept his head. While all around him reacted with the special irrational terror reserved for the supernatural, Josie, at the furthest end of the bar from the door, merely gaped and finished his pint and wondered what the future held for him, now that his hero in devilment had returned to life.

'How are you all?' the ghost said cheerfully, in the voice they all recognized as belonging to the deceased. Then it floated straight to the bar, encountering no obstacle as patrons, who a moment before were glued to the floor, made swift to clear its path. 'Give us a pint, Austin, I've a terrible thirst.'

Austin Glynn, too, despite the fallen glass, had kept his head. He was not a superstitious man: his years in the Irish Republican Army, his bootlegging career in America, his experiences with patron chicanery, had left him with a healthy cynicism about human nature. He had also once been privileged to see the great Harry Houdini perform his magic in New York, which confirmed for him that things were not always what they seemed. So he quickly recovered his equilibrium and concluded that here was no ghostly apparition but the original Martin McDermott in person. Hadn't he had occasional suspicions about the latter's sudden disappearance, particularly when no corpse was ever found? So now, kicking from under his feet the broken glass, he said in that offhand tone he used with all his patrons, 'How are you Martin? We haven't seen you around here for a while.'

'It's a long story, Austin. Which I'll tell you all as soon as I drown my thirst.'

Josie Ryan stepped forward then and punched him lightly on the shoulder. 'Jesus Christ, Martin, is it yourself that's in it?'

Martin grinned at his friend. 'Josie, you old son of a gun, how are you at all?' He grabbed Josie's hand and shook it with gusto.

That did it. The bewildered patrons stopped fearing they had drunk too much. They looked at each other and grinned and raised their glasses to imbibe more courage. Ned Canavan went further, reaching out a hand and touching Martin's broad shoulder. 'Begob, he's no ghost all right,' he announced to his brother drinkers. 'He's a solid man by the feel of him. It's himself that's in it for sure.'

Tongues were then loosed and an avalanche of questions was directed at Martin McDermott. How could it be? Didn't the priest himself say he was dead? Didn't they wake him and pray for him? Didn't they even gain plenary indulgences for him this very evening so his soul could be released from Purgatory? How could he be alive if he was dead? And if he was dead how could he come to life again? The questions were deep and probing.

Martin inhaled half his pint while he listened to the barrage. 'It's a long story, and a difficult one. Did any of you ever hear of amnesia?'

They were as silent then as Alphonsus Finnerty's class on being asked the location of Timbuktu, until one fellow asked, 'Is she a film star or a hoor?' at which not a single drunk so much as tittered.

'It's a problem with the brain.' Martin rapped knuckles on his skull by way of emphasis. 'It's caused by a blow to the head, and it makes you forget for a while who you are. That's what happened to me when I fell into the river that night.'

The room resounded with 'Be Jaysus,' 'Doesn't that beat Banagher?' 'Upon me oath!' 'Did you ever hear the like of it?' And many other profound remarks.

'Are you telling us,' Austin Glynn asked, polishing another glass, 'that you hit your head on something when you fell in the river and it made you forgot who you were?'

'That's right.' Martin drained his glass. 'Give us another.'

Ned Canavan raised his own glass. 'Here's to the health of Martin McDermott, recently returned from the dead.'

'Drinks for everyone.' Martin produced a pound note and laid it on the bar.

While the crowd surrounded the Coshlawn Crann Lazarus – as Jack Kelly dubbed him – and tentatively touched and poked him, Austin, busy pulling pints, shouted above the din, 'So, Martin, where the hell have you been these past several months?'

A sudden hush descended. That very question had been, or sometime would be, on everyone's mind.

'I was in Dublin,' Martin told them, 'working as a hod carrier, if you don't mind. Now, can you imagine Martin McDermott working as a hod carrier if he was in his right mind?'

'Well I'll be damned,' issued from several well-oiled throats.

'And I not remembering a thing about my past life. Not a damn thing. Not a single bloody iota. Not even how I got to Dublin. Until two days ago. And do you know what happened to me then? A brick dropped from a scaffold fell on my head and knocked me out. Honest to the good God. And when I regained consciousness didn't it all come back to me about who I was and where I belonged.'

'Begob I must try that on the missus,' some wag said. 'She forgets everything I tell her.'

They were still laughing at that sally when Aideen walked in from the kitchen. 'What's the joke?' she asked.

All eyes turned on her, then on Martin. She had her mouth opened to say something else when she spotted her one-time fiancé.

They could still hear her banshee wail well after she crashed back through the kitchen door and vanished from sight.

Martin was delighted with the reception he received at Glynn's. Not even Aideen's terrified cries subtracted from his pleasure: he'd talk to her again after her father had explained everything. He was less gratified at his own father's reaction when he walked in the door, suitcase in hand, just after the old man and Rosaleen finished the rosary.

'Musha, God help us,' was all Tom McDermott said. 'Late again. You haven't changed a bit.'

Rosaleen shrieked for joy. 'Welcome home, Martin.' She rushed forward and put her arms around him. 'It's so nice to have you back with us again.' Grabbing his hand she led him to the sofa and made him sit beside her.

Tom McDermott picked up the newspaper and began to read.

'How did you get here?' Rosaleen asked. 'We didn't know if we'd ever see you again. What made you decide to come home anyway? Did you meet anyone on the way? I bet if you did they got a terrible shock. I—'

'I took the train from Dublin and borrowed a bike in Lahvauce.' He patted her hand; it was good to be home again.

'How in God's name are we going to explain you to the parish?' His father's voice fairly crackled with fury.

'I already did.' He told them about the effect of his appearance in Austin Glynn's public house and his amnesia story to explain his disappearance. His father said nothing, just returned to his newspaper. Rosaleen laughed so hard the tears came to her eyes.

'Oh God, I wish I had been there, Martin. They must have thought the porter was making them see ghosts. On All Souls' night, too.' This latter thought set her off again.

Martin laughed with her. 'Poor Aideen was the worst. She went flying back to the kitchen as if old Nick himself was chasing her.'

'Ah, the creature. It must have been a terrible shock to her.'

'I'll go back to see her tomorrow and make it up to her.'

Just then his younger brother walked in. 'Well, honest to God!' Kieran stood there gaping at him. 'The dead arose and appeared to many.'

'How are you, Kieran?'

Kieran continued to stare, as if not quite believing what he saw. 'Right now I'm in a state of shock. You're welcome home, of course, but I wasn't expecting to see you.'

'It's so nice to be here and to see you all again.'

'You bloody bugger.' Kieran's expression darkened. 'Do you have any idea what you put us all through with your fake drowning?'

'Sorry about that.' What more could he say?

'Jesus! Is that the best you can do? We held a wake for you; we had a mass said for the repose of your black soul; we cried our eyes out; half the parish was in mourning for you. And all you can say is, sorry?'

'Leave him be now, Kieran,' Rosaleen said. 'What's past is past; the important thing is that he's home again now with his family. We'll get over it.' She grabbed Martin's hand and held it tight.

Tom McDermott put down his newspaper. 'You'll have to find yourself another place to live, Martin. I'm giving this house to Kieran the day he gets married.'

Martin made no comment; anything he said would only annoy the old man still more. Anyway, Aideen's dowry would set him up as a cattle jobber and he'd soon have a house of his own in Dublin.

He slept in his old room that night: Rosaleen made up his bed and told him over and over how happy she was to see him alive. Next morning he found his racing bike hanging in the barn, the front wheel buckled, the handlebars out of alignment. He borrowed Barney Murphy's ass and cart, took the machine to a bicycle shop in Lahvauce, convinced the mechanic that he was indeed alive, and left his treasured racer to be fixed. Two days later he returned for it, riding the bike he had borrowed. 'Good as new,' the mechanic said. Martin had wheels again.

It took Aideen Glynn a long time to calm down after the shock of seeing Martin McDermott. Hours later, after Daddy had convinced her that what she had seen was no ghost but the living Martin returned after suffering amnesia in Dublin, she lay awake in bed with her thoughts. He'd be back to court her again, wouldn't he? His eye on that dowry, though not on herself. Well, he'd get short shrift this time. Hadn't Rosaleen told her what the black-guard's motive was? Anyway, she was an engaged woman now. About to marry a most respectable man who wasn't marrying her for her money. True, she wasn't in love with Alphonsus in the way Laura Devon's heroines were in love. And if she put Alphonsus and Martin side by side, there was no doubt that the latter stirred her blood a lot more than the former. Nevertheless, she could trust Alphonsus, whereas Martin was totally unreliable. Could she even believe that story of his about amnesia? That such things happened, of course, she knew from her reading: it had happened to a heroine in a novel she once read. But nothing about Martin could be taken at face value. He was a born chancer. So when he came around to court her again she'd tell him where to go, so she would. In no uncertain terms, too.

In the morning, however, as she was getting dressed, another thought struck her. She smiled at herself in her wardrobe mirror. She liked that idea even better.

As she was finishing breakfast, sitting across from Daddy who was reading the paper, the knock came to the front door. Mammy, dusting in the hall, answered it. Then came Martin's voice, followed by Mammy's welcoming response: Mammy knew about his return from the dead, and since she couldn't stand the living sight of Alphonsus she would, out of spite, be cordial to Martin. The pair of them chatted for the longest time while Aideen sat there debating with herself whether to disappear out the back door and make him come round again. Just when she had made up her mind to do that Mammy walked into the kitchen.

'That nice man Martin McDermott is in the parlour, dear. He'd like to talk to you.'

What could she do except go and talk to him.

'I'm so terribly sorry about all that has happened, Aideen.' He stood there, the face St Joseph-statue sad, the arms held out like Jesus welcoming the little children.

'You scared the living daylights out of me last night, you know.'

'I'm so sorry about that, too.' His expression dripped repentance.

'You could have written to me as soon as you found out. After all, I *was* your fiancée.'

It was hard to tell whether his look of surprise was real or fake. 'Was?' He plopped into a chair.

'You don't imagine I was going to wait around for a man I believed to be dead?'

'You mean there's someone else?' With that doleful expression he could get a job in Hollywood.

'I'm engaged to marry Alphonsus Finnerty, Principal of the National School.'

'Well, I'll be damned.'

You will, she thought. Out loud she said, 'The wedding is set for next May.'

His face brightened. 'Ah! That gives you plenty of time to change your mind.'

'I have no intention of changing my mind.'

'You'll change your mind about that, too.' His expression switched to earnest. 'You can't marry that fellow now, Aideen. Not with me back from the dead. I'm your first love, remember? We belong together, you and I. No one could ever love you as I do. Alphonsus Finnerty might be a halfway decent second choice, but now that I'm back—'

'He didn't even ask for a dowry.'

Martin's Adam's apple moved up and down several times. 'I won't either.'

She was enjoying herself. 'Alphonsus is a very talented man, let me tell you. He loves books and he's fun to talk to, and he plays golf, and he doesn't drink any more. And he started going to mass again. And he's going to go to confession for Christmas.' She smiled at her for-one-hour fiancé. 'All round, he's a better man than you, Martin.'

He stood abruptly. 'We'll see about that.' And he left in a hurry.

35

Martin McDermott's return from the dead stirred up more than mere amazement and titillation in the parish of Coshlawn Crann. Those whose lives had been affected by his putative demise were forced to reassess the effect of his resurrection. Aideen Glynn, after years of romantic neglect, found she had a choice of suitors. Her mother was presented with the possibility of a lesser evil since she disliked Alphonsus Finnerty enough to accept Martin as a son-in-law. Austin Glynn considered Martin's return to be extremely inconvenient, now that he had acquired a more suitable mate for his daughter. That suitable mate quailed on hearing that a predecessor fiancé had returned. Nor was the possibly deleterious effect of Martin's revivification lost on Father Donovan: should Aideen revert to her former fiancé, his plan for four marriages might well collapse like a house of cards. Brideen Conway, privy to the secret of Father Donovan's largesse, was equally put out on learning of her future brother-in-law's reappearance.

Resolution of all concerns hinged on Aideen Glynn's reaction to the risen-from-the-dead Martin. Aideen, though she initially gave Martin the bird, by no means ruled him out as a future husband. Of course, she wasn't about to set aside her current fiancé yet: caution was of the essence lest she lose both by precipitate action. She needed advice before she chose. Not the kind of counselling her parents would be only too willing to give. Not even whatever words of wisdom her friend Rosaleen might have to offer. What she needed to know was what her romantic heroines would do in her shoes. Would they choose the virile but scatterbrained and unreliable Martin? Or would they prefer the less robust but intelligent and trustworthy Alphonsus? She consulted her novels, including those of Laura Devon. Practically all heroines chose virility over refinement. She noted, however, that heroes tended to be brilliant as well as manly, though they often masked their intellectual talents until near the end. She doubted that Martin had any hidden brain power. Or that Alphonsus concealed a sterling masculinity beneath his delicate exterior. So which to choose?

Austin Glynn, a man of action when action was indicated, set about looking for a way to influence his daughter. The morning after the black-guard's appearance, he was in the kitchen having breakfast with her when, before he had even time to broach the subject, Martin knocked on his front door. He heard his wife's pleasant chatter with the fellow. He listened to their footsteps going down the hall to the parlour. He said nothing when Christine informed Aideen that 'That nice man Martin McDermott is in the parlour and would like to talk to you.' He waited till Christine went upstairs, then tiptoed down the hall and listened to the conversation in the parlour. What he heard gave him cause for concern. He knew his daughter: playing hard to get with Martin meant she was at least leaning towards accepting him. He also knew that any direct attempt to influence her would fail. He'd have to work on Martin instead. The fellow's interest lay only in the dowry and, if Austin were to deny him that, he'd melt away. Such a raw *coup de grâce*, however, would certainly incur Aideen's fiercest anger, a calamity to be avoided if at all possible. He'd give the matter more thought and try to devise an alternative scheme.

Alphonsus Finnerty noticed a cooling in Aideen's ardour even before he learned of Martin's return. The morning after the risen one's appearance Alphonsus paid his usual visit to his fiancé on the way to school. Hitherto greeted with a warm and wet good-morning kiss, his welcome this particular day was reduced to a skimpy peck on the cheek. Which didn't unduly disturb him at first: he was getting used to the vagaries of Aideen's moods. However, after he spoke with his future father-in-law on his way out, the green-eyed monster nipped at his innards.

'You heard the news, I suppose?' Austin's counterfeit-casual tone indicated something important.

'What news?'

'Martin McDermott came back from the dead last night.'

He knew his future father-in-law as a plain-spoken man, so he could find no sensible way to interpret that statement. 'Sorry. What was that?'

'Martin McDermott. You remember Martin?'

'Of course. The scallywag who got himself drowned a few months back.'

'He didn't drown at all. He says he suffered amnesia from hitting his head when he fell in the river, and that he's been in Dublin ever since. Anyway, he walked into the pub last night.'

'Fancy that!' Interesting story indeed, though not important to Alphonsus Finnerty. 'You don't sound as if you quite believe him?'

'I have my doubts. It will all come out in due course, I suppose. Anyway, *you* should know, Alphonsus, in case you didn't hear it before, that Martin had got engaged to Aideen the night he fell into the river.'

'Good Lord!' He had *not* heard: since he lived in Lahvauce and spent all his time there when he wasn't in school, and since he didn't socialize with the Coshlawn Crann teachers, he wasn't privy to much parish gossip.

'He was round already this morning to talk to Aideen; obviously he hadn't forgotten about *her*.' After which Austin Glynn made a sound that could best be described as a snort.

'You don't think that. . . ?' At which point Alphonsus Finnerty remembered Aideen's peck on the cheek, and the green-eyed monster nipped.

'I don't think, I *know* the blackguard will be chasing her again.'

'She won't go for him.' But above his unwavering tone Laura Devon was screaming, *Of course she will; doesn't the heroine always go for the handsome young muscle-head?*

Austin Glynn wagged a finger at him. 'If I were you, Alphonsus, I'd treat Martin McDermott as a serious rival for Aideen's affections, and act accordingly.'

His aplomb collapsed. A man who rarely sought advice, he now in plangent tone implored Austin Glynn, 'What do you think I should do?'

The publican took a deep breath. 'The way I see it is this: he's a lot younger than you, and he's better looking, if you don't mind my saying so, and he drips what my father used to call manliness. As against that, however, he's wild as an unbroken stallion, he's totally unreliable, and he doesn't have half your brains. Now Aideen thinks a lot of brains: she likes a man who can talk intelligently to her. So you might keep that in mind.'

'You'll put in a word for me yourself?' He hated himself for practically begging the man's help.

'I'd like to, Alphonsus, but I won't, and I'll tell you why. I want you to marry her, of course, but if I were to say as much as one word in your favour, the way Aideen is she'd be liable to pick Martin just to show her independence.'

Alphonsus Finnerty fretted all day. Five times – a record – he left the classroom to visit the outhouse, much to the amusement of his pupils who wondered what disgusting concoction he must have eaten. In the evening, he sat before his typewriter for more than an hour without striking a key.

Then inspiration struck and, neglecting his supper, he typed till the early hours. He was out of bed in the morning after less than five hours' sleep, twice read through what he had written, made some corrections, ate a hasty breakfast, performed an even hastier toilette, and was at Aideen Glynn's door at the usual time.

'I'd like your opinion, my love, on the first couple of chapters of a new novel I've just started.' This after Aideen had repeated the previous morning's peck on the cheek. 'That's if you don't mind reading it?'

'Well, of course, Alphonsus. You know I like to read everything you write.'

He left her the manuscript and went to school. But his thoughts stayed behind, going over and over every sentence he had written, watching her expression, trying to read her mind, fearing she'd see through his efforts, hoping they'd sway her. After class he hurried to her house again.

'She's gone to town, I'm afraid.' Complacency writ large on her mother's face: Christine never took pains to hide her dislike of him. But not once since they had got engaged had Aideen failed to be waiting for him after school. He drove home in the foulest mood. Nearing Lahvauce he spotted her cycling towards him. He stopped the car when they came abreast and rolled down the window.

'Aideen, my dear, I was so disappointed that you weren't home when I called.'

'Sorry about that. I had to do some shopping.' Her tone was cheerful, at least she wasn't mad at him.

'How did you like my new novel? Did you have time to read it?'

'I read it.' She hesitated. 'I was a bit disappointed with Tony.'

'Oh.' That didn't sound good. 'Why was that?'

'Well, at first I was sure he was going to be the hero, he was so virile and strong. But then you made him out to be a real lout.' She cocked an eyebrow at him. 'So unlike you to do that, Alphonsus. What came over you?'

'I thought I'd try something different.' Lame, Fonsie, lame.

'Tony, as you described him, reminded me a bit of Martin McDermott. Did you hear that Martin came back from the dead?'

'Your father mentioned it. I don't know the fellow very well.'

'Well, anyway, I think your heroes should be big and muscular and manly.' She gave him an impish smile. 'That's the way we girls like them.'

He spent the evening awash in misery.

Cait spoiled Father Donovan's breakfast, breaking the news as he was about to top his morning egg.

'Well, you don't say?' Trying to maintain a casual tone while the bells of disaster tolled in his head. 'He said he lost his memory and has just recovered it?'

'That's what I was told. But if you ask me—'

'I've heard of the like, all right. So he's back in Coshlawn Crann, alive and well? Isn't that amazing.' The fellow could at least have stayed out of the way till after the weddings.

'Christine Glynn told me he has been round this morning already to see Aideen. And she engaged to Mr Finnerty. That's not right of him, Father, sure it's not?'

'Not right at all, Cait.' *Martin's only interest in Aideen was her dowry,* Brideen had told him a week after the fellow was supposed to have drowned. He finished his meal in a hurry and dashed across the road to have a talk with Austin Glynn. He found him in the pub, counting the money in the till.

'Don't tell me what's worrying you, Father.' The publican placed his index finger against the middle of his forehead. 'Glynn the magician can read your mind.' He screwed his face into an agonized expression. 'It appears that you're worried about the resurrection of the dead. Something to do with a blackguard called Martin McDermott. The very lad we all wore our knees out for yesterday, praying to get his sinful soul released from Purgatory.' He glanced at the priest. 'How am I doing?'

'Cait told me he's been around to see Aideen already this morning.'

'They say, Father, that sometime in the future every house will have its own telephone. But sure they'll never need the like of that in Coshlawn Crann.' Austin resumed his counting.

'I hope she's not going to cast off poor Mr Finnerty. I'm told she's already had a profound effect on the way he treats his scholars.'

'I'll tell you this, Father: beneath Alphonsus's morose exterior there's a good-hearted man. All he needed was the right woman's touch to cheer him up.'

Father Donovan felt relief course through his body. 'Then you're not going to let Aideen reject him in favour of Martin McDermott?'

Austin Glynn's laugh mingled pity with contempt. 'If you don't mind my saying so, Father, you speak as a man who doesn't have a twenty-five-year-old daughter to contend with. There's no question of my letting or not letting Aideen do anything. She'll do what she wants, regardless of what I say.'

'But if she were to. . . .' The remote possibility that had sent him running to Austin suddenly converted to looming threat.

'If she were to choose Martin over Alphonsus there wouldn't be a thing you or I could do about it.'

Panic clawed at his priestly bowels. 'I trust that if she did it wouldn't make any difference to the dowry we're promised?'

Austin Glynn stopped counting his money and looked at Father Donovan with the tolerance of a parent observing a small child's folly. 'I'm afraid, Father, it would make all the difference in the world. You see, Martin McDermott doesn't have a penny to his name. And left to himself the young scoundrel never will. So if my daughter is foolish enough to marry him I'll have to give them the entire amount I promised you.'

Father Donovan stumbled back to his house, trying to repress an unpriestly despair in the goodness of God. He spent the entire morning in that state of wavering faith that strikes even the most faithful priests at one time or another. He only nibbled at the mutton chop Cait set before him, to the intense annoyance of that fastidious housekeeper, for whom failure to clean the plate was tantamount to personal insult. His divine office he said without attention, his mind on the brewing disaster. Not even the arrival of Brideen Conway cheered him: how was he going to tell her that the return of her future brother-in-law was going to destroy her dream. Her doleful expression matched his own, as if she, too, knew the fate that awaited. Which she did.

'You heard about Martin McDermott's return from the dead, I suppose?'

'Indeed. Wonderful news,' he forced himself to add.

'Wonderful, my eye. The blackguard came back for one reason only: to steal our money.'

'I don't understand.'

'I was talking to Julia Ryan this morning and she told me that Martin told her brother Josie that the only reason he came back was to get his hands on Austin Glynn's money by marrying his ugly daughter – those were his exact words, according to Josie. He wants to become a cattle jobber, he said, and he needs her dowry to get started.'

A faint gleam of hope pierced Father Donovan's gloom. He got rid of Brideen as quickly as politeness permitted and hurried across the road in the rain to see the publican again. Austin was polishing the counter top.

'It's the Holy Hour, Father, so I can't serve you any booze right now.'

Father Donovan waved his disdain for any such thing, though a drink was just what he needed at this moment. 'Listen, Austin, I just got a bit of news that might be of interest to you.'

'I'm beginning to think maybe you're the fountain of all the parish gossip yourself, Father.'

'God forgive me for passing things on, but I have to tell you this. Brideen Conway stopped in just now, and she told me that Josie Ryan's sister told her that Martin McDermott told Josie the only reason he came back was to get hold of the dowry he'd get if he married Aideen – "your ugly daughter", he called her.'

Austin Glynn flushed, the pupils diminished, the lips tightened. He said nothing for a minute. 'Thanks for the information, Father,' he said curtly then. 'And if you'll excuse me now I've got some thinking to do.'

At the end of dinner that evening, Austin said to his wife, 'I wonder if you'd mind the bar for me for a few minutes. I want to have a chat with Aideen.'

Both mother and daughter showed expressions of annoyance. Christine said, 'Only for a very short time, dear; I have things I need to do.'

Aideen said, 'Daddy, if you want to talk about what I think you want to talk about I don't want to talk about it.'

'It's not that at all,' he told her. 'You're going to like what I have to say.'

Christine got up. As she was going out the door she said, 'You can help Aideen with the dishes while you're talking.'

Aideen washed and Austin dried. 'If you decide to marry Martin McDermott,' he said to her back as she leaned over the sink, 'I'll have to give you some means of support. Martin doesn't have a penny to his name.'

'I never said I was going to marry him.'

'Well, if you should decide to, here's what I propose to do for the two of you.' He spent the next ten minutes laying out his plan. Aideen listened in complete silence. When he finished he asked her, 'How does that appeal to you?'

'Fine. Just fine. *If* I decide to marry Martin. Which I haven't yet.'

Austin went out to the bar to relieve his impatient spouse.

36

Martin McDermott saw Aideen's initial rejection as merely a necessary act to maintain her pride. She'd say yes eventually. He saw it in her eyes even as she was saying no. When she said Alphonsus Finnerty didn't ask for a dowry she was merely testing him: Austin Glynn would cough up the money once they were engaged. So he waited two days and went to see her again, at ten in the morning, knowing that Finnerty would be in school.

'Martin!' Christine welcomed him when she opened the door. 'How nice of you to visit us again.'

Aideen was less effusive. Nevertheless her eyes, if not her greeting, gave him hope. 'What brings you here at this time of day? Shouldn't you be out feeding cattle or pigs or something?'

'I came to visit the woman of my dreams.' A line he had crafted and rehearsed.

'Well, aren't you the romantic lad.' Her smile was teasing, but he could see all the same that she was flattered.

'And to ask you again if you'll marry me.'

'I'm already engaged, as you well know.'

'You were engaged to me first.'

'Well, I'll say this much for you: you have Mammy and Daddy on your side; they'd both like me to marry you.'

'There you are, then.'

'I'll think about it. Daddy promised to make things easier for us in regard to where we'd live. You wouldn't have to worry about getting your father's place, he said.'

God! He was on the pig's back. The dowry was his. Martin McDermott, cattle jobber, was on his way. 'So you'll marry me then?'

'I didn't say that. Not yet anyway. But let me tell you what Daddy has planned for us. If I were to marry you – and I mean *if* – he said he'd buy us a fifty-acre farm and build us a new house on it. He has set aside a couple of thousand for me for whenever I decide to settle down, and that's what he's going to do with it.'

Shite! Holy shite! He'd better talk to Austin before taking matters any further. 'That sounds wonderful.' Hoping she didn't notice his discomfiture. 'I'd love to talk to your father about it.'

'You'll find him in the bar, I'm sure. Cleaning up after last night.' Was it his imagination, or was there a mocking twist in her smile?

Austin was setting up a new half barrel behind the counter. 'How are you, Martin?' He looked up at the clock over the mirror. 'It's a bit early for a pint, I'd say. Even for a man like yourself.'

'I was just talking to Aideen.'

'Were you now? You'd need to be careful there, Martin. She's an engaged woman, you know, and her fiancé mightn't take too kindly to a good-looking young fellow like yourself coming around talking to her.'

'She told me you'd like to see *me* marry her.'

'Did she indeed? Well, it must be her imagination. I never said the like. Damned if I did, Martin. Amn't I perfectly happy with the man she's engaged to.'

'You told her that if she married me you'd buy us a farm and build us a house.'

Austin tested the new half barrel by pulling part of a pint and tasting it. 'Good. Up to par, as they say. I was just thinking what would be the best thing for me to do if my daughter was foolish enough to throw over Alphonsus Finnerty and marry Martin McDermott.'

'You were going to *give* me the two thousand pounds the first time.'

'I was, wasn't I? But that was when you were going to take over your father's farm. Now they tell me it's being signed over to Kieran. A sound man, your brother; he'll do well by it.'

'If Aideen were to marry me I'd still prefer to have the two thousand in my hand.'

'You would, I suppose. Why wouldn't you? But it wouldn't be good for Aideen, you see. And Aideen is my main concern. Cattle jobbing is no way of life for a married man, Martin. You'd be always away from home, leaving the missus on her own with the childer. Not to mind the temptations: I've heard stories about cattle jobbers and them loose women up in Dublin that'd make your hair turn grey.'

Shite again. Where on God's earth did Austin Glynn hear about his dream? 'What's all this about cattle jobbing?'

The man's smile was crafty. '*Dubhairt bean liom go ndubhairt bean lei* – a woman told *me* that a woman told *her*. You know how it is around here.'

You can't keep anything secret.'

'Well, it's true anyway. I *am* going to be a cattle jobber.'

He left then, without saying goodbye to Aideen. The dowry was a lost cause.

But vengeance wasn't. The only person in the world he had told about his cattle jobber ambition was Josie Ryan. He brooded on that all day, even while he picked up his racing bike from the mechanic in Lahvauce, and lay awake half the night thinking about it. Anger presented him with horrific images of Josie – decapitated, disembowelled, gibbet-hanging, stretched on a Catherine. He experienced the most intense pleasure from imagining the blackguard's excruciating pain. Morning brought on a more sober perspective. Inflicting physical injury on the gobshite would only bring himself into conflict with the law. Better to do something more subtle that, while causing great pain to Josie, would benefit Martin. He spent the morning cleaning, oiling, tuning the racer while he dreamed up and discarded a score or more ideas. In the afternoon he went for a spin in the rain, and hit on a solution that fitted perfectly with his plans.

Alphonsus Finnerty spent another miserable day at school. He dashed to the outhouse six times – another new record – to the enormous though well-concealed amusement of his pupils. He had visited Aideen as usual in the morning, and was treated to the same – pleasant, though as if she weren't there – attitude by his beloved. That bloody good-for-nothing McDermott was edging him out: he was on the point of losing the only woman he had loved in fifteen years. So deep was his anguish that he paid little or no attention to the mistakes in reading or spelling or poetry recitation or sums of his pupils, to the further delight of those delinquent scholars.

At three o'clock sharp he dismissed the class, got into his car, and morosely decided not to visit his fiancée on the way home: what was the use? He was taken aback then when, passing the Glynn house, his Vauxhall turned off the road of its own accord and came to rest in front of the pub door. With a hang-dog expression he knocked on the front door: might as well get it over with now as later. Aideen opened it immediately and with a little cry of joy flung herself into his arms, her behaviour rivalling his most imaginative description of a romantic heroine in action. She kissed him fiercely on the lips, then buried her head in that most endearing of spots in the human anatomy where the shoulder meets the neck, all the while emitting what Laura Devon would have described as contented sighs.

'My love,' murmured ecstatic Alphonsus Finnerty, who a moment before had been in the depths of despair. 'My love.'

'I've been waiting for you all day, my prince, and it seemed ever so long,' she said, drawing back her head and gazing soulfully into his eyes. 'That horrid McDermott man was here this morning, and do you know what he had the nerve to say to me?'

'If he said anything unbecoming to you, I'll knock his brains out.' Alphonsus Finnerty made a fist of his bony fingers.

'He asked me to marry him, would you believe? Need I tell you, Alphonsus, I sent the blackguard packing in a hurry. He won't forget the dressing down he got from Aideen Glynn for a long time, I can tell you.'

Father Donovan got a somewhat different version of the same event when Austin Glynn turned up on his doorstep in mid-morning.

'Great news for you, Father,' the publican announced, walking in the parlour door after Cait gave him reluctant admission.

'About Aideen?' The priest jumped to his feet – he had been sitting by the fire, searching vainly for ideas to discourage Martin McDermott from marrying the girl.

'She won't be marrying that ruffian, after all.'

'Thanks be to the good God.' The fervour in Father Donovan's gratitude must have impressed even the Almighty.

'I devised a scheme to trap the gold-digger, Father, and by God it worked. The bloody fellow went away with his tail between his legs without so much as saying goodbye to my daughter.' Austin pulled a bottle from under his coat. 'So let's celebrate the event while I tell you all about it.'

Father Donovan got the glasses, then raised a warning finger. 'Only one drink this time, Austin, please. Cait was very annoyed the last time the two of us got somewhat under the weather celebrating. She said it was most unpriestly of me, and even threatened to leave if it happened again.'

'Housekeepers are as bad as wives,' Austin grumped. 'They have to be obeyed. So we'll just have the one.' He filled both glasses to the brim.

It was Saturday before Brideen heard the good news. 'I'm too depressed to do anything this evening,' she told her fiancé after she put the mother to bed and he grabbed her hand, his signal to commence their session of sinful lust. Not having seen him all week she began to relate what Julia had told her about Martin's black intentions and its likely effect on their wedding plans.

'Not to worry, dear,' Kieran interrupted. 'Aideen told Rosaleen yesterday that she had rejected Martin's latest advances and that she's definitely going to marry Finnerty.'

Brideen barely repressed a whoop of delight. She danced her way across the kitchen floor to her bedroom, pulling her clothes off as she went.

Martin McDermott only mildly berated Josie Ryan for that lout's awful indiscretion in disclosing his cattle jobbing ambition.

'Jaysus, Josie, you stupid gobshite, do you know what your big mouth cost me?'

'Honest to the good God, Martin, I only mentioned it to the Mammy, and I told her she wasn't to tell a soul.'

'It cost me the hand of Aideen Glynn in marriage, and two thousand pounds in dowry that would come with her.'

'Sorry,' Josie mumbled. 'I'm fierce sorry, Martin. You know I didn't mean it.'

'But I forgive you anyway,' Martin told him.

Josie looked apprehensive. 'You're codding me, now, aren't you? What are you up to?' Despite being slightly bigger than Martin, Josie was afraid of his friend's ire: on the one occasion that they came to blows years before, Martin had inflicted not-to-be-forgotten punishment on his face and solar plexus.

'Not a thing, Josie. You're my friend and I forgive you. That's all.'

'I'll do anything to make it up to you,' Josie vowed.

37

The year nineteen hundred and forty-seven slipped quietly into the parish of Coshlawn Crann. At both masses on New Year's Day Father Donovan read the list of Christmas dues paid: they were up just a bit from last year, he said, with the biggest donation, five pounds, coming from Austin Glynn; it was noted by the observant – at least half the parish – that Tom McDermott's donation had dropped from his usual three to a single pound. A week later, the country was hit with the heaviest snowfall in years. The daffodils bloomed in time for St Bridget's Day. Tom McDermott bought a bungalow on the outskirts of Lahvauce after selling twenty-five of his best bullocks. Larry Sweeney was rumoured to have got engaged to a woman from the far side of Lahvauce – a farmer's daughter, it was said – but no confirmation of this could be had. It was said there was the best crop of shamrock in years for St Patrick's Day.

In April, the banns of marriage for Aideen Glynn and Alphonsus Finnerty, Liam Conway and Julia Ryan, Brideen Conway and Kieran McDermott, Rosaleen McDermott and Packy O'Brien, were read three Sundays in succession at both masses.

Martin McDermott continued to live at home, even after his father moved into his new house in Lahvauce in March. He spent the time helping his brother with the farm work and re-establishing himself in pub and parish. Not a single wild incident was reported of him in Austin Glynn's public house during the period.

'He's getting old,' Jack Kelly declared sagely. 'Before you know it he'll be getting married like the brother and settling down.'

Even Kieran was impressed with his behaviour. 'You're welcome to stay till the weddings,' he told him. 'Of course, when Brideen moves in I'd just as soon you left.'

On the Sunday that the final banns of marriage were read, Martin went to last mass: he had become a regular mass-goer since his return. Afterwards he waited for Josie Ryan outside the church gate.

'I need a small favour, Josie.'

Josie wagged his tail. 'Anything, Martin. Just ask me and it's done.'

'Let's go for a spin and we'll talk about it.' They got on their bikes – Martin on his racer, Josie on his big upright Raleigh – and took off in the direction of Lahvauce. Martin stopped about a mile down the road, out of sight of houses and persons.

'What do you want me to do?' Josie pulled up alongside.

'Remember how you gave away my secret about wanting to become a cattle jobber, after I expressly told you to tell nobody?'

Josie blushed. 'Sorry about that, Martin.'

'I'm going to give you a chance to make up for it.'

'Josie Ryan's your man.' He squared his shoulders and stuck out his chest.

'I need money to become a cattle jobber.'

'Why wouldn't you.' But a wary look came into Josie's eyes. 'Unfortunately, I don't have that kind of money.'

'I don't want your money, Josie. What I want you to do is steal a few cattle for me and sell them at the fair in Lahvauce tomorrow.'

'Jesus Christ Almighty!'

'Ten bullocks. From Kieran.'

Josie threw his leg over the bar and dropped his bike against the bank of the road, as if it were red hot. 'You can't be serious, Martin?'

'Why wouldn't I be serious? Amn't I entitled to them? Look how hard I worked for the old man all these years? And who gets the place in the end? And what do I get? Don't tell me they're not my cattle by rights.'

'You're dead right, be Jaysus; of course you are. But' – Josie raised protective arms as if he were about to be struck – 'why can't you steal them yourself?'

'Oh I will, Josie.' Martin winked at him. 'I'm going to take another ten myself.'

'But then—'

'Why don't I just take the twenty myself and leave you out of it? Right?'

'Right.'

'But, you see, we don't want anyone to know what we're doing, do we? If I tried to sell twenty bullocks in Lahvauce, everyone in the town would notice me because no one ever sells that many at a time. But nobody will spot a thing if we just sell ten apiece.'

'Do you think?'

'Why would they? We'll have no problem at all.'

'Christ, Martin, what if I get caught? I'll be put in jail for sure.'

'You won't get caught. I'm doing the herding for Kieran these days. He's so busy getting ready for the wedding he won't miss them.'

'He'll miss them sometime,' astute Josie pointed out.

'By that time they'll be sold, and I'll be gone.'

'But I'll still be here.' Josie was half wailing.

'Not to worry a bit, Josie. I'll leave a letter for Kieran, telling him *I* took them all. He's not going to send the guards after his own brother.'

'Jaysus, Martin, I don't know. . . .'

Martin leaned over, tapped Josie on the chest. 'Listen. Remember the hundred quid I promised you before I went to Dublin? Well, if you do this job for me now, that hundred quid is yours.'

That did it. Josie nodded.

That Sunday evening at supper, Martin told his brother and sister he was leaving for Dublin in the morning. 'You wanted me out after the wedding.' He looked significantly at Kieran. 'So I've decided to go live in Dublin.'

'But you're going to stay for the weddings, surely?' Rosaleen looked shocked.

'I'd rather not. Too many bad memories. Aideen and all that, you know.'

Brother and sister nodded. Neither was sorry he was leaving immediately. He had been so quiet since returning from the dead they were afraid he might be reserving his next devilment, whatever it would be, for the wedding day.

After he helped his brother milk the cows and feed the calves, Martin changed his clothes, packed his suitcase, and said goodbye. 'I'm going to stay in town tonight with a friend, so I can catch the early train in the morning.' He attached the suitcase to the handlebars of his bike and rode off.

Monday morning, Josie Ryan was up at three. By seven o'clock he had rounded up, driven to Lahvauce, and sold ten of Kieran McDermott's best bullocks. He met Martin afterwards, as arranged, in Joyce's public house. They retired to the snug for drinks and to sort out the money.

'You sold them?' Martin asked him.

'I did to be sure. Forty-three pounds a head.'

'Good man yourself.'

Josie handed over the money to Martin, who counted it and handed him back a hundred pounds. Josie grinned and caressed the notes before putting them in his pocket.

'Did you sell yours?'

'I did. But I only got forty-one a head.'

'See! I'm a better hand at bargaining than you.' Josie chortled. 'Maybe 'tis I should be the cattle jobber.'

When he got home that afternoon, his mother handed him an envelope. 'A young lad from the town came out on a bike a while ago and said to give this to you.' Josie tore open the envelope.

Dear Josie

I hope you won't mind that the ten cattle I sold today were yours. I figured you owed me at least that much for all the harm you did me, giving the game away on me to Austin Glynn – which cost me two thousand pounds, as you know. Anyway, since I gave you a hundred quid you're only out seven and a half bullocks. You won't think of reporting this matter to the guards of course. If you did, they'd very soon find out that you stole ten bullocks belonging to Kieran.

I'll write to you from Dublin.

Your friend,

Martin

In the morning when Kieran went out to milk the cows, he found an envelope tied with a string to the milking stool. There was a letter inside.

Dear Kieran

I hope you won't mind that I borrowed ten of your bullocks. I'm going into business as a jobber and I need some cattle to get started. I'll return them as soon as I can.

Wishing you and Brideen a great wedding day, and every good health and happiness in your new life together. The same to Rosaleen and Packy of course.

Martin

When Kieran showed Rosaleen the letter, she laughed. 'He's funny. *Borrowing* our bullocks!'

'Dammit!' Kieran roared like a bull. 'I'd have given him the bloody cattle if he'd asked for them. He's entitled to at least that much out of the place.'

38

On Saturday, 3 May, in the year of Our Lord 1947, at 10 a.m., four weddings, with nuptial mass and papal blessing, took place in the most spectacular ceremony ever held in Coshlawn Crann. Austin Glynn, though his wife wanted an exclusive celebration for their daughter, insisted on sharing the great day with the other three couples.

'It's my money and your vision that's making it possible for them all to get married,' Austin told the priest months earlier when they were discussing a date for Aideen' nuptials, 'so I think it's only right to celebrate all the weddings together. That is, of course, if no one objects.'

'I'll enquire,' Father Donovan said. 'Though I'm sure they'll all agree.' He refrained from contradicting the publican by asserting it was De Valera' vision of rural Ireland that made it all possible. Cait had told him that Austin Glynn was a Free Stater in the Civil War and nursed a profound hatred of Dev, which was why she herself couldn't stand the blackguard, the housekeeper added.

Aideen was delighted with the idea. 'What could be more romantic than four brides walking down the aisle together?'

'You have a choice:' the priest told Brideen Conway, 'either to get married on the same day as Aideen, or later.'

Brideen didn't hesitate. Her lust had been gathering force with every day she waited; she'd be willing to get married outdoors on the coldest wettest night of the year if that would speed the legitimation of her libidinous desires. 'Of course; I'd love to get married on the same day as Aideen,' she told the priest without so much as consulting Kieran.

Neither Rosaleen or Julia had any objections either, so the single date for the ceremony was set. Brideen, Rosaleen, and Julia, got together straight away to plan their outfits. After very little discussion they agreed that, since none of them could afford a formal wedding gown, they'd all wear white tailored suits, in the New Look with the longer fuller skirts.

'Do you think Aideen will go for it?' Brideen wondered.

Aideen, though her face showed disappointment, gallantly declared she was willing to forego her romantic dream of a fairy-tale lacy gown with yards of train and settle for what her sister brides could afford. Not so her mother.

'My daughter will marry in a fashionable wedding gown,' Christine Glynn declared. 'Her groom will wear morning suit and top hat, and her father will lead her down the aisle in tails.' From that position the woman could not be budged.

'What does it matter?' Kieran demanded of his distressed fiancée. 'I'll be happy to marry you without any clothes on you at all, not to mind a white gown.'

'You're incorrigible, Kieran.' But she ceased to fret and accepted that it was all right for Aideen to wear her fancy gown while the rest of them wore their modest suits. She did, however, pursue a wedding dream of her own.

'I'd love if the children would throw flower petals at us as we walk out the church door,' she confided to Maura Prendergast. Maura promised to have that dream fulfilled.

Father Donovan told himself he was the happiest priest in the country. He was redressing, if only in a small way yet, the evil of emigration. Wasn't he fulfilling De Valera's dream of developing a people who would be satisfied with frugal comfort, of creating a land whose countryside would be bright with cosy homesteads and whose fields and villages would be joyous with the romping of sturdy children, the contests of athletic youths, the laughter of comely maidens?

On the eve of the wedding, he heard the confessions of those about to be married. Alphonsus Finnerty, having unloaded the guilt of twenty years' absence at Christmas and having confessed again at Easter – under the relentless pressure of his fiancée, of course – had little to say and got a quick absolution. Brideen Conway said it had been just a week since her last confession, and she had only the most venial of sins to relate.

Father Donovan had just returned to the sacristy to put away his stole when the outside door opened and an older woman, heavy in a bright flowered dress and wide-brimmed hat, walked in.

'Good evening to you, Father.'

Her face was unfamiliar. 'Good evening. Can I help you, ma'am?'

'Arrah, not at all, Father; I just came by to pay my respects. I'm Mrs Finnerty, Alphonsus's mother.'

'Pleased to meet you.' Father Donovan suppressed an insane impulse to laugh. There was about the principal a leathery ageless aura that made the idea of his having a mother seem somehow incongruous.

'I came all the way down from Dublin to see what she looks like.'

'Weren't you great to come.'

' 'Twas hard to imagine what kind of a girl would want to marry our Fonsie.'

'He's very fond of her by all accounts.'

'His father used to say he'd never come to any good.'

'Alphonsus is a fine teacher, ma'am.'

'His old fellow used to wallop the daylights out of him when he was a gossoon.'

'That was most unfortunate indeed.'

'The father was a real blackguard himself. A right gurrier, as we say in Dublin.'

'Children are never the better for being beaten, I always say.'

'I met her this evening for the first time.'

'Did you? A fine young woman she is indeed.'

'A pity she isn't a bit better looking. Face like the back of a bus.'

'Ah well, beauty is only skin deep, they say. Aideen has many fine qualities.'

'And 'tis she will need them, God help her. He'll probably wallop her like his old man walloped me, the Lord have mercy on the bowsy.'

'Well, it was very nice of you to come round to see me, Mrs Finnerty.' Father Donovan extended his hand.

When his daughter returned home after confessions, Austin Glynn asked her if she'd take care of the bar for a bit.

'I have to have a chat with Father Donovan about the ceremony tomorrow,' he said. Without giving her time for suspicious questions, he left and hurried across the road to the priest's house. Cait gave him grudging admission.

'I have here a receipt, Father, that shows I deposited a thousand pounds in your account at the Bank of Ireland in Lahvauce. So I've fulfilled my part of the bargain.'

'May God reward your great generosity, Austin.' Father Donovan shook his hand, effusively. 'I won't offer you a drink now, but we'll celebrate in style tomorrow.'

'I have to hurry anyway: Aideen is minding the bar.' On the way back he ran into his wife, who was coming from the church, and they walked home together. 'I just gave the priest his receipt for the money,' he told her.

'Good. As long as you didn't give him the bank robbery money.' Her short laugh was brittle.

'As a matter of fact, I did.'

She stopped dead in the middle of the street. 'Austin! You didn't?'

'I did.'

'Oh no! How could you?' Horror contorted her still lovely face.

'Why not?' He faced her. 'Isn't it about time I did something with that money? You yourself have been after me for years to get rid of it, but you wouldn't let me spend it on us. So what better than give it to the church?'

'Like you'd give the remains of your dinner to the dog. Is that any way to treat your God?'

He threw up his hands in exasperation. 'What do you want me to do? It's been twenty three years since the bloody robbery. And the Bronx is a long way away, and there's no way I can return it to the bank – which anyway, given the way things work in America, is probably not even there any more.'

'But it just doesn't seem right to foist it on an innocent priest. What if he ever found out?'

'How would he find out? The only person who could ever tell him is you. And I hope to God for his sake and the sake of the brides that you won't.'

'What if I have a duty in conscience to tell him?'

'Oh, for God's sake, Christine; you have no duty to destroy other people's lives. And that's exactly what you'd do if you told Father Donovan about the source of the money I gave him.'

She stood there, head bent, for the longest time. Then, incongruously, she laughed out loud. 'Poor dear innocent Father Donovan!' She shook her head and continued walking.

After Austin Glynn had left, Father Donovan wrote a cheque for £1,000 payable to Rosaleen McDermott, and put it in an envelope; he'd present it to her tomorrow after the ceremony. His dream was coming true, thanks be to the good God. He picked up his breviary and began reading Vespers. A minute later Cait stuck her head in the door.

'Brideen Conway is here; she'd like to talk to you.'

'Brideen! Come in and have a seat. I'm sure you're all excited about the big day.'

'Indeed, Father. But I won't sit. I just had to stop in to thank you again for making it all possible. You've been an absolute brick. Without you this wouldn't be happening.' Her smile was ravishing.

'Thank the Lord, Brideen, not me. I was merely His instrument. And do say a prayer for Mr De Valera, too: it was his vision that inspired us all.'

She wrinkled her nose. 'I don't think we owe very much to Dev, Father. Him and his frugal living. Bah! Now, the person we do owe a lot to is Austin – I mean our generous benefactor, whoever he is. Where would we be without that thousand pounds?'

'It was most generous of him indeed. And hard-earned money, too, he assured me. That's what makes his gift so extraordinary.'

'I better run. I have a lot of things to get ready for the morning. Thanks again, Father.' She held out a shy hand. He took it in his. So soft and delicate, yet firm in his grasp. Her eyes were shining; she had never looked so beautiful.

He shook himself after she left. No more of that nonsense. He had passed through his trial by fire and come out a stronger wiser man. Thanks be to God. He resumed his recitation of Vespers. But when he finished and closed the book an involuntary phrase escaped him.

A pity, all the same.